JAN STEELE

Shoes

ON THE

Stairs

a novel

Shoes on the Stairs
First Edition

Cover design by ebooklaunch.com

Acorn editor: Holly Kammier

Copy editing and formatting by Debra Cranfield Kennedy

ISBN—Hardcover 978-1-947392-56-4
ISBN—Paperback 978-1-947392-55-7

To my husband, Scott,

and my children, John, Julia and Jessica.

And...

To those who have suffered at

the hands or words of bullies.

Susan,
I am so blessed to have such a wonderful friend. Thank you for all your support and love. Enjoy the journey!

Jan Steele

Some of us think

holding on makes us strong,

but sometimes it is letting go.

—HERMANN HESSE

Chapter One

"Oh, shit," is all I can manage to utter as I look out my driver's window on an oddly rainy San Diego autumn morning. The shiny, silver grill and the large black Escalade it's attached to are no match for my husband's prized BMW sedan. I lean away from the driver's door and brace for impact. There is nothing I can do to stop the inevitable. My heart pounds furiously, my stomach lurches into my throat and a brief *I don't have time for this,* flashes in my brain before contact.

The initial force of the crash pushes me toward the passenger side. The clunk and screech of metal on metal and the explosion of glass forces itself into my ears. In what seems like a short second, my body whips back toward the door along with my head. There is a thunk as my skull makes contact with something hard, maybe the door that now pushes into my side, and then there is an unfamiliar silence. I strain to open my eyes, my lids carry the weight of deep sleep. I need a little rest, and then I'll try to open them again. My head throbs worse than any headache I've ever had, like someone replanted my beating heart in the center of it. I'm so tired.

Wait, where am I? I need to get up and get the kids off to

school. Why can't I open my eyes? Why can't Brad turn off that screaming alarm? Get up, Claire! The kids need you to get up. The kids need . . . the kids . . .

—

EARLIER THAT MORNING, my loyal alarm clock blared after another night of tossing and turning thanks to my husband's incessant snoring. How is it that his snoring will wake me and not him? How can he sleep through such a loud noise vibrating through his head? I pushed him onto his side and pressed the snooze button. In exactly seven minutes, it would go off again— not enough time to fall back asleep and not enough time to contemplate the meaning of life. When it went off the third time, at 5:59, not only did I not have time for a shower, I had set chaos in motion. I should never have pressed that damn snooze button.

I slid my lethargic body out of bed and propelled it to our midsized, outdated master bathroom of worn honey oak cabinets and white tile countertops. As I brushed my teeth and avoided my reflection in the mirror, my gaze fell upon the once white grout I had scrubbed and bleached yet continued to look as tired and as haggard as I felt.

I threw on my workout clothes, tugging a pair of black yoga pants over my ever-expanding forty-six-year-old ass and tucking in my muffin top. After a brief moment of disgust and another attempt at convincing myself that today I would make it to the gym, I brushed my thin, straight, "L'oreal Red/Blonde Number 8" hair into a ponytail, and lobbed on some makeup I'd recently purchased from the internet promising to make unwanted lines and wrinkles "melt away." The least it could do was hide the bags under my tired hazel eyes. I made a few quick sweeps of mascara and gave my underarms a heavy spray of deodorant before rushing out of the room, noting, of course, that I was still running behind schedule.

A ping of jealousy hit me with the sound of Brad still snoring, oblivious to the arrival of morning. I turned on the hall light, illuminating the beige tiled foyer that leads to the wooden stairs. The walls still wore the pink flowered wallpaper I'd installed shortly after Brad and I bought the house almost twenty years ago. The once cream background was now yellowed, and some of the seams had pulled from the wall. It had been begging to be removed for years, but there never seemed to be time for such projects.

I had no idea why I crept up the stairs when two blaring alarm clocks continued announcing the new day without any resistance. All three children slept, cozy in their beds. Why ruin such a beautiful thing? And why was I always the one to carry out this unpleasant chore? Waking them up was like waking hibernating bears—it wasn't safe.

I strode lightly into Ivy's room, opening the door, and approaching the bed. At fifteen, with long, golden blonde hair, steel blue eyes, and a perfect three-thousand-dollar smile we were still paying off, Ivy was the equivalent of nature's tsunami. Once the earthquake hit, it was smart to run to higher ground.

"Ivy, it's time to get up, sweetheart," I said in a quiet, calm voice. But there was no sound or movement. I filled my lungs and gave my voice more force. "Ivy, you need to get up." She finally stirred and let out a groan. "Come on, it's getting late."

"I know!" Ivy's screech pierced my ears.

Inhaling a deep cleansing breath, I headed to Jasmine's room next.

"Hey, pumpkin, time to rise and shine." I opened the blinds, the October sun as resistant to take on the day as the kids. "Come on, Jazzy. Another fun day of first grade is waiting."

"I don't want to go to school today. I have a tummy ache." She had a tummy ache every school day.

I took in Jazzy's small, freckle-dusted face framed with mashed brown curls. I wished all three of the children could be this small again, rid of the complications and distance the teen years had brought. I kissed Jazzy's forehead.

"You're as cool as a cucumber."

"Please, check again," Jazzy said, sounding like she had laryngitis and grabbing her stomach.

"You're not sick, kiddo. Maybe some breakfast will help."

Jazzy was still in bed grousing when I entered Edward's room at the end of the hall. Teenaged body odor hit me the moment I opened the door. I recoiled slightly before venturing in while breathing through my mouth.

"Edward, time to get up."

As usual, there was no response. I shook him and rocked him side to side, still nothing.

"Edward, get up!" I continued to shake his eighteen-year-old, five-ten frame as if begging a dead man to come back to life. His thick blonde hair sat flat against his head except for the cowlick that stood at attention. I could still see the little boy in him when he slept, the innocence of youth now spoiled by the taunts of others. His laptop and phone sat on the floor next to his bed.

"Were you playing on the computer all night? Is that why you can't get up?"

"No!" he said before pulling the covers over his head.

Regret filled me immediately. I'd been so hard on him

lately. It was difficult to tell who I was more disappointed in, Edward or myself. By now I thought he would have grown out of his awkwardness, like a butterfly emerging from a cocoon. It had to happen, but when? What would it take to pull him out of the insulation I had helped surround him in? I had protected him too much for too long and, in doing so, had failed to teach him how to protect himself.

I gave him a gentle pat and lowered my voice. "Please, just get up."

Buddy, our over-sized, black-ball-of-fur mutt, greeted me in the kitchen. He was the only creature in the house who ever appeared happy to see me in the morning. His bushy tail wagged as he rushed over and nudged me with his thick muzzle. I stroked his velvet ears before opening the back door to let him out. The fresh, invigorating eucalyptus scent intensified by the morning rain, permeated the air. I sucked it in, hoping it had the same effect as chugging a cup of highly caffeinated coffee. I wondered if there would ever be a time when I wouldn't feel so disjointed and exhausted, when life itself would once again be my eucalyptus.

I pulled out some sandwich fixings and a pre-made salad, checked the expiration dates and closed the fridge. From the pantry, I grabbed a can of Chef Boyardee mini ravioli, the only thing Jazzy ever wanted for her school lunch. I opened the can and held it at arms-length as the congealed pasta slurped and oozed into the bowl, holding my breath until it was safely sealed in the microwave.

I loathed making lunches. Each child wanted something different, and each lunch needed to be packed a certain way. But if I didn't make them, the kids would probably starve, and I'm sure, after they hit up enough of their friends for food, I'd be labeled as a "free-range" parent. The very thought makes me cringe. I didn't leave my teaching career to be a "hands-off" parent.

Growing up as a single child with laid-back parents wasn't something I wanted for my own children. I wanted to be involved in their lives and to protect them, and in today's world of raising kids, if I wasn't pushing them and placing the bar of expectations beyond their reach, I wasn't doing my job. Today, kids needed a résumé chock-full of amazing life experiences and achievements to get into college, and it was up to the parents to make sure this list grew by the day. Sports, academics, clubs, community outreach, leadership and more were expected of these kids at an exhausting pace, not only for them but for the parents. There was never time to do anything but push and pull them across the finish line in the hopes they would get into the very best university to get the very best job and live the very best life—and pray they didn't hate you for it.

While Jazzy's food heated, I slapped together a ham and cheese sandwich with mayo and two bags of chips for Edward and then, because Ivy insisted on vegetarian options even though she wasn't vegetarian, I placed the pre-made salad and a piece of fruit in her Lululemon reusable bag.

The microwave pinged and, as I glanced in its direction, its bright green digital clock yelled at me, "It's 6:45, where are the kids?" They needed to leave in fifteen minutes, and they hadn't even eaten breakfast. Craptastic. My body climbed the stairs again. Silence.

"Ivy, get up! You have to leave in fifteen minutes."

"What? Why didn't you get me up earlier?" She flew out of bed. Her voice loud enough to shake her two siblings awake.

At that moment, the house came alive with frantic activity. Showers went on, doors slammed, and worry set in that they weren't going to make it to school on time, again. I put Jazzy's ravioli in her thermos and added some fruit and carrot sticks, that would no doubt come home untouched, into her "Frozen" lunchbox while footsteps pounded above me. Before I lined up the lunches on the counter, I threw a few Hershey's Kisses into each lunch to make up for the kisses I knew I wouldn't have time to give them as they dashed out the door.

Five minutes before the kids were supposed to leave, Jazzy appeared. Her hair was a knotted mess, she was missing her socks, and she hadn't eaten breakfast. My daughter sat at the table and groaned.

"What do you want to eat? You don't have much time, so it needs to be something quick," I said.

"I don't know." Jazzy's voice pitched somewhere between a whine and a cry.

"Well, you need to decide, or you're going to go to school hungry."

"Fine, oatmeal." She lay down across the chairs at the table.

"Jazzy, you need to finish getting ready, you don't have time to rest. Get your socks and shoes on and brush your hair while I make your breakfast."

"I'm tired, Mommy. Don't you even care?"

"The whole world is tired. Now go get ready."

Jazzy huffed as she got up and did what she was asked while Edward entered the kitchen.

"Mom, I need you to sign this." Edward slapped a paper on the white-tiled island countertop.

"What's this?"

"It's nothing. Just sign it, please."

"I don't sign anything until I know what it is." I put on my reading glasses and studied the paper.

Edward shoved his hands in his pockets. "It's a detention, no big deal."

"No big deal? What for?" I resisted the urge to put my hands on my hips and flex my face in exasperation.

"I had a small fight with Zane. That's all."

"A fight? What kind of fight? About what?" I scanned his body, but there weren't any obvious physical signs of an altercation. Still, Zane's name sparked an unfavorable heat to spread through my bloodstream along with an urge to punch him myself.

"I don't want to talk about it, okay? Just sign it. It won't happen again."

"We're going to talk about this tonight. Got it?" I didn't have time to pull answers out of Edward, although even if I did, I'd get an abbreviated version of the story.

Edward ignored my question and went to pack the rest of his things while I scrambled to find a writing implement. I fished a broken purple crayon out of the junk drawer and signed the detention slip, cursing that punk, Zane Goodman, in my head. He was like a cat playing with his live dinner before eating it. I needed to talk to the dean today and get this stopped before it grew out of control again. And if the school wasn't effective, I'd hunt that little shit down myself and teach him a lesson.

"Mom, I need twenty dollars," Ivy said as she rushed into the kitchen like she was being chased by her sister for a hug. She poked into the pantry and grabbed a breakfast bar.

"I just gave you your allowance two days ago." Lately, I was nothing more than a damn ATM to Ivy.

"Yeah, but this is for school. I'm not going to spend my allowance on school stuff." Ivy flailed her bright gel manicure in the air. "Oh, and don't forget the cookies. I need them for tomorrow."

"Why don't *you* make the cookies?"

Ivy's face contorted before she flashed her signature eye roll. "Yeah, right. Like I have time for that."

"Jazzy, you need to get going," I said, avoiding an argument over money and cookies with Ivy. Jazzy had no time now to eat the oatmeal I'd made for her.

"Mommy! Where are my shoes? Who moved my shoes?" Jazzy said.

Ah yes, here we go again.

"Where did you take them off?"

"They were right here." Jazzy pointed to a spot next to the kitchen table.

"Good morning, everyone." Brad flashed a contented smile as he sauntered in, followed by the fresh scent of Irish Spring and citrus aftershave.

He appeared completely oblivious to the drama of the morning playing out right before his eyes. How did he always look so well-rested and perfectly dressed every morning? Not a wrinkle in his shirt, not a blonde hair out of place, his blue eyes bright and wide open. He poured himself a cup of coffee.

"Think, Jazz. Where was the last place you remember having them on?" I asked.

"Right here. I was right here." Jazzy pointed to the same spot.

"Obviously that's not the place, because they're not there."

Jazzy placed her hands on her hips. "Then someone moved them!"

"I didn't move them, and there's no one else in this house who would've possibly moved them because no one else cleans up around here. Go retrace your steps."

Jazzy left in a run. "Great. Now I'm going to be late for flag salute!"

A tornado circulated in the kitchen and Brad stood right in the eye, completely unaffected by the chaos swirling around him. He appeared at peace, with his coffee in hand and engaged in whatever was on his phone. I released a loud sigh, certain my blood pressure was soaring well above normal and hoping my exasperation would catch his attention. The worst part was that this unscripted, yet predictable bedlam happened almost every day, like that annoying movie, *Groundhog Day*. Sure, I'd tried to make changes, but the result always remained the same.

After a minute of searching, Jazzy stomped back into the kitchen, sat at the table and crossed her arms over her chest.

"I can't find my shoes so I'm not going to school."

While I took a measured breath to keep from yelling, Brad turned toward Jazzy.

"Jazz, sweetheart, calm down. Close your eyes and try to picture where you took them off." Brad's warm, calm voice of reason was like honey on a sore throat and one of the things I loved about him.

Jazzy closed her eyes for a couple of seconds before they popped open and she sprinted out of the room, returning moments later with her shoes in hand. This time she'd found them in my closet, so I added that to my mental list of possible places to look for Jazzy's lost items. One of these days, I was going to get Jazzy organized, have her put things in their proper places and avoid this chaos completely.

The kids ran out the door, now almost ten minutes late. As predicted, I didn't even have time to give them a quick kiss before they left, and as the door slammed shut and Edward drove the car out of the driveway I wondered, as I did every morning, how I could make tomorrow go better than today.

Back in the kitchen, Brad stood at the counter, amused by something on his phone while he sipped his coffee.

"Did you see this on Facebook?" He turned his phone screen in my direction.

"I haven't been on Facebook in ages. Too busy for that time-suck."

But truthfully, it wasn't the time that kept me away as much as it was the lives of my "friends", which always sounded monumentally better than my own, that stopped me from scrolling through the pages. The job promotions; the endless pictures of exotic vacations; the perfect children doing perfect things; the perfect, perfect lives everyone seemed to live. Everything and everyone were perfect on Facebook, and although deep down I knew no one lived the utopian life they portrayed on social media, the braggery still ate at me and left holes of inadequacy and unhappiness.

"Bridget Radcliff just published a novel. Isn't she a friend of yours?"

"What?" I glanced at Brad's phone. Bridget's post made its way to his page from a friend of a friend of a friend in the small, claustrophobic world of fake-believe.

"Looks like it made it onto Amazon's bestseller list."

"Wow, fantabulous," I said without an ounce of energy in my voice. "Another smut novel makes it onto the bestseller list. And if you must know, she's an acquaintance, not a friend."

I didn't know if it was really a smut novel, but I assumed it was only because I couldn't imagine Bridget writing anything else. But this, I admit, was one of my flaws. I assumed a lot about everything. I assumed I'd marry a prince and become a princess. I assumed I knew everything there was to know at fifteen. I assumed I'd want sex every day for the rest of my life and my marriage to Brad would be like living inside a rainbow every day. I assumed I wouldn't miss my career when I stayed home to raise the kids. I assumed *my* children would be the best at everything because I assumed I would be the best mother there ever was. But now, even with all I knew about assumptions, about how they are idealistic dreams I refused to prove wrong, I still gave them weight in my life. Why would assuming Bridget wrote something scandalous be any different?

A little jealousy bounced within me. Even with Bridget being a divorced mother of two, she somehow found the time to write a best-selling novel. And that picture of her on Brad's phone, all trim and sunshiny-beautiful holding her book, lit a fuse in me, or maybe it was already lit but had met the nitroglycerine.

In any case, I was ready to explode. I moved to the sink and gazed out the window, counting slowly to ten, fully aware of the emptiness growing within me. Each person's success reminded me of my own career as a teacher I'd willingly given up for *this*.

"All right," Brad said, taking one last gulp of coffee before placing the mug next to the sink. "Time to battle the freeway. What are your plans for the day?"

I had to think about this question. Did he really want to know my entire schedule? He had it on the Google calendar we shared. If he'd looked, he'd know my whole, tedious day was booked, starting in exactly twenty-eight... twenty-*seven* minutes.

Oh, I thought I'd go to the spa today, you know, and get one of those head-to-toe pampering deals. And then, since I'll have nothing to do until the kids get home, I'll curl up on the couch and read a book by the fire while I stuff my face with the soufflé I plan to whip up, and chase it down with a refreshing glass of prosecco. Scratch that—maybe I'll just fill out that application for the teaching job Brenda begged me to apply for. Maybe, then, I'd actually feel accomplished and appreciated and not so damn empty.

I wanted to say it; see if Brad was really listening, if he'd hear the growing discontent of my current life trajectory. But I couldn't put that on him. He worked hard, harder than most, to keep the family comfortable, which was no easy feat in Southern California. If he felt the pressure of that responsibility, he never showed it. I owed him the same in return.

"Oh, the usual. Nothing glamorous," I said. "What about you?"

"Meetings. The next few weeks are going to be busy. A lot of late nights at the office while we push to make our delivery date on the new product."

My heart sank a little. Brad took his job as a director of engineering at a small tech company seriously. I often pictured his job as a helpless, flailing newborn who needed constant attention. If the baby cried, he ran to it; if it cooed, he smiled with pride. And when the baby grew up, a new one was born. There was no end to the neediness of his job, and like an older sibling, I was often jealous of all the attention it received.

"Going solo, am I?" I said omitting *again* in my question.

"Just for the next month. Hopefully, if all goes well, I can take a little breather for the holidays." Brad placed some paperwork on the kitchen island in front of me. "Would you be able to get this smog check taken care of? It's due today, and I'm not going to have any time to do it."

"Today?"

"If possible."

"I'll need your keys," I said, holding back the dramatic sigh.

While I stared at the smog check request, Brad put his

laptop in his bag and zipped it up before handing me his keys, his face apologetic.

"I know I said I'd help Edward with his college apps, but I'm not sure I'm going to have enough time right now. Could you get him started?"

I bit hard on my lower lip to keep myself from making a comment I'd regret later. But there was no stopping what was stewing inside from bubbling out of me.

"Really? I mean, it must be nice to only have to focus on work. Claire will take care of it, she has nothing else to do, right? Edward won't care either, it won't bother him that his dad is once again putting work before him." I flailed my hands like I was directing some god-awful symphony.

Brad's once calm face looked tortured, and the veins in his neck bulged.

"You're overreacting a tad, don't you think?"

"No. I'm finally *reacting* for a change. We can't live like this anymore. *I* can't live like this anymore. Edward's having issues at school, Ivy never wants to be home, Jazzy complains of a stomachache every school day, you're at work more than you're home. Who the hell are we anymore?"

"We're an American family with a lot of shit on our plate. Nothing out of the ordinary."

"Stop that! Stop normalizing everything. We need to make some changes."

"Look, I don't have time for a lengthy conversation about things you think we need to change."

"And that's why nothing ever changes. I can't keep this up. Sometimes I wonder what would become of this family if I wasn't here. What would you do then, Brad?"

Brad glanced at his watch before pinching the bridge of his

nose. "Let's talk about this tonight."

I swear I could feel bubbles of boiling blood popping in my veins as I cocked my head.

"I promise. Tonight." Brad kissed my pursed lips. "I love you," he said before leaving.

I leaned against the door jamb and watched him pull my minivan out of the driveway. I'd survived another morning in the jungle without nearly enough gear, and Brad's ability to look past it, or push it to the side until he had time to tackle it, which seemed to be never, was turning my disappointment into anger.

Was this it?

My life was measured in smog checks, kid's lunches, laundry, and all those things no one else either wanted to do or didn't have time to do. I envied Brad and his career. Hell, I even envied Bridget with her successful smut novel.

I couldn't stop the discontent in myself from surfacing. I even questioned my vigilant parenting which wasn't, in my opinion, producing ideal results. It was clear the kids were as disconnected and possibly as lost as I was. "For the love of God, snap out of it," I said out loud. *I can fix this.* It's never too late to make changes unless, of course, you're dead.

I repeated *I can fix this,* in my head, trying to convince myself of its truth as I sat down at my computer, like I did every morning, to respond to emails. But this time, instead of committing to another school fundraising event pleading for my help, I declined.

It felt good, so good that any email asking me for something was responded to at first, with an, "I'm so sorry, but unfortunately I have another commitment that day," to, "sorry, I can't," to a big fat, "No." A tickle filled my stomach. I was making changes already, and I felt lighter, freer and a little empowered.

After responding to emails, I returned to the kitchen. Throwing Jazzy's uneaten oatmeal down the disposal, my eyes fell on the signed detention slip still on the counter. Fantastic. If Edward didn't turn it in, he'd receive another detention.

Oh, yes, the smog check, too. My morning schedule looked like a scattered deck of cards in my head, and my damn-good-I'm-going-to-kick-ass feeling I'd acquired a few short minutes ago turned back into angsty frustration. I tried to move the to-dos on my list around like one of those number-slide puzzles where you have to get the numbers in order. But I was never good at that game, always unable to get that last number in the correct slot. With no time to waste, I stuffed the papers into my purse, gave sweet Buddy a kiss on the top of his furry head, and ran out the door.

Rain in San Diego was like snow in Atlanta, causing more accidents than the police could physically assess, even though the average traffic speed slowed to a toddler's crawl. Growing up in the Midwest with torrential downpours and blizzards, this Armageddon-style of driving was completely baffling. And irritating.

As I drove out of our dated, Mediterranean-inspired subdivision, I tried to lighten my mood, forcing a few audible laughs at the sight of my distraught, dog-walking neighbors. It was only rain, for Heaven's sake, but you'd have thought they were being chased by a swarm of killer bees as they scurried down the street shielding their heads and side-stepping puddles.

Despite my ridiculous neighbors, my agitation continued to climb, especially when thoughts of my unproductive conversation with Brad popped into my head, followed by the in-your-face gleaming smile of Bridget Radcliff. I pushed the pedal of Brad's beloved BMW with a heavy foot. Its acceleration, insanely more responsive than my tired minivan's, had me exceeding the speed limit until I'd hit a pocket of traffic. "Come on! Gas is on the right!" Wasn't anyone else in a hurry this morning? What could I cut from my bloated schedule? The St. Mary's Halloween Carnival committee meeting, Jazzy's six-month dental cleaning, Buddy's annual vet visit, the weekly schlep to the grocery store? Certainly not the smog check. It would have to be the over-due chat with April at Coffee Heads; a luxury always first to get knocked off the list. Over-scheduling was another habit I needed to change. My phone chimed. There was a text from Edward.

FORGOT MY IPAD CAN U BRING TO SCHOOL MUST HAVE

He hadn't even realized he'd also forgotten his detention slip, and I was already halfway to the school. A loud groan escaped my lips before I found the next street where I could make a legal U-turn. The last thing I needed was to be pulled over by the police.

Thanks to the sloth-speed of the Prius in front of me, who somehow managed to maneuver through the intersection while the light turned red, I responsibly stopped rather than risking death. I'm pretty sure I'd been stopped by every light since I pulled out of the driveway. Why did this always happen when I was in a hurry? At least I was first in line so I could move quickly when the light turned green. With this car's gusto, I'd be through the intersection before the guy excavating his nostrils in the pick-up next to me realized the light had changed. I grabbed my phone to text Edward back:

GOING HOME TO GRAB IT. WILL DROP OFF AT ATTENDANCE OFFICE WITH DETENTION

I looked out of the corner of my eye. The light was green, at least I thought it was. Before I pressed "Send," I punched the gas and propelled the car into the intersection. Something felt terribly wrong. The blare of a horn coming from my left gave me only a micro-moment to turn and see the Escalade barreling toward me. There was no time to react. Zero chances to change the course of my decision.

"Oh, Shit."

Chapter Two

When I regain consciousness and open my eyes, I'm hovering over my broken body. My face is drenched in blood, a bone protrudes from my left arm, and my head hangs limply to the right while the seatbelt still holds my five-foot-seven frame upright. My body isn't moving. I look . . . dead. I should be freaking out, but I'm not.

Such a strange . . . feeling. There's no pain in my arm or head. In fact, all those aches and pains familiar to my forty-six-year-old body are gone. I feel like I'm lounging on a fluffy cloud.

"We'll have to pull her out of the passenger side. Let's secure her neck," someone says. I can't remember where I was heading before this unfortunate event. The post office? The dry cleaners? My memory is as unresponsive as my body until I glance at my purse, now on the passenger floor.

Half of its contents has spilled out along with a familiar piece of paper. Of course. I was bringing Edward his detention slip he had forgotten at home this morning. I need to snap out of this, there's too much to be done. Edward must have his iPad and slip—and Jazzy, oh Jazzy. If I don't pick her up for her dental appointment, she'll be waiting in the office long after all the kids have gone home. She's always worried one of us will forget to pick her up since the one day I lost track of time last year and picked her up an hour late from Kindergarten.

"Call my husband. He needs to pick up Jazzy," I say, but my mouth doesn't move, and they don't appear to hear me while they load my limp body into the ambulance.

"It doesn't look good," one of the young paramedics says. His lack of optimism is more than concerning. Yes, I'll probably sport a bulky cast on my arm for a couple months, pink if Jazzy has anything to say about it, and have quite a headache, but I'm breathing. I'm not even close to being dead. Besides, shouldn't being an optimist be a prerequisite for paramedics?

I follow them into the ambulance and sit on the bench next to one of them. They fuss with equipment, rip open sealed supplies and attach me to a heart rate monitor. My face is the color of Jazzy's morning oatmeal.

"She's coding. Get the paddles." They cut my tight workout top down the middle and my breasts spring out like trick snakes from a can before flopping to my sides. Good gravy, no wonder I could barely breathe in that thing. They place the paddles on my bare chest, but I can't feel them, thank God for that. The jolt would be painful. It's like I'm watching an episode of *Grey's Anatomy* in the comfort of my family room. All I'm missing is a bowl of salty popcorn and an ice-cold beer. But watching myself, instead of some actor I could care less about, makes me increasingly worried about the outcome. I need to survive.

"Clear," one of the guys says, and then there's a jolt followed by another. After a few more attempts, the heart rate monitor beeps and a relieved "We got her back," is uttered by the paramedic next to me.

—

THE AMBULANCE PULLS up at the hospital, and within a few minutes, my body's whisked to the ER. I follow behind as a swarm of activity circles my stretcher. Once we reach the compact room, the team of doctors and nurses are so in sync with each other, it's like watching a ballet without tights. The team has this whole mess under control, so I take the opportunity to check the waiting room for Brad.

Walking the hallway, everything is so vivid. What once seemed almost black and white and gray, is now in full HD color, the sounds crisp and clear even from a distance. There is the distinct ticking of a man's watch from down the hall, the gentle tapping of someone's foot I can't see, and the beating of hearts from beyond closed doors. But what I can't sense is the physical feeling of what's around me.

I reach for the wall, but there's no contact with its hard surface. I can see my hand, so it's there, but I can't feel anything with it. Moving down the hall, an older man and a woman young enough to be his daughter, pass me. I smile at them and say, "Hello," but they don't respond. Usually, I'd think this was rude, but I'm beginning to understand this strange limbo state I'm in.

I reach the cafeteria, a place infamous for its foul smell of peas and bland potatoes, and wait to grab at my nostrils, but again, there's no smell. Not being able to smell would've come in handy this morning when I was accosted by a rotting presence in the fridge, but now it concerns me. What if I never get to smell the comfort of fresh baked cookies, the sugary scent of Jazzy's hair after she wakes, Ivy's exuberant use of perfume? I think I'd even miss Edward's signature pungent scent.

Without any sense of time, I have no idea how long I roam the hallways. I'm not tired as I move up and down stairs and walk, or float, from one end of the hospital to the other. I peek into the nursery and check on the little ones, so beautifully pink and new; their cries rhythmic and musical; their heartbeats rapid and purposeful.

But now I sense my family's here, and like metal to a magnet, I return to the room where my body is lying. It's hooked up to about a dozen machines. There's a breathing tube down my throat; an accordion behind my head rises and falls, rises and falls; beeps come from different machines, and as I gaze at my body, all I can think of is *holy shit, you look like crap.*

Brad enters the room, and I rush to him. I wrap my arms around his hunched shoulders, but he walks right through me. He comes to the side of the bed and grabs my hand, the real one.

"Oh God, Claire," he says, covering his mouth with his hand.

"I'm going to be fine," I say, but he doesn't reply. All I want is to reassure him, to let him know I'll be on the mend in no time. I don't want him to worry, but his face is bleached of color and his hands tremble.

The doctor who'd directed the well-rehearsed ballet enters the room.

"Mr. Blackwell, I'm Doctor Hess." He reaches out and shakes Brad's hand. "Your wife is a fighter. She's stable." Doctor Hess clears his throat. "What we're most concerned about is her brain injury. She took a significant blow to the head."

"How bad is it?"

"I'm not getting any response from her right now. She's not reacting to any stimuli."

"What does that mean?" Brad asks, but he knows. We've

watched enough ER shows together to understand.

"We need time right now. We've relieved some of the pressure building in her brain. Now we need to wait and see."

"How long? Until we'll know something?"

The desperation in his voice makes me feel something I haven't in a long time—a sense of being needed, and more importantly, wanted.

"It could be days, weeks. The brain is a very complicated organ, and everyone handles trauma differently," Doctor Hess says.

Brad nods. "Can the kids see her?"

"Yes, but not for long."

After the doctor leaves, Brad ushers the kids into the room. The girls' eyes are red and wet. Edward walks behind everyone, his eyes focus on the floor. Jazzy runs up to my body and grabs my hand.

"Oh, Mommy! Wake up, Mommy!" she says. Jazzy's love wraps around me like a warm, cozy blanket. She's always the one who can make me smile on my worst days. The overwhelming surge of love that flows through me is painful, like the first bite of something overly sweet stabbing the muscles in my jaw. I want to hold her and kiss her and tell her Mommy will be just fine.

Not a sound comes from Ivy or Edward. The two of them stand at a distance while Brad attempts to comfort Jazzy until she calms down.

"Why don't you tell Mommy about your day?" Brad says.

"Can she hear me?" Jazzy asks.

"Of course."

"Mommy, today was a good day at school." She looks at Brad, and he nods. "I got only one wrong on my math test. And you know that bully girl, Samantha, who kept teasing me? I did what you told me—you said to kill her with kindness, so I gave her one of the kisses you put in my lunch and guess what? She said I could sit with her at lunch today." Jazzy frowns. "But then Daddy picked me up because you had an accident, and now I can't have lunch with her."

"You'll have other opportunities to have lunch with her," Brad says, putting his arm around her little shoulders. "Ivy, Edward, do you want to say anything to Mom?" he asks.

They both shake their heads, neither saying anything. But their eyes reflect fear.

Chapter Three

Earlier today, I watched my body for hours and didn't see one twitch or eye flutter. I unsuccessfully attempted to climb back into my body multiple times. I can't connect with it, like there should be an outlet in my body I can plug into and, presto, I'm back. I have to figure it out, because Brad and the kids need me. I shudder at the thought of what the house must look like after three days of me being gone. I can picture the floors and countertops cluttered with discarded items, Buddy's shedding fur floating across the tile like tumbleweed, the sink overflowing with dirty dishes, the refrigerator's rotten stench intensifying.

While Brad and the kids are gone, the chatty nurse, Carol, with red-framed glasses and streaks of royal blue in her blond bob-styled hair, enters my room and talks to me as she checks the machines and takes notes. "Nice day outside, Claire. A perfect day for trick-or-treating." She checks the IV bag and writes something down on her clipboard. "My son, Joey, is dressing up as a shark. I bet Jazzy has an amazing costume. You strike me as the type of mom who'd made it from scratch weeks ago. My kids are lucky if I make it to Party City before they're sold out." She makes her way around the bed. "How are you feeling today?"

I love how she asks me as though I'm going to respond.

"Knock, knock," Brad says as he enters the room. He's been here most of the time, taking business calls in between reading me the book from my nightstand, *The Husband's Secret* by Liane Moriarty. He makes me laugh as he acts out the characters and editorializes each chapter.

The kids stop by after school each day. Ivy and Edward mess with their phones in silence while Jazzy draws pictures of bright yellow suns and colorful rainbows and tapes them on the hospital room walls. She also sings silly songs she makes up and tells me about her day.

I want to grab the phones out of Edward's and Ivy's hands and say, "Hey, look at me and tell me what's happening with you." I want to know how school's going, how they're feeling and if they're eating. Instead, I get silence except for the incessant tapping of Ivy's nails on her phone screen.

"Hello, Blackwell family," Carol says. "I'm just checking a few things, and I'll be out of here."

"No rush," Brad says. Ivy and Edward take seats in chairs near the window, their phones in their hands, while Jazzy sticks to Brad like sap on a tree.

"Jazzy, why the sad face today?" Carol asks, and immediately Jazzy cries. "Oh, what's the matter?"

"Her mom did something with her costume, and now we can't find it," Brad says.

"It's at the tailor, Brad, the one on Citrus Avenue," I say, but no one looks at me; no one hears me. "It's at the tailor!"

"I was going to be a huntress," Jazzy says and sniffs.

"Oh wow! A huntress. Well, I'm sure your mom put it somewhere safe. What if I find you a pair of small scrubs just in case? You can be a doctor. How does that sound?"

Jazzy nods and wipes her eyes.

"Thanks, Carol. I think Jazzy would make a great doctor," Brad says. "Any change since this morning?" he asks in a lowered voice.

"No change, but she's holding steady. I'll be back later," she says, adjusting my pillow before leaving the room.

There's a rap on the door.

"Mr. Blackwell," Dr. Hess says as he enters the room. He reaches to shake Brad's hand.

"How's she doing? Any change?" Brad asks.

"Can I meet with you in the hall?"

Brad's eyebrows furrow as he studies the doctor's face. "Sure. Kids, stay with Mom, okay?"

I follow Brad and Dr. Hess out to the hall. Brad's heart drums rapidly like it's going to burst from his chest any moment. He follows a few paces behind Dr. Hess with his hands fisted in his pockets and his shoulders raised nearly to his ears. Dr. Hess's heart rate increases as he motions for Brad to take a seat in a green plastic chair that looks about as comfortable as a concrete slab. He sits in the other seat and faces Brad.

"I'm going to be honest with you here. Claire's brain is showing no signs of activity. She doesn't respond to any stimuli. We ran a second EEG earlier this morning to test the electrical activity in her brain. There was nothing. All the tests indicate Claire's brain is dead."

What? I can't be brain dead. I'm processing everything around me. I am not dead! I sit next to Brad and try to clutch his hand.

"This doctor doesn't know what he's talking about. I'm here, Brad."

"Aren't there some other tests you can do? Maybe she

needs more time to heal? You said it could take weeks." Brad's face whitens as he teeters on the edge of his chair. He's going to pass out. Dr. Hess motions to one of the nurses who retrieves a cup of water and hands it to Brad. Brad lifts the shaking cup to his mouth and drinks. I place my hand on his knee, so desperate to connect with him, to let him know I'm still here.

"We've run multiple tests. If I thought there was even a minuscule chance I was wrong, I wouldn't be sitting here telling you this. She's gone. She's been gone since the accident. I'm so sorry." Dr. Hess places his hand on Brad's trembling shoulder.

"No, Brad. I'm going to be fine," I say, patting his leg, wanting desperately for him to see me; hear me.

"We need to give her more time." Brad stands and runs his fingers through his disheveled hair. "There've been cases where people wake after years of being in a coma—when there was no hope. Claire could be one of those miracle cases."

"I understand your fear. If a second opinion would help you, I encourage it. It's important to feel you're making the right decision."

"I'd like a second opinion."

Brad has bought me more time. I need to get myself back into that middle-aged mess of a body of mine before they run more tests.

—

"WHAT DO I do now?" Brad whispers.

The past few days, I diligently forced myself to connect with my body. I kept thinking how cool it will be when I open my eyes and surprise everyone, but no matter how hard I tried, I couldn't unite with my body.

He sits alone in my room, his face lost in painful thought,

with the organ donation pamphlets in his hands.

I kneel in front of him and rest my hands on his knees. "Let me go," I say, wanting nothing more than to stay. But this isn't a way for any of us to live. He and the kids need to move on, and they won't as long as I am lying here. And not having any physical connection with them is a torturous existence for myself.

When the kids visit after school, Brad stays strong as he talks to them about the results of the tests.

"The doctors have done all they can, but Mom's brain just can't recover."

"What are you saying, Dad?" Ivy says, her voice shaky.

"It's time to let her go. She's never going to wake up."

Edward slowly lowers himself onto the chair by the window and covers his face with his hands. Jazzy clings to Brad's legs. Brad picks her up, and she rests her head on his shoulder.

"You said she was going to be fine. You even joked the other day about how upset she'll be when she sees the mess we've left for her to clean when she gets home. Now you're telling us she's never coming home?" Ivy's face is an angry tomato red. Her squinted eyes bleed tears she quickly wipes away with the palms of her hands.

"I'm sorry, Ivy. I'm just as shocked as all of you are. One of the things I wanted to discuss with the three of you is organ donation," Brad says.

"What's that?" Jazzy asks through her sniffles.

"It's where you give your organs, like your heart or your lungs, to someone who needs them," Brad says.

"Can I have her heart?" Jazzy asks.

"It doesn't work that way. You see, there are lots of people who have bad hearts or other parts of their body that don't work right and need to have them replaced. So, with your mom, those parts of her are healthy, and they can help someone who wouldn't live without them. Do you understand?"

"So, it's like the library, where they borrow it for a while and then give it back?"

"More like a bookstore, where they get to keep it forever."

"How much does a heart cost?" Jazzy asks.

"It's free. We give it away for free." Brad's voice catches.

"Mommy would like that. She never likes people to pay her back for anything," Jazzy says.

Not being able to hold them, console them when they feel their world crumbling under their feet, is akin to being torn to shreds by lions and still alive while they consume me.

Chapter Four

The moment my mom sees me, she breaks out in a horrendously loud sob. Our relationship has never been super chummy, but I'm certain she's felt we're closer than we actually are. I love my mom and dad, but they weren't exactly the most diligent or doting parents. Both worked full-time while I grew up, my mom was a secretary for an attorney while my dad often traveled as a regional salesman for a lawn care equipment company. Neither of them was ever home before 6:00 pm, forcing me to be a latchkey kid by third grade.

My mom was never a room mom or a chaperone for any of my field trips, nor did she ever bring in special treats to share with my classes on my birthdays. I grew jealous of the other kids whose parents volunteered or surprised their kids with a special lunch or walked home with them after school. I wanted *those* parents. Instead, I got Dot and Frank, who both loved me but had always struggled to show it, at least in the way I needed them to.

But, despite how I was raised, I want to embrace my mom and wipe the tears from her eyes. The pain of losing a child is a torture I can't begin to fathom, no matter the circumstances. I reach out and try to touch her. My mom stills then looks up and around.

Did she feel it?

She wipes her face and leans in to kiss me. "Oh, darling. Dad and I are here. We love you," she says, brushing her graying chestnut hair behind her ear. Brad hands her a tissue, and she dabs the corners of her puffy, red eyes before blowing her nose.

"I'm right here, Claire Bear," my dad says as he gives my shoulder a gentle pat. My dad's a man's man, strong as a palm tree in a hurricane. He'd always been strong, played football in college, hunted, chopped and stacked wood for winter, shoveled our long driveway every time it snowed and spent hours every Saturday during the tortuous humid Chicago summer heat tending to our yard. He showed me how a man was supposed to be, told me the man must be the rock in a relationship, show no sign of weakness. Never once did I see him cry, not even when his parents were killed in a car accident when I was eight. Now, there are tears in his eyes.

"You don't have to be afraid, Claire. I've seen the white light. It's there," Mom says.

My dad grimaces. "Dot, please stop with that."

My mom never misses an opportunity to talk about the white light she claims she saw when she "died" during her appendectomy years ago. She said she saw her grandmother, Gertie, and felt so peaceful. Ever since then, my mom's been at peace with death, telling friends, family, even strangers at the supermarket, not to be afraid, that death is not something that should be feared, but rather, something everyone should look forward to.

There were times I'd be mortified when my mom would insert herself into strangers' conversations to tell them her story. After a while, I learned to ignore it rather than get the lecture on her need to share her faith in the afterlife. There's nothing more I want right now than to believe what she saw was real, that when I go, there's something more waiting for me and someday we'll all be reunited.

My parents sit quietly by my bed. My dad's large, calloused and age-spotted hand holds mine, while my mom brushes my strawberry-blonde hair coming out below my bandage-wrapped head. With a white washcloth, Mom wipes my face, like some ceremonial ritual—preparing the body. She pulls lotion from her purse and rubs it into my hands, lingering on each finger. She dots my pale cheeks with her lipstick and rubs it in and then puts a little on my lips.

"You turned out to be such a beautiful woman," she says as she continues to primp my face. Mom runs her fingers through my hair, creating little curls at the ends. "I love you, Claire."

My dad allows tears to slip down his cheeks.

"We love you, Claire. Safe travels," he says as he breaks down with a shaking sob. Once again, I picture the pride of lions, ripping pieces of me from my bones. They consume my skin, muscles, and organs as I watch and still breathe knowing they will eventually kill me—there will be so little left of me that my body will cease.

My mom rises and leans over me, her nose nearly touching my forehead. She takes a long, steady inhale as though she's drawing in my scent and holding it. On the exhale, she places a kiss on the bridge of my nose. "I'll see you in Heaven." Dad places his arm around her shoulder and guides her out of the room.

———

AFTER GIVING ME last rites, the priest leaves my room. Brad and the kids stand around my bed with heavily thumping hearts and tear-soaked eyes. I study each face, memorizing the curve of each nose, the length of their eyelashes, the texture of their skin. They're all beautiful, and even though they're hurting, they're alive.

Jazzy places her adored stuffed animal in the crook of my arm.

"Here, Mommy. You can have Pink Kitty just in case you get scared," she says. Jazzy loves Pink Kitty, and I'm touched she'd think it would comfort me. But she's going to need it more than I am. I hope Brad will take it back later. She won't be able to live without her stuffed animal for too long before she realizes the mistake she's made giving it to me. "I love you, Mommy. Grandma says I'll see you in Heaven, but she says it will be a while."

"Bye, Mom, I love you," Ivy says and kisses my cheek. It's the most affection I've received from Ivy in months, possibly years.

Edward moves near the head of my bed and leans, close to my ear. His heart beats wildly and he works to control his short, quick breaths. Brad places his hand on Edward's back, but Edward shrugs it off. "I'm sorry, Mom. It's all my fault. I'm so sorry," he says.

"What? Wait! No! No! It's not your fault!" I yell, but he can't hear me; no one can hear me! Why does he feel it's his fault? It was *my* fault. I was the one driving the car; I was the one texting when I shouldn't have been. Oh, God! I was texting *him*. I never got to send it. It was probably on the screen after the accident. The cops must have told Brad, and somehow it got back to Edward. This is not how I want to leave. I don't want anyone, especially one of my children, to feel they're to blame for my death. This is *not* how this is supposed to end.

———

THE MOMENT THE doctors take my heart from my chest, I feel my own tug. I'm officially dead. There's no way to come back now.

Sadness consumes me. While I hope my harvested organs

make other's lives last longer, it's the definitive end of my life; my hopes, dreams, and so much of the time that should have been. How could this be it? Regret fills me so fully I want to scream. *No! I want another chance. Please, God, just one more chance.* But I know it's not possible and God doesn't answer. I look for the light my mom promised would be here, but I can't find it. I circle the room looking for my exit, but for the life, or *death* of me, I can't seem to locate it.

"I'm going to talk with the family," the doctor says.

I follow him out of the sterile operating room, glancing at my body one last time. As I walk down the gray linoleum tiled floors of the long hallway with the doctor, he pulls his gloves and mask off and throws them in a bin before exiting the double doors leading to the waiting room. Brad's slouched on the olive, thin-cushioned couch, alone. He looks so lost, so defeated, and now he's going to be told I'm gone.

"Brad," the doctor says.

Brad glances at the doctor, and a guttural sob escapes him and rips through the air. The cry travels through me and shakes me. The doctor takes a seat next to him.

"I'm sorry," he says. He pauses, allowing Brad time to pull himself together. Brad's blotchy, red face glistens with tears and the contents of his nose run down and over his top lip. He pulls a tissue from his front pants pocket and wipes his nose.

"The organs?" Brad asks.

"They're on their way to their recipients. She had a good, strong heart."

"I know," he says. I sit on the other side of Brad and put my hand on his. I know he can't feel it, but it's all I have to offer.

Where the hell is that white light? Where's my exit? Why must I stay and watch Brad in so much pain and not be able to console him? I stand next to him as he signs the remaining paperwork and then watch him walk out of the hospital. The weight of his loss pulls his sturdy shoulders down. The automatic doors open and swallow him. Panic overcomes me.

"Wait! Come back!" But the doors don't open. He's gone. *I'm* gone.

Chapter Five

The visitation is a terrible thing. Everyone gets to look at you—dead. I'm personally not a fan of all the hoopla. It's the one event no one wants to go to, but everyone feels obligated to attend. That stupid tradition where everyone wears dark, depressing clothes, speaks in hushed voices, and stands around with nothing to do, saying stupid things to try and make the bereaved feel better. I'd prefer everyone go to a bar and get wasted. People could say what they really felt and then pass out and forget the whole thing ever happened. That's just my two cents, of course. I now wish I'd discussed this with Brad and had him agree to it so this pervasive display could have been avoided.

After Brad left the hospital, I returned to my body thinking, at some point, the light would appear. But I'm still here. Imagine that. It's not the first time I've ever gotten lost, but this is a big one. *Seriously, Claire, you can't find the big white light?*

I'm curious if there are other spirits here at the funeral home who are lost, but as I roam the dimly lit rooms, I don't spy any. It's just me and the bodies. Mr. Clemson's in the Serenity Room. He's at least eighty, and from the looks of him, with his wrinkly, age-spotted skin and rotund stomach, he enjoyed his time on this planet. Ms. Seamen, who I already feel sorry for having to live with that name, is in the Tranquility Room. Her bald head and puffy cheeks make me believe she battled cancer. She's beautiful, even with all that her sickness took away. There's a picture poster of her propped up on an easel near the foot of her casket, obviously taken during healthier days. And then, there's me, Claire Blackwell, in the Harmony Room, not looking anything like my former self. For a moment, I question if they have the correct body since the makeup is all wrong. My face is too pink, like someone mistook the blush for foundation, and then painted the same baby-pink color on my pursed, prissy lips. The least they could've done was give me a small, satisfied smile.

—

FROM THE MOMENT the visitation begins, the funeral home is packed. There's even a line out the door for the viewing. I'm confident I didn't have this many friends in real life. I don't even recognize a lot of these people. Are they funeral crashers? Is there really such a thing?

None of the kids are dressed properly, but Jazzy's outfit is straight out of the street urchin catalog with her pink and black striped sequined shirt, faded, mid-shin length leggings, and black scuffed-up flats. Her hair is barely brushed. I fear this will be the norm now that I'm gone.

And let's discuss the damn lilies. They're everywhere, like the weeds in my rose garden, if I ever had the time to have one. I can't stand lilies. For starters, they make me sneeze. They may be pretty, but they stink worse than Buddy after a lost battle with a skunk. They probably smell like death because it's one of the most common flowers in funeral arrangements. And now, every ornate bouquet in this room has lilies in it, which proves my point. It's a good thing I can't smell, or I wouldn't be able to stay at my own visitation.

I remain in the room as the long day progresses. Brad and the kids stand in line by my pink casket. Well, it's not pink-pink. It's more of a rose metal contraption with shiny pink satin trim on the inside. Brad at least picked out one in my favorite color, showing, despite the lilies, he's been thoughtful with the difficult decisions. These types of details are not his thing, so I know he's trying to give me the best send-off he can. But the casket is open, which is completely ridiculous. I don't like the idea of people looking at me. They cock their heads and stare at a face that doesn't even look like mine, still battered and slightly swollen from the accident and painted with clown make-up. What are they thinking as they shake their heads?

Ivy must have picked out my outfit, thank goodness, because I'm wearing my favorite royal blue, form-fitting cocktail dress paired with a silver and pearl necklace and pearl earrings. My broken arm is covered with a pink paisley patterned shawl.

Brad goes through the motions as people come by the funeral home. In our twenty-two years of marriage, I've never seen him so weary, so broken. Some of the kids' friends filter through, which seems to help them break into a smile from time to time. I visit the circles of people talking in hushed voices. One, in particular, intrigues me—I barely knew these women. They are from the high school charity event committee.

"Such a shame. Those poor kids," the platinum blonde woman says.

"I heard she was texting while driving. We need to arrange a speaker at school to prevent this from happening again," another blonde says, shaking her head.

"She always seemed to be in a hurry. Probably spread herself too thin, and . . . ," the brown-eyed, brown-haired woman says. "Could have happened to any of us."

"Well, if this has taught us one thing, besides not texting while driving, life's too short not to enjoy the little things that make us happy. Do you think she was happy?" Blonde One asks.

"Have you taken a look at her husband? I'd be more than happy," Blonde Two says as she fans herself—she's fanning herself! Seriously. I'm not even in the ground yet, and she has her eyes on my husband?

"Yeah, I suppose you're right, but she never seemed to be smiling when I saw her. She was always so serious, always checking her watch, and running out of our committee meetings right after adjournment," Brown Eyes says.

Blonde One leans into their small circle and lowers her voice. "Well, she did have her hands full. Edward's always had issues at school. Andrew told me that, just last week, he got in a fight with Zane Goodman. Edward punched him and threw him into a locker."

I find this impossible to believe. How could Edward punch Zane? Zane's built like a bulldozer and could probably flatten Edward with one hand. Plus, Edward avoids confrontation, even when someone physically takes a shot at him, especially Zane. What Blonde One's saying doesn't make any sense. There must be more to the story.

"I'm so glad I don't have those issues with my kids," Blonde Two says while the other two nod. I actually feel sorry for them. They must suffer from Severe Delusional Disorder. Maybe they're living in that perfect world bubble I'd always tried to infiltrate, but never could, because, hello, there's no such thing. Even if there were, bubbles eventually pop.

I've heard enough from women who barely know me and move to my friends, Brenda and April.

"I hadn't spoken to her in a while. She's always so busy," Brenda says, dabbing her dark blue eyes with a tissue. She combs her right hand through her chest-length, ombré hair.

"We were supposed to meet for coffee the day of the accident," April says, before taking a sip of bottled water. It drips onto her green silk blouse. Brenda quickly hands her a tissue and April blots the area. Normally, April would freak at the potential for a water stain on her designer shirt, but she barely gives it a glance.

"Oh, I didn't know. I'm sorry."

"I feared something like this would happen. Not that she would die, but she seemed so distracted the last time I saw her. She nearly backed into a car in the parking lot." April's razor-sharp blonde bob swishes as she shakes her head like she's in a shampoo commercial. She raises her perfectly shaped eyebrows. "I wish I could have done something."

"Hey, what happened was an accident. It's not like she killed herself and we didn't see the signs. Should we have told her to slow down a little? Sure, but she wouldn't have listened. I just can't believe she's gone," Brenda says.

"I can't either. I'm expecting her to hop out of that casket any second and tell us she doesn't have time to just hang around and do nothing."

Brenda lets out a little laugh. "And then she'd scold Brad for letting Jazzy out of the house dressed that way."

"God, I feel so horrible for Brad and the kids," April says and cries.

Brenda wraps her arms around April and hugs her. They know me all too well. My two dear friends in a sea of acquaintances. I will miss them.

—

IT'S BEEN HOURS of what I can only assume has been pure torture for Brad as he listens to people relay their sympathy, tell stories, or offer advice as though they've been through the exact same thing. He graciously smiles, but I can hear his heart thump heavily in his chest like it's trying to pound its way out and flee.

He hasn't sat down once and has only occasionally taken a drink of water from the bottle my mom gave him hours ago. His own parents couldn't make the trip. His dad's poor health has kept them close to home in the suburbs of Chicago for the last two years, but I'm sure Brad wishes they'd walk through that door any minute. Many of his coworkers and friends from various stages of his life pay their respects. His current friends are limited. Just like me, there was never much time to devote to hanging out with friends.

There's no longer a line worming around the room, and the crowd dwindles. I move to Brad's side, wishing I could somehow hold him up, to take some of the weight he's carrying on his shoulders.

And then, Bridget, the best-selling author arrives.

She makes her way toward Brad like she's the fresh air he's been waiting for. She looks as perky as her Facebook picture Brad ogled that morning when everything fell to hell. If he hadn't seen that picture or made a comment on Bridget's successful book, maybe the morning wouldn't have gone the way it did; maybe I wouldn't have yelled at him and acted like a jealous lunatic causing me to carry my angst with me in the car. Maybe, I'd still be alive. I'd never had much of an opinion about the divorced mother of two, at least nothing worth my time or attention. But now there's a negative association I can't shake, and as Bridget closes in on Brad, a faint flicker of jealousy ignites within me.

Bridget's long, ebony hair cascades down the back of her black midi, form-fitting dress. The belt accentuates her narrow, envious waist. Her boys must be adopted because there's no way that body's gone through labor. She's a physical marvel with her wide, white smile and her warm cinnamon eyes surrounded by smooth, sun-kissed skin.

She's the type of woman other women love to scrutinize, trying their dang best to find some flaw to make them feel a tad better about themselves. In fact, I think her nose is slightly too wide for her narrow face. The thing is, she's so sickly sweet, it's hard to hate her. Hell, I got suckered into a few committees because I couldn't say no to her. And now, I'm utterly helpless as Bridget, the beautiful, talented and very single mother of two, stands in front of Brad.

"Brad, I'm so, so sorry," Bridget says as she latches her hand on his biceps and squeezes. "Claire was a wonderful woman. We'll all miss her terribly."

"Thank you . . . Bridget, right?"

"Yes," she says, with a look of surprise. "You have a great memory."

Of course he does.

"You just published a book if my memory serves me correctly. Congratulations. That's a big accomplishment. Claire and I saw it on Facebook—" Brad bites his lower lip and swallows. "Claire was so happy for you."

Well, that's certainly stretching the truth, but Brad tends to put a positive spin on things. There's no doubt he didn't want to mention it started World War III and led to my demise; that would be awkward.

"Oh, thank you. How are the kids doing? Grayson's so sad for Jazzy. He's been missing her at school."

"They're doing okay. It hasn't really sunk in yet, for any of us. Claire's parents have been a big help, especially with Jazzy, but they'll be leaving after the funeral."

"I can't even imagine..." Bridget shakes her head. "If there's anything I can do, please don't hesitate to call me."

"That's very kind of you."

Bridget pulls a business card out of her Kate Spade purse and hands it to Brad. Listed on the card are her name, email address, and cell number printed over a muted picture of a group of kittens.

"Here. Please call if y'all need *anything*," she says, turning my flicker of jealousy into a hot, well-fueled flame.

Brad glances at the card.

"I mean it. I can drive the kids, grocery shop, cook meals, do laundry, anything really."

"Thank you," he says with a small grin and slips it into his pocket.

Bridget rubs his arm with her hand and gives him her bright smile, which can only mean she drinks wine and coffee from a straw. "Take care," she says.

Brad's eyes follow her as she saunters over to the casket, makes the sign of the cross, and stares at the body in the metal box. She shakes her head and wipes a tear from her face. I want to reach my arms out of the casket, grab her by the shoulders and scare the shit out of her. If only I had that power. Brad's eyes move back to the rest of the visitors in the short line to pay their respects. His grief-filled face brings relief to my worry. As much as it pains me to see him suffer, it would be far worse to see him falling under Bridget's spell, especially when he's so broken and vulnerable.

When the last mourners leave the room, Brad, the kids, and my parents are alone with my body. Jazzy's curled up on one of the floral couches in the back of the large room; a dark blue, hand-knitted afghan covers her, making her appear smaller than she is. Edward and Ivy sit in the back row of the rattan chairs set up for guests. Ivy stares at her phone while Edward rests his head in his hands as he leans his forearms on his thighs. My mom walks among the three, checking on each one over and over. She sits down next to Ivy and puts her arm around her protectively.

"Do you want to say goodnight to your mom?" she asks. Ivy shakes her head as a lone tear slides down her cheek. "It's okay. You don't have to." My mom reaches over with her other hand and pulls Ivy's face toward her so Ivy has no choice but to look her in the eyes. "You know she's here with you, right?" My mom says it with such conviction I wonder what she saw when she passed on that operating table years ago. How does she know I'm here?

"Grandma," Ivy says as though the idea of me being here is wholly absurd. "She's gone. GONE," Ivy hisses into her grandmother's face before getting up and marching out of the room. My mom sits for a moment, still and contemplative.

"Claire, dear, how can I convince them?" she says. "I know you're here. I can feel you. I only wish they could feel you too." She moves to the casket and fixes the scarf covering my arm before touching the crystal rosary wrapped in my hands. "Good night, dear," she says before returning to Brad and offering him more water.

My mom poses a good question I don't have an answer to. How can she convince them I'm still here? How can *I* convince them?

"Let's get the kids home," my mom says to Brad, as though he needs a push to encourage him to move from the space he's occupied for the last several hours. "Frank, take Jazzy and the kids to the car, will you?" My mom's not asking, and my dad, a man of few words, nods before walking to the couch. He tries to wake Jazzy, but she's sound asleep. He motions for Edward to pick her up, which Edward does before they exit the room.

"Do you need some time alone?" my mom asks Brad.

"I don't know *what* I need right now." His eyes peer at the casket. "I don't think I can leave her."

Enveloping him in her arms, my mom allows him to sob. She guides him to a chair, and they both sit, still embracing. Brad's so out of character, so uncontrollably emotional. He made decisions based on reason where I'd let my personal feelings interfere. Nothing seemed to faze Brad, not even when the church was double booked on our wedding day, some clerical snafu I lost my shit over, turning me into a true bridezilla. He kept his cool, sent the groomsmen out for alcohol and set up a bar in the reception hall until the other wedding was done and out. Even with the kids, he's been level-headed when all I could muster was a shouting match that usually ended with slamming doors and an "I hate you." But now, his foundation is anything but solid as he sways and teeters and loses his footing.

"Brad, you'll get through this—I promise you," my mom says. His body continues to convulse with his sobs. "She'll always be with you. She's here, Brad. Don't you feel her?"

Almost immediately, he stops crying and pulls away from her. His face tilts slightly to the right, and his eyes, mere slits, sit under his narrow brows. His mouth scrunches as though someone's punched him in the gut.

"No, I don't feel her," he says in a strained voice. "She's gone, Dot. She's never coming back."

"But I've been on the other side and watched on. She's here—"

"Stop. I don't believe in that bullshit. She's not here and I..." Brad pinches the bridge of his nose and takes a deep breath. He looks back at my mom, who appears to be unaffected by his reaction. "I'm sorry. I'd just appreciate it if you wouldn't say things like that, okay? Not to me and not to the kids. We need to get through this without, you know..."

"I'm sorry if I upset you. I'll be out in the car with Frank and the kids." She squeezes his hand before leaving the room.

Brad glances once more at my body, lowers his head and follows my mom. It takes me only one beat of Brad's heart to realize I'd much rather go home with them than stay one more night in this creepy funeral home.

Chapter Six

I t's the morning of the funeral Mass. The house wears its usual calm before the storm. Brad's alarm clock blares before he pushes the snooze button. Seven minutes later, it's a repeat. I wonder how many times he'll press that button before he decides to get out of bed. He has three children to wake and supervise while they get ready.

Finally, after the third snooze, I hear the crackling of his bones and shortly after, the spray of the shower. What's going through his mind right now? If it were Brad who'd died, I don't think I could have gotten out of bed, let alone make it through the day.

It doesn't take him long to get ready; at least it doesn't seem long to me. He exits the bedroom wearing my favorite dark gray suit, the one with a slight sheen to it, a white shirt, and a navy-and-black-striped tie. His eyes squint at the sun streaming through the beveled glass front door. Gently, he wakes each child, starting with Ivy, then Jazzy, and then Edward. There's no screaming today, no frantic slamming of doors, no harsh words; only silence.

The kids trickle down to the kitchen. Jazzy's the first one downstairs in a dress I've never seen before. It's a flowy pink chiffon with a satin, rose embellished sash. It looks like a flower girl dress, but I like it; it's Jazzy, and it's perfect. Ivy wears a shorter-than-I-would-like black skirt with a burgundy, definitely-showing-too-much-skin tank top. I wait for Brad to say something, but he hides his face behind his coffee cup. Edward has on the only suit he owns. The arms are an inch shy of his wrists, and the hem of the pants rests above his ankles. He must've had a significant growth spurt in the last six months because I don't remember him having a problem fitting into that suit on Easter Sunday. I think I would have noticed this.

They all linger silently around the cluttered kitchen island. No one even attempts to speak until the doorbell rings.

"I'll get it," Jazzy says, rushing to the door. "Grandma! Grandpa!" She opens the door and lets them in.

"My, my, don't you look beautiful," my mom says. "Doesn't she look beautiful in the dress we got her, Frank?" She nudges him in the side.

"Oh yes, very beautiful," he says, distracted. "Where's the rest of the family?"

"In the kitchen," Jazzy says.

"Brad," Frank says, offering his hand. Brad shakes it.

"Did you two sleep okay last night at the hotel?" Brad asks.

"Well, the mattress was—"

"Yes, we did," my mom interrupts. "How were things here? Everyone okay?"

"Oh yeah, fabulous," Ivy says.

"Ivy," Brad says with a sapped warning.

"What time does the car get here?" my mom asks, eyeing my dad as he moves to the counter and rummages through the pile of baked goods that have been showing up at the front door.

"Nine. It should be here any minute. Can I get you something to eat? Drink?" Brad asks.

"Coffee," my dad says.

"Oh, for heaven's sake, Frank, get your own damn coffee. Brad doesn't need to wait on you right now." My mom flicks her hand like he's a fly on the countertop.

I never understood how my parents remained married for over fifty years. They bicker more often than a vegetarian farts. But, somehow, someway, they still love each other and therefore put up with each other. I admire them for sticking to a commitment, even if it might send one of them to the insane asylum or the slammer.

The doorbell rings again. There's a black stretch limo in the driveway, and Jazzy's eyes grow wide.

"Wow. That's a big car," she says. "Can we go in it, Daddy?"

"Yes, get your shoes on," he says.

Jazzy searches for her shoes, but as time passes and her pace around the house quickens, Brad becomes impatient.

"Jazzy, we need to go."

Jazzy shouts from the kitchen, "They're not here. Who moved my shoes?"

Ivy crosses her arms and leans against the wall in the entry. "Here we go again. Same shit, different day."

"Ivy!" Brad clenches his jaw and runs his hands through his hair.

"We go through this almost every day, Dad," Ivy says, with an edge of irritation.

"Doesn't matter. And watch your language."

"Oh, I almost forgot," my mom says. "Frank, go get the bag out of the car."

My dad shuffles to the car. When he returns, he hands the bag to my mom who pulls out a shoebox and hands it to Jazzy.

"We thought these would go better with your dress."

Jazzy opens the box, and her face lights up. "Wow, these are pretty!" She pulls a pair of glittery pink shoes from the box and slides them on her little feet. "Mom will love them."

"Maybe you won't lose these," my mom says.

Jazzy puts her hands on her hips. "Grandma, I don't lose them. Someone keeps moving them," she says. "Or it could be a ghost."

"Or maybe you just need to remember where you put them in the first place," my dad says.

"Maybe." Jazzy's distant voice is contemplative, like the ghost explanation as a viable possibility.

I join everyone in the limousine, taking a seat between Brad and my mom. After all, I should attend my own funeral. Maybe the white light will appear at the church, maybe everyone attends their funeral before they depart for good.

Jazzy pushes all the buttons and opens all the compartments. "This is so cool, Daddy. Look." She presses a button and neon lights illuminate the inside.

"Okay, Jazz, let's calm down. I think we all need some quiet time." Brad turns off the lights and then settles back in his seat. Jazzy crosses her arms in front of her and scowls.

Much of the ride is silent. No one looks at each other. My mom fiddles with something in her purse and then pulls out a tissue. She fiddles again and takes out a handful of mints and offers them around, but no one's interested. Ivy and Edward stare out the darkened windows, and not one glance is made at their phones.

My dad takes a snooze; a loud snore escapes his open mouth as his head pitches forward in an awkward position. My mom reaches over and places her hand under his chin and closes his mouth, but it pops open at his next exhale, followed by a snort. She closes his mouth two more times before she sighs. He's a chronic insomniac which causes him to fall asleep multiple times during the day. Dad really can't help it, but it drives my mom to the brink of madness.

Mom lets out an irritated sigh. "Frank!"

"For God's sake, what?" he says.

"You were snoring again."

"So what?"

"So what? No one needs to listen to you sawing away like a chainsaw."

I'm usually the one to run interference during their spats, but now I can't. Brad doesn't even look at them. He stares disconsolately out the window with a face I've only seen one other time in our two decades together, at his best friend, Luke's, funeral almost four years ago. Luke took his own life after his wife asked for a divorce. Brad kept thinking he could have done something to prevent it, but none of us knew. Luke never let on he was struggling. Brad never got over Luke's death, and now he's faced with another tragedy he couldn't stop from happening. His lips press firmly together while his jaw muscles pulse like an erratic heartbeat.

The car pulls up to the church, and Brad and the kids get out, followed by my parents and me. The church parking lot is full, and the hearse is parked around the corner. Honestly, I'm relieved to see my body made it here. I used to always joke about being late to my own funeral. Good to know, for once, I'm on time.

My family moves down the center aisle of the church and I follow. The sun streams through the stained-glass windows, casting a celestial glow on those sitting in the pews. The casket rests prominently at the front of the church, draped in a spray of perfect pink roses. We take a seat in the front pew, all eyes resting on Brad and the kids. I gaze at the patchwork of people filling the seats while light organ music plays in the background. Some are here to say goodbye to me, others to show support to Brad and the kids, others were just part of one of the many circles I dabbled in. Tissues dab wet eyes while light whispers fill the air.

"Here I Am Lord" is sung by the angelic voice of Marcie Bell, the church soloist, as everyone stands up and Father John walks down the center aisle.

The mass is typical. Catholics can almost recite it in their sleep, and some do as they sit in the pews every Sunday, but today they all appear very much awake. After Communion, Father calls up Brenda to give the eulogy. Brenda ambles reverentially to the lectern. She clears her throat a couple of times and unfolds a piece of paper with shaking hands. Her heart thumps as though it's in a hurry.

"If any of you ever had the opportunity to ride in the car with Claire, you'd have certainly heard her say, 'Gas is on the right.'" Brenda pauses as a few chuckles escape and heads nod. "Well, that's exactly how she lived her life. Claire never slowed down—she was always squeezing every second out of the day. If she wasn't driving her kids to all their activities or doing any number of things stay-at-home parents do, she was volunteering for charities, joining committees, making a meal for a sick friend or parishioner, or helping do whatever it was she was asked on a daily basis. Claire could never say 'No.' 'No' was not in her vocabulary."

I find the irony of being broadsided on the same day I started saying "no" almost laughable; sadly, tragically laughable. So was the idea, *I can fix this*, that I repeated like a mantra to convince myself it was true. But it *is* too late, I can't fix any of this, and what I've left behind will suffer because of it. Brenda could have shortened her eulogy to one short sentence saying, Claire was always late, always lost but always trying her damnedest not to be. That would've summed me up perfectly.

Brenda continues with all the gooey friendship stories and builds me up to look like the best person who ever walked the planet. Funny, I can't picture the do-gooder, sacrificial lamb Brenda describes. I'd felt more like a firefighter during fire season; putting out one fire as three more ignited. I could never let my guard down, not even for a second.

After Brenda sits, Brad takes a slow walk to the front of the church. There's no sheet of paper in front of him as he grips the sides of the lectern with both hands and leans in, surveying everyone.

"I want to thank all of you for being here today and showing your support for me, Edward, Ivy, and Jasmine. Many of you have gone above and beyond, bringing us food, sending us cards, dropping off care packages for the kids. It's really overwhelming and comforting to know we're not alone. So, thank you." Brad clears his throat before he continues.

"Claire was my soulmate, my one and only."

I look to the women who ogled Brad at the visitation, hoping they get the message of, "my one and *only*." I stare longer at Bridget, who sits a few pews behind my family and needs to understand this more than any of them.

"We met in college our freshman year and fell in love and never once considered not spending the rest of our lives together. Our wedding day was the happiest day of my life, even if it did throw us a curveball. She sacrificed a lot in our marriage. Probably more than I ever gave her credit for. When we had kids, she stopped teaching to stay home and raise them. She was the true heart of the family. She was the glue that kept everything together." Brad chokes up, and Jazzy runs up to him and holds his hand.

This is all too dramatic. Where are the jokes, like the ones at Luke's funeral? Everyone was crying at his funeral, but it's because they were laughing so hard. That's what I want. I want to see my kids smiling, laughing. I want them to remember the good stuff, not the sappy, sad reminder of their loss.

"What do you do without the glue?" he asks and pauses, and then a small smile appears on his lips but never quite travels to his eyes. "Well, if you were Claire, you'd find a way to make new glue. You would search the internet and find a solution, something that may not be the same but would work. We'll now have to do just that, find some other form of glue to hold us all together. I will miss her more than the flowers miss the sun and the parched earth misses the rain. I will forever miss you and love you, Claire," Brad says and dissolves into tears. This time, he walks away, Jazzy firmly grasping his hand, and takes a seat while everyone wipes tears from their eyes.

I place my hand on Brad's. "Thank you," I say. "But you need to remember some of the funny stuff, or this is going to be a longer road for all of you." I want to tell him everything will be fine; he will be fine; they will all get through this, but I'm not so sure. What I am sure of is that this definitely would have been much better in a bar.

Bright light streams through the church skylights. This is it! Thank God! I was beginning to think I'd be stuck here forever. I move into the light and wait. I look at my family and those sitting in the pews, taking it all in one last time before I leave. But nothing happens, and then the light dims and disappears behind a cloud. This is ridiculous. Could I be stuck in some form of Hell; stuck here to watch my family fall to pieces without any way of comforting or helping them?

—

AT THE END of the graveside service, everyone forms a line and gives their condolences to Brad, the kids, and my parents before taking one last ceremonial look at my casket and walking away. The cars drive down the gravel road, leaving a nebula of dust and the seven of us behind. This should be it. This is where I walk off and into the light and my family moves on with their lives, but again, there's no light to walk into. Where the hell is it? Maybe I'm missing it or not looking in the right direction. I pan the cemetery and then up to the sky, and yes, down to the ground (it could happen), but there's nothing. *I'M STILL HERE!*

"Hello, God?" I say, moving past my grave site and waving upward as though I'm directing an incoming airplane. "It's me, Claire Blackwell." I peer behind moss-covered gravestones, thinking God might pop out from behind one of them and say, "Aha, you found me." But I come up empty.

"Surely you can't leave me here," I say. "Okay, let me rephrase that. *Please* don't leave me here."

As I continue to search for my exit, a strong gust of wind plucks crimson leaves from a nearby Sweetgum tree and blows them to the ground. Jazzy shivers and Ivy pulls the collar of her jacket over her ears.

"Let's go," Brad says. He wraps his arms around both girls and guides them to the car.

I don't know what to do. Do I stay and wait for God to take me Home or is He telling me, in a slightly passive-aggressive way, that I have unfinished business? Do *I* think I have unfinished business? An audible sigh escapes me as a more forceful gust of wind etches a leaf-free path to the car. It's not the red carpet, but I interpret it as a sign. I follow my family to the car, and seeing no other option, join them on the drive home.

Chapter Seven

The bed Brad and I made love in countless times, conceived our children in, and made plans for our future together in is a crumpled mess; it probably hasn't been made since the day of the accident. Brad fixes the covers and Jazzy climbs in on my side. She puts her head on my pillow and inhales deeply.

"It smells like Mommy. Smell, Daddy." Jazzy holds my pillow up to Brad's face as he tries to get her to sleep. He turns his head away but takes a small breath and winces.

Once Jazzy is settled, Brad's heavy feet propel him to the kitchen. He selects one of our expensive bottles of Phelps Insignia from the small wine fridge and takes it to the counter. As he opens the bottle, tears stream down his face and I can't wipe them away. He fills a wine glass with the deep red liquid, swirls it around for a few seconds, and then takes a long drink. He turns on the outdoor music; Pink Floyd's *The Wall* streams from the speakers. Exiting through the back door, his glass in one hand, bottle in the other, he walks the short distance to the fire pit and puts them both down on the small table before lighting the pit, taking a seat, and looking up at the stars. With my parents back at the hotel and heading home to Florida tomorrow, he's very much alone.

Besides our bed, nights at the fire pit enjoying a bottle of Cabernet after the kids were in bed was one of our favorite places to be. It was our time to reconnect, to make plans, and to become more intimate with each other with each glass of delicious grape nectar. We'd stargaze, recount our days, worry about the kids, worry about ourselves as a couple. Sometimes, when the wine went to our heads, we'd make love in the fresh night air, feeling like we were back in our twenties and less encumbered with responsibilities and schedules.

It's been a few years since the outdoor lovemaking, probably because of my inability to contain my angst, especially after a glass or two of lip-loosening truth serum. I would place blame on everyone but myself for feeling stuck in an unthankful job. Brad would nod and tell me he understood, but it felt like my words, my confessions, were lost in the darkness between us. His demanding job and my compulsive over-scheduling to make myself feel needed and appreciated had, without us realizing it, slowly pulled us away from each other. If only I would have stopped focusing on the what-ifs, and just been thankful for *what was*.

But, tonight, Brad sits alone, and I can only imagine the what-ifs running through his mind. It doesn't take long for his thoughts to escape his lips and cut through the brisk night air.

"What now, Claire? What do I do now?" He takes a few large gulps of wine and pours more into his glass. "We were supposed to do this together, remember? Now it's all fucked up. I don't know what I'm doing. I don't know how to talk to the kids. I don't know where anything is in the house. I don't know how to pull this shit together." He downs the rest of the wine in his glass and fills it back up. "We were supposed to drink this wine together. It's your favorite."

I imagine the velvety texture, the scent of dark ripe berries, currants, and vanilla; the rich, juicy black plum kissed with cocoa floating on my tongue, and the warmth the liquid masterpiece leaves behind. I miss this. I miss all of what I can no longer have; the scents of life, the taste of sweet and sour, the feel of skin, touch; human touch.

Brad lifts the glass to the sky before taking another drink. He brings the glass to his chest and lets out a sob, one that comes from deep within; one I've never heard before, even when Luke died. "How could you text and drive? All those times you yelled at me for doing the same thing. Ridiculous. You're a hypocrite, you know?" He finishes the remainder of the wine in his glass before throwing it into the fire pit. The glass shatters. He puts the bottle to his lips and drinks directly from it until it's empty. "Damn it!" he says.

"I don't know what to do with the kids. How am I going to work and take care of them? Edward and Ivy barely talk to me, and Jazzy won't let go of me. What do I do now?"

He leans his head back and stares at the cloudless sky. Tears escape the far corners of his eyes and trickle past his temples and into his hair. He closes his eyes and his angry breaths slow to an even, calm rhythm. I want to help him, offer advice that will make everything better, but even if he could hear me, I don't have any answers for him.

Screams from inside the house rouse Brad from his wine-induced snooze. His head whips up, but when he tries to rise from the chair, he's unsteady from the alcohol that has infiltrated his bloodstream. He stumbles to the door and trips over the threshold.

"No! No! No!" Jazzy's scream pierces straight through me,

as though Jazzy's right next to me. Something's terribly wrong. I beat Brad to the room. Jazzy's sitting up and shaking. Her glassy eyes stare across the room as she continues to scream. "No. You can't leave me. You can't leave me. Don't go!"

I reach for her, but I can't make contact, and my chest aches from not being able to comfort my daughter. Being stripped of the ability to comfort and control is unbearably painful, yet I have no choice but to endure this torture.

Brad finally makes it to the room, his body not completely in his control.

"Hey, Jazzy." His speech is slow and slurred. "What's wrong?"

Jazzy continues to cry and yell. Brad shakes her, but she doesn't budge.

"Jazzy, wake up, wake up for me. It's just a dream."

"No, don't go. Why?" She screams and stretches her arms in front of her, reaching for something that isn't there.

After a few unsuccessful attempts to wake her, Brad picks up the water glass next to the bed and pours some of it on Jazzy. She screams again, but now her eyes appear awake.

"Daddy! Why did you do that? I'm all wet."

"I'm sorry, I'm sorry," he says wiping her face with a blanket. "You had a bad dream. I couldn't wake you."

"I want Mommy."

"I know you do." He pulls Jazzy into his arms and rocks her until her cries fade. "I want Mommy too."

Eventually, she falls back asleep. Laying her back down, he goes to the bathroom and grabs two towels. He gently pats her hair with one of the towels. Pulling off her wet clothes, he wraps her in the other towel and moves her to his dry side of the bed and covers her up with the top comforter.

Brad crawls onto the wet side of the bed and pulls up the covers. He nestles his face into my pillow and takes a large inhale and silently cries himself to sleep.

Chapter Eight

The doorbell chimes and Buddy runs to the door, barking his ferocious Labrador bark. I move to the door and peer through the glass. Oh hell no. It's Bridget Radcliff. Bridget primps her hair and then irons down her top and tight pencil skirt with one hand while holding a casserole dish in the other.

The days that have passed after my funeral can be equated to sitting in a rowboat in the middle of the ocean without any way to save the people drowning around me. I lack even an oar to extend outward, to give them something to keep their heads above water. Brad struggles to get out of bed and allows the kids to stay home from school. They sleep all day. The house is quiet until someone sobs from behind a closed door. If only I could tell them I'm here.

I'm relieved no one comes to answer the door. Like usual, everyone thinks someone else will answer it. Maybe Bridget will deposit the dish into the cooler next to the door like everyone else and be on her way. But she presses the bell again and Ivy eventually stumbles down the stairs in a daze and opens the door.

"Oh hi, Ivy. I didn't mean to bother you," Bridget says. Ivy doesn't say anything. Bridget bites the bottom of her full, sparkly lips and fusses with the tin foil covering the casserole dish. I admit I'm finding some pleasure at Bridget's uncomfortableness.

"I brought y'all some dinner." She holds up the dish in her hand.

Ivy reaches for the dish. "Thanks."

"Is your dad here?" Bridget peeks around Ivy to catch a glimpse of my family nightmare while still holding on to the dish.

"I think he's resting."

"Oh," she says with a slight disappointed frown. "I was hoping to talk with him and see if there's anything he—y'all need."

"I think we're fine right now, thanks," Ivy says void of energetic pleasantries. "Thanks for the dinner."

"You're welcome. It's a special southern recipe from my Nana. None of you are allergic to nuts, are you?"

"Nope."

"Whew. That would have been a disaster." Bridget finally lets go of the casserole dish and reaches into her purse. She pulls out another card, a duplicate of the one she gave Brad at the visitation, and hands it to Ivy. "Just in case y'all need anything, just give me a ring, okay?"

Ivy glances at the card and then back at Bridget. She nods and gives Bridget a small smile.

"Yeah, sure. Thanks again for the food."

Just as Ivy is about to close the door, Brad exits the bedroom, five steps to the left of the front door.

"Who's at the door?" Brad asks.

"It's Mrs. Radcliff. She's dropping off some dinner."

Shirtless, Brad scurries to the front door. His tousled hair and low hanging gray sweatpants make him a sexy sight to behold. He should at least put on a shirt before Bridget hooks her eyes on him.

"Bridget," Brad says. "Thanks for the meal. Care to come in?"

Bridget flashes her brilliant smile. "I don't want to intrude. I'm sorry if I woke you."

"Come in, please. I could use a distraction—some adult conversation."

"Are you sure?"

Brad waves her in and closes the door. "Excuse the mess," he says kicking littered clothes, shoes and other items out of their path in the entry. "I haven't been much of a housekeeper."

"Totally understandable," Bridget says surveying the house as Brad leads her to the grungy kitchen scattered with dirty dishes and empty food containers. Two full bags of trash sit on the floor waiting for someone to take them to the outdoor bin. The small visible bits of countertop are covered in crumbs or other food particles. It would take me hours to clean up this mess. I'm concerned someone's going to get sick.

"Beer?" Brad asks opening the fridge and grabbing two Sculpin IPAs hidden behind a stack of half-eaten casserole dishes.

"Sure." Bridget scrunches her nose. "I hope you're not eating some of that food in there. Smells like something's past its expiration date."

Brad closes the fridge, opens Bridget's bottle, and hands it to her. "I know I need to clean it out. It just hasn't been on the top of my priority list."

"Why don't I tidy it up for you?"

Brad shakes his head. "I wouldn't wish that job on my worst enemy. I'll get it done. Soon."

"No, seriously, I don't mind. It wouldn't take me long. You need room for the new stuff."

Brad takes a swig of his beer. I can't tell if he's considering it or ignoring her valiant attempt to squeeze her way into my family. He better say no.

"I'll come over when everyone's gone, so you won't even know I've been here. Except for the absence of those science experiments in the fridge," she says and points her beer in the direction of the refrigerator with a small laugh. She then takes a drink never moving her ridiculously long-lashed eyes off Brad.

Brad raises his hands in the air. "Alright. At this point, it's an offer I can't afford to refuse."

Brad opens the junk drawer in the kitchen holding everything that doesn't have a home. Cleaning that drawer was always on my perpetual list of things to do. He fiddles around and grabs a pencil without a tip. Shaking his head, he throws it back into the drawer and fishes out a pen along with a piece of scrap paper he rips from a used envelope.

He tests the pen. When nothing comes out, he draws circles until the pen lets go of its blue ink. "Here's the garage code to let yourself in," he says handing her the small piece of paper. "The kids go back to school tomorrow, and I'll be at work, so anytime."

"Like I said, you'll never know I've been here," she says and winks.

What I'd give to have some powers at this very moment and scare her perfect little ass right out the door. I know Brad needs help, but why can't it be some eighty-year-old woman with whiskers, missing teeth, and cankles? Or even Brenda or April who would never pursue Brad. Why, of all people to come to the rescue, does it have to be Bridget?

As they finish their beers, Brad asks Bridget about her book and her boys, and she gushes as he compliments her on her success. Their playful banter makes me want to vomit. It's too soon for any woman to make Brad smile. I'm sure I'm acting selfish here, but it's a feeling I can't control, and I don't need Bridget distracting Brad away from our kids right now.

After my still shirtless husband says goodbye to the eager homewrecker and closes the door, I stick my head out. "They're just fine, no need to come and clean, or come anytime, really, ya hear?" I mimic her sickly-sweet southern accent and wish like hell she could hear me. But Bridget doesn't turn. Instead, she saunters to her car and drives away.

—

AFTER A WEEK at home, Brad insists the kids go back to school. At seven, he notices they're all still in bed when they should be pulling out of the driveway. The tornado hits, but this time, Brad's not in the eye; he's in the whirling storm, and visibly frazzled.

"Let's go, let's go, let's go!" he says clapping his hands.

"I can't find my sweater," Jazzy says.

"You'll have to go without it. You're already late."

"But I haven't had breakfast."

Brad retrieves a granola bar from the pantry and hands it to her. "Here."

"I don't like these."

"Then don't eat. You need to go," he says, nearly pushing her to the door.

Edward and Ivy zoom down the stairs and out the door, not even saying goodbye to Brad.

"Hey! Don't forget your sister," he says as he gently nudges Jazzy out the door.

"My shoes!" Jazzy swiftly turns away from the door and sprints toward the kitchen.

Brad lowers his head. "Same shit, different day," he says under his breath before beginning his own search for her shoes.

Once her shoes, the pink ones she wore for the funeral and not her proper school shoes, are located under the family room couch, he watches Jazzy hop into the car before Edward darts out of the driveway. He closes the door, leans his hands against the thick wood and lets out a frustrated growl before pushing away from the door. He packs up his laptop, grabs his keys, and heads out of the house. I should follow him to work and make sure he's all right. But, with no way to get home on my own, the best place for me is right here. I'll be around when the kids return. They'll need me, or rather, I'll need them.

—

IT'S SO QUIET. I can't ever remember being in the house when it lacked chaos and the echo of life bouncing off the walls and into my ears. Even when I was alive and alone in the house, there was always the sound of the dishwasher, washing machine or some other device filling the empty space. Now, I can hear the soft sounds of the house itself; the creaks of the settling frame, the hum of a left-on light, the whoosh of the furnace as it blows warm air around the empty house. My hearing is hypersensitive. Maybe this is what it's like to be a dog. Does Buddy hear the same things I do?

I need to test my presence, see what I can and can't do. Last time I checked I couldn't persuade anything in the physical world. But my increased ability to differentiate between Brad's and the kids' unique heartbeats could mean I'm connecting with them on a deeper level that will eventually lead to a physical reunion. I run my hands through the thin, dated drapes in the living room, but they don't move. Each time I try, my hands flow directly through the fabric, not even creating a slight shift or sway. Nothing I attempt to touch, no matter how hard I concentrate, is influenced by me.

When I test my mobile ability, it's clear I don't possess the lightning speed like those vampires in the movies. I can't move any faster than when I was alive, and I can't snap my fingers and be transported to where I want to go. Instead, I must travel the same as everyone else. When I sit, I don't make an indentation on the cushion. It's like I'm not really here. Where are my ghost, or whatever I am, perks? There should be at least some. Instead, I have no presence here. I can't affect anything, so why would I possibly be here if I can't control the physical world around me?

Buddy follows me around the house. I'm unsure if he can see me, but it sure seems like he at least senses me. He usually sleeps all day, but he walks next to me as I move from room to room. The house is a mess. The kids have mostly been living in their rooms for the past two weeks.

I'm about to go upstairs to the kids' rooms when the rumble of the garage door stops me. Maybe Brad decided to work from home today. The door to the garage opens and in pops Bridget in a sunny yellow, form-fitting, V-neck top and black leggings. Her perfectly painted face and loose ponytail look like she's about to go out on a casual date. She can't possibly think Brad will be home.

Buddy barks at her twice and then wags his tail as he greets her with an affectionate nudge. Some attack dog, he is.

Bridget leans forward and pets him, her tatas in full view. "Aww, you're such a handsome boy," she says in a high-pitched, syrupy voice. "Are you going to be my helper?"

Bridget moves to the kitchen and surveys the carnage of

what weeks without anyone giving a shit can do. It doesn't look much different than when she was here yesterday, except for another bag of trash on the floor and a few new dirty plates added to the counter. I think Brad's going to need a housekeeper or they might end up on an episode of *Hoarders*.

She peers under the sink, moving around the cleaning supplies. "Ah-ha!" she says pulling out my yellow rubber gloves. She grabs a trash bag, also under the sink, and goes to the refrigerator. She takes a deep breath before opening the door. Her face dons a permanent scrunch as she plucks items from the fridge, checks them and throws them in the bag. She lifts the lid of a plastic container and gags, and I can't help but be delighted at her misery and my inability to smell. I suppose I could consider this as a ghost perk.

In less than fifteen minutes, she has cleared the fridge of everything spoiled or questionable. She rinses the containers she can salvage, loads the dishwasher and starts it. I'm ready for her to leave, ready to have my house back and her out of it, but she continues cleaning with the energy of a barista after her fifth shot of espresso. She clears off the counters and wipes them down before taking the bags of trash out to the bin.

When she returns, she opens the junk drawer and goes through it, testing pens, throwing out the ones that don't work, and organizing everything. Once she's done with the drawer, she floats from room to room, tidying up, putting things away that I'm sure no one will ever find again.

She enters the master bedroom and pauses as she looks at the disheveled bed. She doesn't belong in here; she's invading my domain and now her scent, which I'm sure is strong and flowery, is overpowering what is left of me in this room. She makes the bed, dusts the side tables and picks up the clothes on the floor, adding more of her scent to everything she touches. Already, I'm being replaced.

—

UNABLE TO CONTINUE watching Bridget leave her essence around *my* house, I retreat upstairs. I enter Jazzy's cheery room decorated in rainbows and butterflies. Barbie dolls, stuffed animals, and princess dress-up clothes that once filled her shelves and bins now conceal the worn carpet. Her small round table's set for a tea party. Only three months past her sixth birthday, she's still young enough to believe there's mostly only good in the world. Like Edward and Ivy, it won't be long before she believes differently.

There are pieces of paper everywhere, notes to me and God:

> *Dear Mommy,*
> *I hope you are happy and having fun in heaven. Do*
> *you see angels? Is everyone nice there? Can you give*
> *my hamster Skylar a kiss for me? I love you and I*
> *miss you soooo much! Love, Jazzmatazz.*

> *Dear God,*
> *Why did you have to take Mommy to heaven?*
> *Grandma said it was because you needed more*
> *angels, but I think it is because you want to taste her*
> *yummy cooking. Could you send her here to visit?*
> *Love, Jasmine Blackwell*

I have the urge to clean her room, to put everything in order like it was before, but the impossibility of this task reaches further than putting a few toys back on their shelves, and if I could weep, her toys would float in my tears.

I leave Jazzy's room and enter Ivy's. Clothes are everywhere, some stacked in knee-high piles. I haven't taken a good look at this room in months, and now I know why. Not only is there nowhere to walk, but it could pose a fire hazard. Gone are the Disney posters and American Girl dolls. Instead, posters of bands I've never heard of drape the teal walls; some look questionable and eerily dark. Mountains of makeup take over her desk which no longer shows signs of being used for homework.

Peeking out from one of the piles of clothes are shorts of the very *short* variety and a cropped, see-through black tank top I've never seen. And there it is, the red, low-cut bandage dress that comes just below the butt cheeks—the dress she'd borrowed from a friend and I'd told her there was no way on God's green Earth she'd ever be allowed to wear. I should've said, "Over my dead body," because then I'd understand why it's in her possession. It appears to have been worn. White deodorant stains reside under the armholes and I can't imagine when or where she would have sported it.

I need to be honest with myself for once. Ivy never received the attention from me she deserved. Compared to Edward, she was easy. Edward consumed so much of my time, and then, when Jazzy came along and devoured the remainder of what I had, there was almost nothing left for Ivy; scraps. Ivy got the scraps. I can't blame her for finding attention elsewhere, for spending more time at her friends' homes than here where she probably felt invisible.

I knew a girl who felt invisible, whose parents were too consumed in their own lives to worry about their only child. I know how hopelessly empty she was, how she searched to fill that growing void, for the attention she so desperately craved. She was so hungry for attention it didn't matter who gave it to her; back-stabbing friends, abusive boyfriends, low-life bosses.

She learned the hard way that it's nearly impossible to shake the feeling of being invisible once you've been treated that way. She could never shake that feeling.

I've made Ivy invisible. I did this, and now I'll never be able to fix it.

Deciding I haven't been tortured enough, I head to Edward's room at the end of the hall. A trail of ants feast on a stash of dishes on his floor. Both his dirty *and* clean clothes are strewn across the carpet, his usual mode of clothing storage. I don't even know why I bothered buying him a new dresser six months ago; he doesn't use it, at least not for clothes.

Eight model fighter jets hang from the ceiling. When he was younger, he spent hours at the kitchen table building each one, paying attention to every detail. My memory retreats to when his passion for the Air Force began, on a sunny October day at the Miramar Air Show. Even I got caught up in the thrill of the jets flying overhead, the sound of immense power vibrating through my body.

"I'm going to fly one of those someday," Edward had said, pointing to one of them.

"You want to fly fighter jets?" I had asked.

"More than anything!"

It's been years since he's mentioned this dream. I don't know what he dreams of now. He doesn't seem like the same boy I held hands with that day at the air show, the boy who had hopes and dreams.

A hoard of papers, books, and empty Coke and Mountain Dew cans blanket his desk. There's a partially crumpled note tucked halfway under his calculus book. I try to read it, but some of the text is hidden, and I can't move the book out of the way.

*Hey Edweirdo the homo, you are a . . . Now that
your mom can't stick up for you, watch your . . .
You never know when . . . more than one way to
skin a cat.*

I'm certain he hasn't told Brad about this note, and I'm
pretty sure that little shit, Zane Goodman, sent it to him.
There's nothing *good* about Zane; he's been bullying Edward
for years. Every time I'd brought my concerns to Edward's first
school, the reply was always, "We have our hands tied. There's
no concrete evidence." Instead of letting Edward suffer while I
unsuccessfully begged for intervention, I moved Edward to a
different school in fifth grade. He was finally happy again, and
I could move on. I thought those days were behind him.

Zane transferred to Edward's high school his sophomore
year. I assumed Zane had grown out of his bullying ways and
Edward never indicated otherwise. The last time I received a
call from the school regarding an altercation with Zane, it was
what I considered fair play or Edward "holding his own." I
brushed it off like a few harmless crumbs, thrilled Edward was
sticking up for himself. But that last detention I signed the day
of my accident set off my internal momma bear alarm, and
these letters prove that Zane is once again torturing Edward.
And, just like with Ivy, there's nothing I can do to fix it.

There's a lot about my children I don't know. Somehow,
they've grown up without me being present. Where was I?
How could I have missed so much? How did I not know
Edward still struggles with Zane, or that Ivy has morphed into
the invisible, attention-seeking child I, myself, could never
escape? I had no idea what was happening under my own roof
as I went on with my busy life, trying to fill my own void. It was
my one job, and I've failed miserably.

Chapter Nine

The moan of the garage door breaks me out of my punishing thoughts. Thank God, Bridget's leaving, I can have my house back.

"Jasmine, you need to calm down," Brad says as he enters the house and I head downstairs.

Jazzy's breathing heavy. Her eyes are barely open as she struggles to pull in breaths.

Bridget rushes to them. "What happened? Jazzy, what's wrong, sweetheart?"

I'm too concerned about Jazzy to dwell on Bridget's choice of words.

"She had a difficult day at school. She just needs some rest," Brad says. "Let's get you on the couch. You can watch TV, okay?" He settles her on the beat-up tan leather couch and drapes the fuzzy purple blanket loaded with dog hair over her.

"I . . . can't . . . breathe . . . Daddy. Maybe . . . I'm dying," she says through her uneven breaths.

"You're not dying. You're having a panic attack. You'll be fine. Good as new."

Bridget brings Jazzy a glass of water. She sits on the edge of the couch and rubs my daughter's arm. Conflict erupts in my mind, and I try to push it away. I should be grateful Bridget's comforting Jazzy, but this is my job. I'm her mother. I'm the one who should be caressing her face and telling her she's going to be okay, not Bridget. Especially not Bridget.

"If you need to go back to work, I can stay and take care of her," Bridget says.

"Thanks. I appreciate the offer, but I'll just work from home today." Brad scans the room. "The house looks amazing. You didn't need to do all this."

"It was nothing. I'll head out and let Jazzy rest. There's a load of towels in the dryer and dinner in the fridge. Feel better soon, Jazzy."

"Thanks for everything," Brad says.

"You're welcome. Anytime." She rubs his arm and stares into his eyes. They smile at one another before she unhooks her hand from his arm and lets herself out.

I sit on the edge of the couch and watch Jazzy breathe. Buddy's right at my heels.

"Hi, Buddy." Jazzy's breaths slow as she pets Buddy's furry head. "Wanna come up?" She pats the couch, and he jumps up and makes himself comfortable, resting his big head on her legs. "Thanks for being my buddy, Buddy."

—

AN ENDLESS LOOP of dysfunction plays at the house. It's day two of school, more than a week after the funeral, and the same chaos ensues as the kids get ready for school, sleeping too late, missing shoes, the rush out the door. And then, late morning, the garage door rumbles, and Brad and Jazzy enter the house. Jazzy, again, has difficulty breathing, and Brad, again, puts her on the couch and goes to his office. I wonder if taking her to the doctor or a therapist has crossed his mind.

I enter Brad's office while he's on the phone with his mom. With Mom and Dad Blackwell unable to travel anymore and being over two thousand miles away, phone calls are the only way of contact now.

"I don't know what's going on with her, but I can't keep leaving work," he says. "I know she's upset about Claire. I don't expect her to act like it never happened, but I'm barely getting any sleep because she's waking up in the middle of the night screaming. I don't know what to do." He closes his eyes and leans his head back.

"No, I haven't gotten the kids to a psychologist. When do I have time to do that? I have a company to help run." Brad's exhausted voice, the darkening bags under his eyes, and his thinning face make him appear as though he's aged five years in the last couple of weeks.

"You're right, I'll call and make an appointment," he says to my relief. "I'm fine, Mom, fine. Look, I need to get some work done. I'll call you tomorrow. Love you too. Bye." Brad hangs up, leans back in his chair, and rubs his face with his hands.

"Damn it. I don't even know who their doctor is. Where would you keep that info, Claire?"

He leaves his office and slogs to the kitchen. As he looks around for the doctor's information, I play the hot and cold game I used to play with the kids. "You're getting warmer," I say as he walks over to my overflowing basket sitting on the kitchen countertop. He rummages through it, picking up papers and scanning them before going to the next. "Warmer," I say, his hand brushing my address book that holds the kids' important information including the pediatrician's number.

"Hot, hot," I say when he puts his hand directly on it. He lifts the book and flips through the pages until he comes to the back of the book containing the business cards of all the services I've used.

"Well, wonders never cease. I actually found it." He returns to his office and picks up his phone. I want to tell him to put my address book back where he found it when he's done, but that doesn't really matter anymore. It's his; everything of mine is now his. He schedules an appointment for Jazzy later in the day with her pediatrician. I'm proud of Brad. I know how hard this is for him to admit he needs help, that the kids need help in getting through this and moving on.

—

I JOIN BRAD and Jazzy on their ride to the doctor's office.

"Am I going to get a shot?" Jazzy asks. Fear cracks in her voice.

"Probably not. You're not really sick."

"If I'm not sick, why do I need to go to a doctor?"

"Sometimes our head is sick or sad, and it makes it hard to do other things."

"Isn't your head sad, Daddy? Do you need to go to the doctor too?"

"Yes, my head's very sad. Maybe I need to see a doctor too. But first, let's take care of you, okay?"

Shortly upon arrival, we're ushered into the exam room. Probably the shortest wait I've ever had at this office. Brad firmly holds Jazzy's hand and swings it as if it will release the nerves in both of them. The nurse has Jazzy sit on the exam table and puts a thermometer in her mouth.

"I'm not sick."

"It's just procedure. We do this with all our patients," the nurse says. The thermometer beeps, and the nurse looks at it. "Yep, no temperature."

"See?" Jazzy says.

"Jazzy, calm down a little, okay?" Brad flashes the nurse an apologetic raise of his eyebrows.

"I'll let the doctor know you're waiting," the nurse says and leaves the room.

Unable to successfully pace in the small room, Brad studies the anatomy pictures on the walls as he chews on his lower lip. I can't remember Brad ever taking any of the kids to the doctor. In his eighteen years of being a parent, he's never had to deal with our children's health concerns. Every fever, rash, wart, and immunization had been handled by me. Each time the kids needed a shot, I was the one who held them down while hot tears threatened to spill forth as they begged, "Please, Mommy, don't let them hurt me, please."

"Mr. Blackwell, I'm Dr. Sanchez," the short, dark-haired woman in a crisp, white smock says, entering the room and extending her hand. She's at least a foot shorter than Brad, and her naturally calm demeanor visibly relaxes him.

"Nice to meet you," he says.

"Jazzy, what seems to be the trouble today?" she asks.

"She's not sleeping. She has these nightmares I can't wake her from, and she's having problems at school where she can't breathe, and I have to pick her up," Brad says in one rushed breath.

"I see." She looks in Jazzy's eyes with her little flashlight. "If it's okay with you, Mr. Blackwell, I'd like Jazzy to tell me. I always encourage my patients to tell me rather than the parents." She cups her hand around her mouth as though she's telling a secret to Brad. "I only speak kid language," she says loud enough for Jazzy to hear and winks at Brad.

"Got it," he says.

"So, not sleeping well, huh?" the doctor asks.

"I'm sleeping fine, but Daddy keeps waking me up. One night, he poured water on me."

"He did? Well, what's going on at school?" she asks while casually listening to Jazzy's lungs with her stethoscope.

"I miss Mommy, and sometimes when I think of her, I get really sad, and then I feel like I can't breathe." Tears slide down her face.

"I heard about your mom. I'm so sorry. That has to be very difficult for you."

Dr. Sanchez sits on the exam table next to Jazzy. She places her hand on Jazzy's knee and pats it. "You know, my mom died when I was eight. I was just a little older than you."

Jazzy's eyes light up as she looks at Dr. Sanchez. It's as though they both belong to some secret club, the "My Mommy's Dead" club I wish she never had to belong to.

"For real?" Jazzy asks.

"Yep. And I missed her a lot, just like you."

"But you look happy." Jazzy looks confused.

"I'm a lot older now. But, when I was little, I didn't think I would ever be able to live without her."

"How did you get fixed?"

"I said a lot of prayers, and I made sure I did one thing every day that made me happy."

"What kind of things?"

"Anything that made me laugh or feel better, like watching a funny movie, drawing a pretty picture, eating my favorite ice cream, or jumping on a trampoline. All those things made me feel normal and for a while, happy."

"But then you were sad again?"

"At first, yes. But after a while, I was less sad and more happy. Does that make sense?"

Jazzy nods.

"Good." Dr. Sanchez pulls out a prescription pad from her smock pocket and writes something down before handing the piece of paper to Jazzy. "Here's a prescription for you. You must do something that makes you happy every day for thirty days or as needed. And, whatever you do, you must not skip a dose," she says. "Let me know if you need a refill."

Dr. Sanchez writes another prescription and hands it to Brad.

"Here's a seven-day prescription to help her calm down and hopefully ease some of her anxiety. I only want you to use it for the next few days, just to give her a chance to get some sleep and get through the rest of the school week. I'll call you on Friday to see how she's doing."

"Thank you."

"She'll be okay. She needs time to sort things out. Kids are resilient. I'll have my nurse give you a list of child psychologists who deal specifically with parental loss. I encourage you to make an appointment sooner than later."

—

WHEN WE RETURN from the pharmacy, Brad's in a hurry to get the medication in Jazzy's system. It's interesting that he's so hasty to medicate, considering how much he fought me on medicating Edward for his ADD years ago. Funny how, when *he's* forced to deal with it, it's easier to provide the "quick fix."

He immediately gets a glass of water for Jazzy and pulls a pill out of the bottle.

"Here, take this," he says.

"What do I do with it?"

"You swallow it."

"I've never swallowed a pill before. Mommy always gave me liquid medicine."

Brad combs his fingers through his hair.

"It's easy. You just put it on the back of your tongue and swallow some water with it."

Jazzy narrows her eyes.

"Try it. Really, it's easy." He hands her the glass of water. Jazzy places the pea-sized pill on her tongue and makes a disgusted face. "Good, now, take a big drink of water to wash it down."

She takes a swig and tries to swallow but gags and spits the pill and all the water onto the kitchen floor.

"What's the problem?" Brad raises his voice.

"It got stuck. It won't go down."

"Let's try it again." He picks the pill up off the floor. It's already falling apart. He throws the pill in the garbage and retrieves another one from the bottle and hands it to her. "Remember, put it in the back of your mouth, as far back as you can, and then take a quick drink."

The second try is as unsuccessful as the first.

"Jazzy, you don't need to make this so difficult."

"I'm sorry, Daddy," she says and cries.

"It's okay. I shouldn't have raised my voice. Let me see if there's a better way to do this."

Brad scans Google on his phone. There are oodles of hits on how to teach children to swallow pills, and he lets out short puffs of air from his lips as he clicks on different sites.

"Okay, sweetheart, let's try taking the pill with your favorite juice. That should work." He pulls the juice out of the refrigerator.

"How about some OJ?" She puts a new pill on her tongue and takes a drink and immediately coughs and gags.

"Let's try it with food." He takes a small piece of soft bread and places the pill in the middle and gives it to her along with her glass of juice.

After a couple of seconds, she jumps up and down. "I did it, Daddy. I did it." She opens her mouth to show him it's gone.

"Good job, Jazz."

—

FOR THE PAST few hours, I've watched Jazzy go from a happy, bouncy little girl to a completely zoned out blob in front of the television.

"Time for bed, Jazz," Brad says. Jazzy doesn't say a word as she slides off the couch and lumbers upstairs to her room. With her day clothes still on, she climbs into bed.

Brad tucks her in while she yawns.

"Daddy, do you think Mommy's watching us?"

"I don't know, but you know she's right here," he says pointing to her heart.

"Yeah, but I heard they watch us. Like Santa Claus."

"Who's they?"

"The dead people who love us. I hope they're right. I hope Mommy's watching us. I hope she sees how good I'm trying to be for her. I don't want her to be mad at me."

"Jazzy, Mommy would never be mad at you. I'm sure she's very proud of you."

"If she saw me yell at Camille at school yesterday, she wouldn't be proud. She'd be mad."

"Why did you yell at Camille?"

"Because she told me I was a crybaby."

"Mommy would be proud you stuck up for yourself." Brad pulls the covers to her chin. "It's time to get some sleep. See you in the morning."

"Good night, Daddy. I love you."

"I love you too." He places a lingering kiss on her forehead before leaving her room.

Jazzy pulls her hands together and prays. I sit at the foot of her bed, gazing at her sweet, moonlit face.

"Hi, God, it's me, Jazzy again. How's Mommy? I really, really, really miss her, but I don't want to tell Daddy and make him sad. I'd do anything to have her back. I would keep my room clean forever and sell all my stuffed animals and put all my money in the Sunday basket if you let Mommy come back. Please?"

An overwhelming surge travels through me, a feeling of warmth I haven't experienced before.

"Mommy? Is that really you?" Jazzy says. She's looking right at me.

"Can you see me?" I ask, not thinking it's possible.

How do I know this is real? The medicine could be altering something where she sees and hears me, but it's only an illusion, a coincidence. I'm overthinking this. I'm here, and she sees me! How long? How much time do I have with my baby girl?

"I knew it! I knew you were here all the time." Jazzy gets to her knees and bounces on the bed. Finally, someone can hear me and better yet, see me. I'm making some kind of unmeasurable progress, but for what, I have no idea. Jazzy reaches for me to wrap her arms around my neck but falls right through me.

"How come I can't touch you?"

"I don't know. But you can see me, right?"

Jazzy nods.

"And you can hear me?"

She nods again.

"Then that's pretty special, isn't it?"

Jazzy's bright face changes to worry. "But we gave away your heart. What are you going to do without it?"

"I guess I don't need it if I'm here without it, do I?"

"Are you mad we gave your heart away?"

"Oh no. I'm so proud of you for making that decision. I'm happy someone else has it. I know how hard that was for all of you to make, but you did the right thing."

Jazzy's concern melts from her face. "Whew! I'm glad because I don't think the people would like it too much if we told them we needed it back," she says. "We need to go tell Daddy you're here!" She climbs out of bed.

"Let's wait a while for that, Jazz. I don't know if Daddy will be able to see me yet. Why don't we keep it between you and me for now."

"Like a secret? 'Cause you don't like it when I keep secrets."

"More like a surprise. We'll save it for a special time, okay?"

"I love surprises, and this is a really, *really* big one. Maybe we could blow up balloons and put up streamers, like a birthday party."

"You always have such great ideas."

"Mommy?"

"Yes, Jazzmatazz?"

"What's Heaven like?" She yawns and struggles to keep her heavy lids from closing.

"I don't really know, sweetheart. I haven't gotten there yet."

I wish I had an answer to Jazzy's question so I can tell her how wonderful it is, but I can't lie. And I certainly wouldn't want to tell her that maybe I'm in Hell. But Jazzy being able to see and hear me is changing my thoughts on where I am and why.

Jazzy falls asleep before I even finish the sentence, but there's a smile on her face, a pure smile I've missed seeing. She hugs tight to Pink Kitty as the rest of her body relaxes. How amazing. Jazzy can see and hear me. Will the rest of the family be able to do the same? Morning can't come fast enough. I want to talk to my family. There's so much I need to tell Brad.

Chapter Ten

I t's six in the morning. I couldn't help but watch Jazzy sleep most of the night. Jazzy didn't have one night terror, and even though I'm sure the medicine helped, my appearance transformed her back into her bouncy, happy self. I hum Journey's *Don't Stop Believin'* as I watch the sun make its debut outside Jazzy's east-facing window.

"Mommy, you're still here!"

"Did you have a good sleep?"

"Very good." Jazzy hops out of bed. "I'm going to get ready for school," she says. "Will you come to school with me today?"

"Sure. I'd love to see what you do all day at school."

"This is gonna be fun." She hurriedly puts on her uniform, which I'm grateful she wears to school every day. Jazzy's fashion sense ... well, she has none, really. I always marveled at the outfit or combination of clothes she'd don before descending the stairs on nonschool days. She reminds me of a modern-day Pippi Longstocking.

I follow Jazzy downstairs.

"Can you make me some oatmeal?" she asks.

"I'm afraid I can't do that. I can't seem to touch anything."

"That's okay. I learned to make it myself, but your oatmeal is better than mine."

Buddy circles me. He nudges my leg, but I can't feel it, and I don't think he can feel it either.

"Jazzy, why don't you turn off the alarm and let Buddy out."

"I don't know how."

"I'll teach you."

I instruct Jazzy how to punch in the code on the panel by the door, and it chimes indicating it's now disarmed.

"Cool. Come on, Buddy. Go outside." She opens the door and lets him out. "Can you teach me more things, Mommy?"

"Sure, what do you want to learn?"

"How to cook pancakes."

"I think I can do that."

I direct Jazzy around the kitchen, telling her which bowls to use, what ingredients to measure, and how to turn on the stove. Jazzy does an excellent job pouring the batter onto the griddle. I'm excited to teach her all the things I didn't when I was alive.

"Jazzy! What are you doing?" Brad says as he enters the kitchen.

"Hi, Daddy. I'm making breakfast." Her face is covered with flour and pride.

"No, no, no, this is too dangerous," Brad says, turning off the stove.

"Hey, what're you doing?"

"You can't just come into the kitchen and start cooking without an adult. You could burn the house down."

"I have an adult. Mommy's helping me." She looks over at me. I shake my head and raise my finger to my lips reminding her of our secret. "She taught me before she died. I wanted to surprise you."

"She taught you?" Brad asks. A large dose of skepticism fills his voice, which is completely understandable. I never took time out to teach the kids anything around the house. It was always easier to do it myself than to show them and then redo it because they didn't complete it correctly. But now I can change all of that. I'm going to teach them everything I can.

"And remember my perscrip—you know, what the doctor gave me? She told me to do at least one thing that makes me happy every day. Making pancakes makes me happy."

"I'm glad it makes you happy. Let me help you finish," Brad says.

Once the pancakes are done, Brad marches up the stairs to wake Ivy and Edward. Thanks to the sweet scent of pancakes wafting up the stairs, they're quicker to rise and get ready. By 6:40, all the kids are downstairs and eating at the table. This is something that never happens in our home, so I inhale the moment in the hopes I can take the memory with me.

"What's Buddy's problem?" Ivy asks, irritated.

"What's he doing?" Brad asks.

"He keeps rubbing his face in that chair and wagging his tail. It's like he's possessed or something."

"That's 'cause Mommy's sitting there," Jazzy says and then slaps her hand over her mouth. Everyone looks at her like antlers just spouted out of her head.

"That's not even funny," Ivy says.

"Well, it's true. I wasn't supposed to tell you, but she's here. She's sitting in that chair watching us right now." Jazzy looks at me and shrugs. I knew it would be hard for Jazzy to keep this to herself.

"Dad, seriously, there's something wrong with her." Ivy rolls her eyes and rises from the table. Edward doesn't say a word as he finishes his food and takes his plate to the sink.

"Jazzy, maybe you should keep stuff like that to yourself, so you don't upset your sister," Brad says. He studies the seat I'm sitting in. He must want to believe I'm here, but he doesn't see me.

"Yeah, sure. Mommy's and my secret," Jazzy says. "But you believe me, don't you?"

Brad takes a moment before answering. I can hear him grinding his teeth as he thinks of a response.

"Sure, Jazz, I believe you," he finally says. "Now go and brush your teeth."

—

I CLIMB INTO the car with the kids. Okay, I don't need to climb; I kind of float. I sit in the back seat with Jazzy while Edward and Ivy are up front.

"Mommy, put your seatbelt on," Jazzy says in a whisper.

"I don't think I need one of those."

"Yes, you do." Jazzy gets on her knees and reaches over to grab the seatbelt. She attaches it and then sits down and puts on her own.

"What are you doing?" Ivy asks.

"Nothing."

The music blares within the enclosed space. How can Edward focus on driving with the electronic thump of the music pounding wildly in his ears?

"Isn't that music a little loud?" I ask Jazzy.

"I'm used to it. He does this all the time."

Edward's speed is too fast as he zooms around cars and narrowly avoids hitting a car slowing down for a right turn.

"Tell him to slow down," I say to Jazzy.

"Edward, Mom says to slow down."

Edward's squinting eyes are visible in the rear-view mirror.

"What the hell?" he says. Ivy turns and glares at her.

Jazzy shrugs. "I knew they wouldn't listen to me." She sinks back into her seat. "I'm so excited you're coming to school with me today." She lowers her voice, but Ivy looks back at her.

"I hope you don't do that at school. Everyone will think you're crazy," Ivy says.

"I'm not crazy. She's really here, honest." Jazzy crosses her heart with her hand.

"Just stop with that. It's not funny. Don't be a freak," Ivy says.

Jazzy quiets and tears form in her eyes.

"It's okay, Jazzy. Your sister's just upset. She didn't mean it," I say, but the tears fall from Jazzy's eyes and down her cheeks.

"I'm not a freak!" Jazzy shouts at Ivy.

"Yeah, okay, whatever you say, *freak*."

There's a burning in my chest followed by an excruciating ache. It's hard to understand why such hurtful words are thrown around like dice at a craps table, especially with all they've been through. They should protect each other, understand each other's pain. If Ivy could hear me, I would let her have it and tell her how much Jazzy needs her.

When we reach Jazzy's school, Edward pulls up at the designated drop-off curb and gets out of the car to help Jazzy with her backpack. He leans over and whispers in her ear, "You're not a freak. Don't listen to Ivy, okay? Have a great day at school." He pats her on the head before getting back into the car and driving away.

Another *ghost* perk, this one far better than not being able to smell the rotten fridge. Not only can I hear Edward's heart, but I can also see it. I had no idea it was filled with such compassion and love for his little sister. All I ever saw was how he ignored her, ignored all of us from day to day. Yet, here he is, showing Jazzy how much he loves her. Ivy doesn't even look at her sister, her blue eyes glued to her phone as though her entire world resides in that small rectangular, I-wish-they-were-never-invented device. Maybe she just needs time.

I accompany Jazzy to her classroom. She keeps her head down as she walks, not looking at the other kids who pass by.

"Good morning, Jazzy," her teacher says.

Jazzy's face perks up. "Hi, Ms. Walters."

"Well, you seem happy today," Ms. Walters says, looking too put-together and fresh for this time of the morning. She's dressed in a rather stylish burgundy pencil skirt and blazer combo with black pumps. Her light, sandy, shoulder-length hair is pulled into a sleek, low ponytail.

"Yes. My—" Jazzy starts to say, but I place my finger on my lips. "Just in a good mood today, that's all."

"I'm so glad to hear that. Why don't you get ready. The bell's going to ring soon."

"Yes, Ms. Walters."

The kids stream into the classroom, and when the bell rings, they all file into a crooked line by the door and make their way outside for flag salute. I trail at the back of the string of children, but Jazzy is toward the front and holds out her hand, wanting me to walk with her. I shake my head and gesture for Jazzy to continue with her classmates. She presses her lips tightly together and raises her eyebrows as she waves me up.

"What are you doing?" one of the kids asks.

"Nothing. Stupid bugs," Jazzy says and pretends to swat them away.

The students pray and recite the Pledge of Allegiance followed by the announcements. When they return to their classroom, Jazzy sits at her desk, and I occupy the chair at a desk next to her, where a classmate, Cameron, tries to sit.

"Hey, you can't sit there. My mom's sitting there."

"What are you talking about?" Cameron says.

"My mom. She's in your seat, and now you're squishing her. Get up!"

"That's crazy," he says. He stays in his seat and gets his pencil case out of his desk.

I get up and lean over toward Jazzy. "It's okay. I'll sit somewhere else. Remember, it's our little secret, right?"

"Oh yeah. Sorry, Mommy."

"Who are you talking to?" Cameron asks.

"No one."

"You're weird," he says and goes back to focusing on his desk work.

At recess, Jazzy follows me around the field.

"You should go play with your friends."

"Nope, I just want to be with you."

Together, we watch the boys on the field tackle each other, time after time as though they are on replay. I often wondered how some of my friends with a brood of sons stayed sane. Their boys never remained still, and it would drive me to near madness to watch them. My friends probably consumed more alcohol than I did when their boys were little, though I think I caught up when Ivy became a tween.

After recess, we head to the auditorium for a special presentation. All the students are seated in rows on the floor. Jazzy sits and pats the floor next to her for me to take a seat. Before I arrive, another girl with long burnt-orange ringlets and a full face of freckles stands in the spot Jazzy has already reserved for me.

"You can't sit here. I'm saving it for my mom."

"Your mom? Didn't she die?"

"I said you can't sit here." Jazzy's face reddens, and her wide eyes shrink into slits. She gets to her feet and pushes the girl so hard the girl falls on two kids already sitting on the floor.

Ms. Walters runs to the girls. "What's going on here?"

"She pushed me." The girl points at Jazzy.

Ms. Walters crouches. "Is that true? Did you push Katie?"

"Yes, but she sat in my mom's spot." Jazzy puts her hands on her hips. "Why didn't you just listen?"

"Even if your mom was here, you can't save spots—it's the rules," Katie says.

"Oh yeah, well, you're just rude." Jazzy leans in, her face close to Katie's.

"Well, you're double rude."

"Girls, that's enough. Jazzy, apologize to Katie for pushing her," Ms. Walters says.

"But I'm not sorry."

"Jazzy, come with me." Ms. Walters takes hold of Jazzy's arm and guides her out of the auditorium. "What just happened in there?" she asks once they're outside.

"She took my mom's seat and was being rude."

"Jazzy, that wasn't nice of you to do. You could have hurt her. You need to apologize."

Jazzy looks at me. My presence is causing more harm than good.

"Your teacher's right. You need to apologize. I don't think me being here is a good idea. I'm going to go until school's out, so you don't get into any more trouble, okay? I'll be waiting for you after school."

"No, Mommy, you can't leave." Jazzy reaches for me. The teacher tilts her head and scrunches her face.

"Jazzy, you don't seem yourself today. I think we need to call your dad and have him pick you up," Ms. Walters says. "Let's go to the office and give him a call."

"Fine with me," Jazzy says. Brad's not going to be happy about picking her up early from school, *again*.

—

JAZZY'S LEGS DANGLE from one of the office chairs. I take a seat next to her while I listen to the brief phone conversation between Ms. Walters and Brad. After Ms. Walters hangs up the phone, she gives Jazzy that, *you poor child* look.

"Your dad's on his way. Ms. Mills will be here in the office to watch you until he arrives. I know this has been a hard time for you. Maybe we'll see you tomorrow?"

Jazzy lowers her head while a tear rolls down her face. After her teacher leaves, she cries harder.

"Daddy's going to be so mad at me," she says.

"He's not going to be mad at you. He's going to be worried, that's all. You need to stop talking to me around other people, sweetheart, or they're going to think there's something wrong with you."

"But I can't. I want to talk to you. I want to tell you everything."

"And that makes me so happy, but some people won't understand."

"How come only *I* can see you?"

"I don't know. I heard somewhere that children are more capable of seeing angels and spirits, so maybe that's why."

"Then why don't *all* the kids here see you?"

"I really don't know," I say wishing I knew the answer to that question.

Brad enters the office. He presses his lips together while he scratches the back of his neck.

"Jasmine, what's wrong now?" he asks.

"I guess I'm having another bad day, Daddy."

"That makes two of us now." He signs her out. "Let's go. I have a meeting in twenty minutes."

"Mr. Blackwell, could I have a word with you?" a voice says from the principal's office. Brad rolls his eyes and then checks his watch.

"I don't have much time," he says.

"It will only take a minute." Principal Fry gestures for Brad to enter her office. "Jasmine, your father will be right out."

I enter the office with Brad. Principal Fry walks around her desk and takes a seat. She steeples her aged, rail-thin fingers and places them under her chin. Her dark, wide-set eyes and heart-shaped nose remind me of a seal.

"Mr. Blackwell, I know you've been through a terribly tragic event, as has Jasmine. I can understand there's a transition period while you all deal with your loss, but I am greatly concerned for your daughter. She hasn't been to school on time in weeks. There are days when she misses the beginning of a lesson, and then the teacher has to take time out to show her independently."

"I understand. We'll work on getting her here on time." Brad glances at his watch again, and his right knee starts to bounce. This was always my job, meeting with the school's administrators. Any time I'd asked Brad if he could join me, he'd used his job to excuse himself. But I learned from his mother, that he was quite the rebellious pupil who made multiple trips to the principal's office until he pulled his act together in high school. It's hard to believe Brad was ever a troublemaker with how disciplined and level-headed he is today. I would laugh at his mother's stories and tell her she was pulling my leg, but then his father would confirm them, and Brad would sport that guilty-as-charged look on his face. I would once again be mildly shocked and highly intrigued to learn there was a bit of a wild side to my husband.

"That's not all, Mr. Blackwell." Principal Fry looks at Brad sternly. "Before today, she had panic attacks. Now she's telling everyone her mother is here with her, that she can physically see her. She pushed a girl down today for trying to sit in a spot she had saved for her mother."

"I'm sure this is one of her ways of coping. The doctor put her on some medicine, so maybe it's making her see things that aren't there." Brad's face reddens and sweat forms on his forehead.

"We can't have it here at school. If this continues, she'll need to stay home until she gets this under control. It's causing too much of a disruption," Principal Fry says.

I want Brad to find his wild side right now and stick up for Jazzy. He needs to ask, no, demand accommodations like a counselor who can talk with her. We pay a shit-load of money, given up vacations and house repairs for a private, nurturing education for our kids. The least they can do is offer to help Jazzy rather than send her home. They can't possibly think, with time alone, Jazzy will return to her old, pre-accident self.

"I apologize for the problems you're having with Jazzy. I'll talk to her about this, and she'll be better tomorrow." He gets up and exits the office.

"Mr. Blackwell," Principal Fry says. Brad turns at the door. "We do care about Jasmine, but we also have to protect the other students. I hope you understand."

I don't understand and neither should Brad. *Protect* them? What happened today was an isolated incident. Jazzy wouldn't hurt anyone. She'd catch a spider and set it free rather than kill it. And I don't like Principal Fry's tone; she seems rather bitchy.

"No, not really."

Brad exits the office and Principal Fry follows.

"Jazzy, we hope to see you back here tomorrow," Principal Fry says. She looks at Jazzy's shoes. "And perhaps, when you come back, you can wear your black school shoes?"

"But these are special," Jazzy says.

"If I let you wear your special shoes, then I have to let all the kids wear their special shoes."

"Or maybe you can just tell the kids that her mom died, and these shoes make her feel better," Brad says, his voice both strained and irritated. "Come on, Jazzy. We need to go." He takes her hand and they leave.

The car ride is silent for the first five minutes. I'm next to Jazzy in the back seat. Brad drives the familiar roads to his office. He taps his right thumb on the steering wheel, which means he's deep in thought. I always knew not to say a word if he was tapping on the steering wheel, not to interrupt him while he stewed and stirred something around in his head.

"Daddy, can you turn the radio on?" Jazzy asks.

"No, I want it quiet. I need to think."

"About what?"

"About how I can't keep getting you from school every day. About how this may have cost the company an important customer. About how I'm going to be able to do all of this without..." He shakes his head. He must hear the sniffles from the back seat.

"I'm sorry, Daddy. I don't want you to get in trouble at work."

He takes a deep breath and exhales.

"It's not your fault. I didn't mean to yell," he says in a calm, apologetic voice. He reaches his right hand back through the seats and pats her knee. "It'll be all right."

"Do you believe in angels, Daddy?"

"Sure, do you?"

"Oh yes. Mommy's an angel." She looks at me and grins.

"I'm sure she is."

Chapter Eleven

"Why can't you come with me?" Jazzy asks me as she pushes around her spoon on the kitchen table. Brad's a few feet away making her breakfast.

"Come where?" Brad asks.

"I'm talking to Mommy, not you." She folds her arms in front of her chest with a defiant frown.

"I told you. I want to see what Ivy and Edward are up to at school."

"I don't know why you're whispering, Mommy. No one can hear you anyway."

Brad turns around and looks at Jazzy.

"That's enough of that. You can't be pretending to talk to your mom. We discussed this last night. If you do it again at school, they're going to send you home for a long time."

"It won't happen today because Mommy won't go to school with me. She's going to Edward and Ivy's school instead."

"What's going on?" Edward asks entering the kitchen.

"Mommy's going to school with you two today and not me."

"Huh, yeah right." Edward grabs his medicine out of the kitchen drawer. He takes five pills from the bottle and puts them in his pocket.

"Dad, I need more meds. I'm almost out."

"What medicine?" Brad asks.

"For my ADD, I need them. Mom always makes... made sure I had enough. I only have two left."

"Great. Leave the bottle on the counter. I'll see what I can do."

Ivy breezes into the kitchen. Her shirt and skirt are a wrinkled mess, and her face is caked with makeup. Her eyes have never been so dark, with smoky gray eyeshadow and thick black eyeliner.

"Whoa, what's with all the makeup?" Brad asks.

"What's wrong with it?" Ivy asks, clearly pissed at the question.

"It's a little much don't you think?"

"Yes, it certainly is," I say, relieved Brad's noticed.

"Mommy agrees with you, Daddy," Jazzy says.

Ivy turns to Jazzy, her face tense and her hands now fists.

"Would you stop with that, you little freak? She's not here. Mom is dead! Get that through your tiny skull and stop!" Buddy whimpers at Ivy's yelling and hides under the kitchen table.

Tears cascade down Jazzy's cheeks while Ivy stares at her as though she could kill Jazzy with her eyes if she tried hard enough.

"Ivy, that was not appropriate. Apologize to your sister." Brad places Jazzy's oatmeal in front of her and kisses the top of her head. She pushes the bowl away and gets up from the table.

"I'm not hungry." She runs from the room and yells, "You're so mean!"

"Why do I have to apologize? She's saying stupid things."

"She's going through a rough time, Ivy," Brad says.

"We're all going through a rough time. But making up stuff? Really?"

"Hey, let's go," Edward says. "Dad, don't forget my meds."

"I'll see what I can do."

After another frantic last-minute search for Jazzy's shoes, we all get into the car. Jazzy and Ivy are still upset. I look at Jazzy and put my finger to my lips. I don't want her to talk to me and upset Ivy anymore. I know how Ivy works. Popularity is the most important thing to her right now, and she's worried Jazzy will ruin all of that with her "Mommy sightings."

Ivy turns around and gives Jazzy the evil eye.

"If you can really talk to Mom, then tell her to butt out! I don't care what she thinks, got it?" Ivy turns back and gazes out the window. A single tear slips down her cheek that she swiftly wipes away.

Edward drops Jazzy off at school. He gets out of the car again and helps her with her large backpack. "Just keep it cool today, okay?"

"Mommy's watching you, so you better be good."

Edward shakes his head and gets back in the car and drives away.

"What, the, hell." Ivy says.

"She's losing it," Edward says.

"She's a fucking freak. I can't listen to her anymore. She's going to drive me insane."

We pass through a boxy, pristine neighborhood showcasing homes that look like carbon copies of each other yet cost at least twice as much as mine. Women push strollers in their form-fitting workout wear, runners dodge cars as they cross the street without barely a glance, and dogs bark incessantly at each other from across the street. A typical San Diego morning. It isn't until we exit the neighborhood and pass the packed drive-up Starbucks two miles down the main drag that Edward speaks.

"Did you ever think that maybe she *can* see Mom? What if we're all wrong?"

"Are you kidding me? She's delusional. I thought she was going to be normal, but she's turning out to be just as weird as you."

"You think I'm weird?" Hurt fills Edward's voice.

"Duh. You barely have any friends and play video games nonstop. You do that weird blinking thing that makes you look like you've got some mental illness. Yeah, I think you're weird. My friends think so too."

"You used to think I was cool. We used to do everything together."

"Yeah, but you changed."

"*I* changed? I think *you* changed. Always wanting to be popular."

"I don't want to be at the bottom of the food chain. Everyone wants to be popular. I just happen to *be* popular," Ivy says. "At least at school, people actually pay attention to me, like I'm a big deal, like I'm important."

I wish I could change this, turn back the clock and do things differently so Ivy didn't seek attention in a way that could potentially harm her. How could I let the same thing that happened to me happen to my own daughter? I can feel her emptiness just as I can feel how hard she's trying to fill it, to stuff herself with anything she can to make the painful void disappear.

"I don't want to be popular. I'd prefer to be invisible than be like you," Edward says.

"Well, you're doing a good job at that."

They pull into the school parking lot loaded with brand new BMWs and hand-me-down luxury Mercedes. I feel like I'm on the set of Beverly Hills 90210. Edward parks in his assigned space next to a sparkling white Range Rover. Ivy hops out and disappears in the mob of students making their way to the school gate.

Edward leaves the car running, as though he's going to leave, and takes a big breath. Frustration and a hint of sadness are etched on his face. I assume it's from his conversation with Ivy, but I'm not quite sure. He seems to be carrying some extra weight on his shoulders. There's a tap on his window, and Edward rolls it down.

"Hey," Edward says.

"You got 'em?" a clean-cut boy in school uniform asks.

Edward pulls out the five pills he'd stuffed into his pocket and holds out his hand to show the boy.

"Five? I wanted ten, dude."

"It's all I got right now. I'll give you the other half when I get more."

"I'm only paying you for five then."

"Fine." Edward holds out his other hand for the money.

The boy slaps two tens and a five in Edward's hand and grabs the pills.

"I'll be waiting for the other five," he says and walks away.

My heart I no longer possess, aches.

Edward shoves the money in his pocket and takes another long breath before turning off the car and pulling the key from the ignition. He exits the car and I follow him, trying to figure out why he would sell his medication and put himself in danger. If he gets caught, he'll be expelled or even arrested. What is he thinking?

He opens the trunk and snatches his backpack, but then stops. It takes him a short second to throw it back in the trunk, get into the car, and drive away, leaving me standing in the empty parking spot. Why didn't I get back in the car? Where in the hell is he going?

If I hadn't gotten out of the car, I'd be riding with him; I'd know where he's headed and what he's about to do. Dread's thick hold latches around my throat and threatens to strangle me. I have no control over this physical world. I can't pick up a phone. I can't yell for someone to stop him. I can't tell Brad or even have Jazzy tell Brad because he would never believe her. Then, God, why am I here?

—

I HEAD TO the school campus, hoping to find Ivy in the throng of perky, fresh-faced students. If I'd actually paid attention when Ivy got her schedule in August, I'd possibly know where her first class is. What is she taking this year? Geometry? English, World History? Biology? I have no clue. If I'd only paid more attention. Ivy was always so well behaved and such an attentive student there was never any reason to worry about her. I wasn't called into the principal's office or had to hold her down for an hour-long meltdown. Ivy's always had friends, and she kept herself busy with one activity or another. She was the opposite of her brother, who required much more of my time and energy every day. I believed Ivy was God's peace offering. A way of saying, "Sorry about the first kid. I'll make up for it this time."

Even though the kids wear uniforms, they all try their hardest to stand out with their multi-colored socks and shoes. The girls' skirts appear shorter than they should be, and I wonder if their mothers know they're hiking them up after they walk out the door. I'm certain, after seeing Ivy's makeup and hearing her in the car, she hikes hers up as well.

"Ivyyy!" Someone yells from across the common area. Ivy

emerges from a gathering outside the library and runs to the girl calling her.

"Ashley," Ivy says as she hugs her.

"You coming to my party on Friday? It's going to be lit."

"Wouldn't miss it."

"Zane Goodman's going to be there. You know he has the hots for you."

"Hmmm, your party's sounding better by the minute." Ivy's eyes brighten as she flashes her straight-toothed smile.

I must have heard that incorrectly. There's no possible way Ivy would even want to be in the same room as Zane knowing how cruel he's been to her brother for years. She knows all we've been through, icing black eyes and swollen lips, insisting on classroom changes, and ultimately moving Edward to a different school. No possible way.

"No parents either, they'll be in Palm Springs. Leaving Michael in charge." Ashley gives Ivy a knowing wink.

"Can't wait. Can I stay over?"

"Of course! Like always."

"Awesome. Gotta get to class. See you at lunch."

I finally get to be that fly on the wall as I join Ivy and endure the languid teaching in her first two classes. What happened to teachers teaching instead of telling the students to get on their iPads and work on an assignment they threw together the night before? The teacher in Ivy's first class gives them the assignment and then goes to her desk and surfs the internet. This is what I'm paying for? Only three out of twenty-six students work on the lame assignment, while the others chat on their iPads about the big party Friday night. How does the school have such high scores on their standard-ized tests when I can't see much learning happening? If I could,

I'd tell Brad to change Ivy and Edward's school. This is a waste of our money.

It's lunchtime and Edward's nowhere in sight. Ivy's familiar heartbeat pulses loudly while Edward's is nonexistent. He must not have returned after he left this morning. Ivy is so animated and happy interacting with her friends at the lunch table. No one would ever guess she buried her mother less than two weeks ago.

"What's going on with your sister, Ivy? My little brother said she's telling everyone that her mom's with her at school," one of the girls with straight, long blonde hair and a slight breakout on her tanned chin asks.

Ivy's face cocks in annoyance, but her eyes dart around the table as if she's assessing everyone's reaction. News travels fast through siblings, and there are still quite a few at the feeder school Jazzy attends. Last year one of the boys at Jazzy's school threw up in front of the class when he had to give an oral book report. Nearly overnight the news had spread to the high school, and the students were targeting the boy's brother saying, "Hey, what's up, Chuck?" or making it a point to dodge out of the way as they passed him in the halls. Ivy had told me how pathetic it was, really making a point of how they shouldn't be judged by who their siblings were or what they did. At that time Ivy was most likely touching on Edward, but now I worry about Jazzy too.

"She's just making it up, obviously. Trying to get out of school and all that."

"Weird," one of the other girls, another long-haired blonde, says.

"Yeah, like your brother, Edweirdo. How'd you get to be so normal?" another says. They all look so similar, like they're from the same family.

"Don't really know. I think I'm adopted," Ivy says. "So, what's the plan for the party?"

"Loads of alcohol and hot guys, that's the plan," Ashley says.

"You going to hook up with Zane Friday night?" one of the other girls asks. Now I wish I knew their names and who their parents are. These girls are not the same friends Ivy had in grade school. Back then, I knew Ivy's friends and their parents; many of the parents were good friends. But as the girls went their separate ways, sadly, so did the parents. I miss those days.

"He's going to drive me to the party. Look, he just sent me a text," Ivy says with a shit-eating grin.

"You'll give us the lowdown after, right?" says one of the others.

"Maybe. Depends on how good it is." Ivy raises her eyebrows, forcing me to walk away. I can't continue to listen to their plans, Ivy's intention to possibly do something she'll regret later. And worse, do it with the very boy who's bullying her brother. My chest aches again. I'm unsure if it's my brain remembering the feeling or if my ghostly body is actually feeling it, but it hurts, and I'm now filled with worry and regret. This is beginning to feel like an episode of "This is Your Life," or the devil's version of "A Christmas Carol" starring Claire Blackwell.

At the end of the school day, Edward is back in the parking lot waiting for Ivy. Ivy and I get into the car, and then we head to Jazzy's school. Ivy is on her phone while Edward visits another world inside his head, relaxed, different. Jazzy climbs into the car.

"Why are you all sweaty and gross?" Jazzy asks.

"I'm hot," Edward says.

Jazzy plugs her nose. "Yuck, it smells like stinky pits."

Ivy rolls down her window and Jazzy does the same.

Edward glances at Ivy with a curled lip as though he's irritated, yet his eyes reflect something entirely different—hurt.

Ivy scrunches her nose. "Don't you use deodorant?"

"Stop talking," Edward says, looking straight ahead.

"What's up with you?" Ivy asks, turning to take a closer look at Edward. "Did you even go to school?" She waits for a response, but Edward doesn't say anything. "Holy shit. You skipped school?"

"Stop talking," Edward says through clenched teeth.

"Fine, I don't really care what you do. If you're going to fuck up your life, that's your problem. Just leave me out of it."

"You said a bad word. I'm telling Dad!" Jazzy says.

"Go ahead. I don't fucking care!" Ivy says.

"I never invited you into it," Edward says.

Ivy crosses her arms and looks out the passenger window. "Fine."

Edward follows with his own "Fine," and it's over. All that bounces around the car now is the headache-inducing pound of Edward's electronic music.

His eyes droop as he drives and, as he blinks, his lids stay closed longer than they should.

"Jazzy, keep an eye out while Edward's driving. He seems a little tired and might not be paying attention." Jazzy can at least alert him if he swerves off the road since Ivy's eyes are glued to her phone.

Something's up with Edward, something serious. And now he's putting the girls and himself at risk. Why would he risk another tragedy? Is he self-destructing? Is my death too much for him? Is he punishing himself, because he thinks he caused my accident? Oh, dear Lord, please help me out here.

It has crossed my mind a few times as I'm subjected to this emotionally painful, ghostly state, whether God really exists. Why hasn't He come to take me home? Why am I still here? Why am I forced to watch my kids crumble? Would a God put me through all of this? What would be the purpose? I've been a faithful person my entire life, all forty-six years, never questioning my beliefs. But now, postmortem, I can't help but question His existence.

Jazzy's eyes focus out the front window for the remainder of the ride home. I'm more than relieved when Edward pulls into the driveway—they're safe. Once we enter the house, the kids scurry like cockroaches to a safe hiding place. Even Jazzy disappears into her room.

I find refuge in the neglected, mostly dead flower garden with Buddy in tow. I'm still confused at my odd limbo state, and the excitement of Jazzy seeing me wanes each time it causes problems for her at school or at home. I worry my presence will generate more harm than good. Jazzy's too young and fragile to suffer more than she already has. I want to stay, but if the rest of my family can't see or hear me, nothing good can come from lingering, and there's no way I'd use Jazzy to try and connect with them because they'd never believe her.

And the pain, the physical torture continuously surging through my body that doesn't even exist, is far more excruciating than anything I'd experienced when I was alive. I can't taste, smell or touch, but my other senses are significantly intensified. I'm trying hard not to convince myself I'm in Hell, but if I were to create what Hell would be like for me, this would be pretty close; rid of control, of pleasure, of touch, of life's delicious scents, of being held by my husband, of caring for and protecting my children. All of what I took for granted has been stripped from me.

What does this all mean? I need a little guidance, please. Isn't there a handbook to life after death? A *What to Expect When You're Dead* brochure would come in handy right about now. I don't know the reason for all of this but, for now, I'm going to embrace this journey, not that I seem to have a choice, and try to reach the rest of my family. I have so much to fix.

Chapter Twelve

I t's Friday night, the night of Ashley's party. Even though I no longer have a stomach, a familiar twisting of my gut persists as I watch Ivy get ready. Ivy told Ashley on the phone she plans to be out of the house before Brad gets home, probably so he won't see what she's wearing, or *not* wearing.

Ivy has on a dreadfully short, sequined skirt and a thin, white, form-fitting crop top. On her feet are my silver, strappy heels, the ones I nearly broke my neck wearing on a rare night out with Brad. Dark eyeshadow and berry blush paint her face. She applies a glossy burgundy lipstick and smiles at her reflection in the mirror. From her Strawberry Shortcake jewelry box, she plucks a pair of large, dangly earrings and attaches them to her ears. On long, bare legs, she teeters to the full-length mirror on the back of her door and makes a full turn, hiking up her skirt a little before grabbing her toy-sized purse and leaving her room.

Buddy barks at the chime of the doorbell.

"I'll get it!" Ivy says as she wobbles down the stairs and nearly falls before arriving at the bottom. She smacks her lips together spreading her lip gloss, paints a sickly-sweet smile on her face, and opens the door. Instantly, her face drops.

"Oh hi, Mrs. Radcliff."

"Wow. Don't you look like you're ready for... a night out," Bridget says and clears her throat. She scans Ivy from head to toe before clearing her throat again. "I brought some dinner. Guess you have other plans. Where are you going all dressed up?"

"A party."

"Must be a pretty fancy party."

"I guess." Ivy reaches for the dish. "Thanks for the dinner."

"You're welcome. Is your dad home?" Bridget asks, but she must know Brad would never let Ivy walk out the door looking like she does. If there's one thing Brad wouldn't allow, it's his daughters dressing in skimpy, streetwalker-style clothing. He also wouldn't let her go to a party, but Ivy seems to be a master at telling him what he wants to hear. And really, it appears Brad has been avoiding any type of confrontation with the children since the funeral.

"No, he'll be home late. Business dinner or something."

"All right, I'll be heading out then. Have fun at your party." Bridget waves and turns to leave but then stops and turns her head around. "Just be careful, okay?" she says, but Ivy doesn't acknowledge her comment and closes the door.

I poke my head through the door and yell, "Thank you." But of course, Bridget doesn't hear me when I could use her help to knock some sense into Ivy.

A few minutes after Bridget leaves, a car horn blows outside. Edward, who finally leaves the confines of his cocoon, peers out the window and then rushes down the stairs.

"You're going with *him*?" he says, his voice higher than usual.

Thank God he's going to stop her!

"Yeah, he's cool," Ivy says.

"You think he's cool? He's an asshole. You can't go out with him."

"Oh yeah, are you my dad now?" Ivy puts her hand on the door handle.

Edward slaps his hand on the door and leans his weight against it. "Ivy, seriously, he's not a nice guy."

"How would you know? You're so stuck in your own world, you don't even know who my friends are."

"I've heard things, bad things. And you know our history. Please, don't go." Edward's voice is firm as he pleads with his sister.

"Well, he's changed, and I like him."

Zane honks the horn again. That little shit can't even get out of the car. I'd knock him over the head if I could. I'm hoping that's what Edward will do.

"He'll screw you and then leave you," Edward says.

"Nice," she says. "But, if he does, he won't leave me. I'm the best he'll ever have." Ivy pushes Edward out of the way. He resists and continues to hold the door closed.

"Please, don't go."

"Pa-leeease, get a life."

He hesitates before stepping away from the door. Without another word, Ivy scampers out of the house and slams the door behind her.

I join Ivy in the car. The asswipe doesn't bother himself to open her door. After Ivy latches her seatbelt, she picks at her fingernails.

"Hey," she says.

"Hey."

Great conversation so far. He seems bright. At least he's

combed his blonde waves out of his brown eyes and dons an unwrinkled, light blue and white striped button-down shirt and khakis. His appearance gives the illusion he's a good boy, like he came from an evening church service.

"Was that your brother in there?"

"Yeah, he's watching Jazzy."

"Fuckin' loser," Zane says under his breath.

"What?"

"Ready for an awesome night?" he asks.

"Ashley's parties are legendary, so, yeah."

We arrive at Ashley's house in less than ten minutes. Her house is slightly secluded, back in the valley of a small mountainous area. Her closest neighbor is a few acres away, which makes it a perfect setting for an underage party. There are only a few people here so far.

"Yay. You two are here." Ashley's long, shiny, dark curls bounce as she runs to Ivy and Zane and gives them both hugs. She's wearing a duplicate of Ivy's borrowed bandage dress except it's royal blue.

"Damn. Good thing I didn't wear my dress tonight," Ivy says.

Ashley's eyes widen. "Totally. Love your shoes. Well, let's get our party on! Beer's in the back. I've got some shots to start us off."

In the kitchen, Ashley hands them each a shot glass while some kind of hip-hoppity music blares through ceiling mounted speakers.

"Here's to . . . well, here's to getting fucked up!" Ashley says, winking at Ivy before they all down the shot. Ivy's face relaxes and then a smile forms on her glossy lips.

"That shit burns so good," Ivy says slamming her shot glass

down on the gray veined, white marble countertop.

"Just how we like it, hot all the way down," Ashley says.

"That's what I'm talking about. You girls know how to par-tay," Zane says.

"Damn straight, we do. Fill'er up, please," Ivy says.

They down two more shots before moving to beer.

This is obviously not Ivy's first party or her first experience with alcohol. How did I not know this? The sleepovers with friends to paint nails and watch movies was all a ruse, a lie I allowed myself to believe. I should have seen something, some sign, some hint she'd sent me. She never gave me any reason to question her. Of all people, I should have known.

—

WITHIN A HALF hour, it looks as though the entire school is here except Edward. Beer after beer is consumed. Multiple couples proudly display more than casual kissing, their bodies meshed together, their hands snaked under shirts and skirts. In a dark corner, one girl's head bobs in a guys lap, and I have to look away. It's almost like they one-up each other, showing how daring and uninhibited they are. Ivy slurs her words while clutching Zane's biceps like he's the only thing keeping her from face-planting on the floor.

"Hey, babe, why don't we find someplace quiet?" Zane says.

"Shhure."

Zane practically holds her up as they climb the stairs and enter the master bedroom. A heavy boulder of dread sits on my chest. Ivy's so drunk, there's no way for her to defend herself. "Ivy, don't go up there," I say, but she doesn't hear me. My deep desire to leave and avoid seeing what no parent should see is bulldozed by my protective instinct even though there's nothing

I can do to help her. Zane closes the door and locks it while Ivy plops on the bed. He takes a seat next to her.

"I've been waiting for this all night. Just you and me. Alone," Zane says.

"Really?" Ivy's gaze bounces around from the alcohol.

"Yeah. I want to get to know you better." Zane puts one hand on her bare knee and slowly moves it between her legs. "You get me?" he says.

Gradually, his hand travels up her skirt as he kisses her until he's where he shouldn't be. Ivy moans. He grabs her hand and places it on his crotch. A hammer pounds at the solid dread within me, releasing a fear too painful to endure. I want to leave, but the fear freezes me in place.

"See how much I want you?" he says.

Ivy's own fear, sadness, insecurity, regret and loneliness blaze and sear me. I feel all of it, bringing me back to when I was her age, when I did what she's attempting to do to fill the emptiness.

"Ivy, don't do this, sweetheart," I say. For a second, Ivy stops. But then she touches him again, and he reclines her on the bed, her blonde hair splays out like a fan. He pulls her skirt up past her hips and exposes her pink underwear.

"I want you. I *need* you, Ivy," he says. He stands up and takes off his pants before getting on top of her.

"Ivy, please, don't do this, sweetheart. You deserve better than this," I say. Ivy stops again and looks over Zane's shoulder. "Push him off. Don't let him take what doesn't belong to him."

"Zane, stop," Ivy says. But he doesn't listen as he tries to push her underwear down and force himself on her. "Ouch, Zane, stop! I don't want to do this."

"You know you don't mean that," Zane says, continuing his quest.

"No, no, no!" I continue to yell and attempt to pull him off Ivy, but my hands go right through him. Damn it! "Fight him, Ivy. Push him, kick him."

Ivy pushes him, but he's too strong. He grabs her arms and holds them against the bed. She squirms underneath him. She squeezes her leg between his and knees him harder than what I would expect in her inebriated state.

"What the fuck?" He lets go of her hands and clutches his crotch. "Fuck! You fucking tease!"

"I told you to stop." Specks of spit fly from Ivy's mouth as tears form in her eyes.

Still holding on to his crotch, Zane's rage-filled stare sends a horrifying chill through me. His eyes have a frenzy about them, a wild animal before the kill.

"Run, Ivy. Get out of here," I say. Ivy scans the room. She gets off the bed as swiftly as she can and runs to the bedroom door, her gait unsteady. She pulls on the handle, but it's locked. Before her shaking hands can unlock it, Zane whips her around and pushes her against the door.

"No one fucks with me. Do you hear me? No one. I should've known you're a loser just like your brother. You made a big mistake. By tomorrow, everyone will hate you," he says and spits in her face. He pushes her to the side and leaves the room.

Ivy falls to the floor and sobs. All I want to do is wrap my arms around her.

"Ivy, you did the right thing. I'm proud of you," I say. Ivy glances around, her mouth slack and her eyes fearfully wide.

Ivy looks right at me. "Mom?"

"You can see me?"

Ivy breaks down again with shaking sobs. "No, no, I'm

seeing things," she says, burying her face in her hands.

"I'm proud of you, Ivy."

"And hearing things."

Ivy slowly peers up at me, as though she's expecting not to see me this time. She covers her face with her hands and shakes her head.

"Proud? I almost had sex with him. How could you be proud of that?"

"Because you didn't. Because deep down, you knew it wasn't right."

"How can you be here? How is this possible? Oh, God!"

"I guess you needed me."

"But I don't. This isn't real. It's not real."

"Real or not, I'm here."

"So, what do I do now, huh?" she asks, her speech still slurred. "I . . . I thought he was going to kill me. He's probably waiting for me."

"You did what you had to." If only I could reach over and ease her fear, pull Ivy into my arms and never let her go. "Why don't you call Edward and have him pick you up?"

Ivy shakes her head. "He'll just say, 'I told you so.'"

"He only wants to protect you."

"I don't need to be protected."

"Ivy, everyone needs protection, no matter how old they are. Call him."

Ivy walks to the house phone on the side of the bed and calls, barely able to hold the receiver. Once she hangs up, she wraps her arms around herself and shakes like she's suffering from a high fever.

"He's coming. What do I do now? I can't go down there."

"I'll tell you when he's here, and then you can sneak out."

"So Jazzy wasn't lying?" Ivy says.

"No."

Ivy reaches to touch me, but her hand passes through me. She stares up at me with a mix of fear and confusion.

"You aren't real. I can't touch you. I'm hallucinating or something. It's the alcohol. Zane must have put something in my drink." She puts her hands over her ears and closes her eyes. "Wake up, wake up, wake up."

"Ivy, calm down."

She opens her eyes. "I don't know what to believe. I want you to be here, but it's not possible. Is it?"

"I'm here, sweetheart, so I guess it's possible."

Edward doesn't school Ivy like she feared he would when he picks her up from the party. Instead, he gives her a remorseful glance before driving home in silence.

Chapter Thirteen

It's Saturday morning now, the house is quiet. Buddy is beside me on the couch dreaming as he whimpers and moves his paws. I would love to run my hands through his silky fur.

The shuffling of feet and the flush of a toilet from upstairs indicate the first signs of life this morning. Jazzy must be up. She's the early riser in the family. With her pink, My Little Pony night shirt rumpled and one of her rainbow striped socks missing, Jazzy descends the stairs looking like she's in an intense game of hide-and-seek.

"Oh, there you are," Jazzy says.

"Good morning. Did you have a good sleep?"

"Yeah, I get tired with the medicine Daddy gives me." Buddy jumps off the couch and greets her. "Hey, Buddy, are you hungry?" she says as his tail fans the air.

Jazzy shuffles into the pantry and scoops out some food and walks it to his dish. Pride swells within me. "You're growing up so fast."

"Not fast enough. I don't like being the baby."

"Being the baby has its advantages."

"What do you mean, advantages?"

"Good things."

"Like what?"

"Like learning from the older kids' mistakes, having fewer responsibilities, and always having someone to stick up for you. You probably even get away with more than they do."

"Ivy doesn't stick up for me. She's mean."

"She can be . . . unkind sometimes, but I bet she'd be there for you if you really needed her."

"Maybe. It's still not fun being the baby."

"I wish I was the baby," Ivy says, entering the kitchen. "It sucks being the forgotten middle child." She opens the pantry and searches for something to eat. Her eyes are puffy, and her face looks younger without all the makeup.

Jazzy ignores Ivy while she lets Buddy outside.

"Good morning, Ivy," I say.

Ivy turns and looks at me in surprise, but then quickly changes her gaze away from me.

Jazzy puts her hands on her hips. "You can see her, can't you?"

"See who?"

"Mommy. You can see Mommy."

"Uh, no. I don't know why you would even ask such a ridiculous question." Ivy snatches a strawberry yogurt from the fridge before stalking out of the kitchen and back to her room.

Jazzy sighs. "I think she can see you, Mommy."

"Maybe she's just not ready to admit it yet."

"I don't get her at all." Jazzy rolls her eyes like a parent talking about her teenage daughter.

"Sometimes teenagers are hard to figure out. Just wait, you'll be one someday." I smile at the thought of Jazzy being a teenager, but my smile fades, and a fist-punching sadness hits me in the chest. I will probably never see her as a teenager. I will miss so much of Jazzy's life, all of their lives.

"I'll never be like Ivy. She's, you know, like you always said, com . . . comp . . ."

"Complicated?"

"Yeah, and moody. I'll never be like that."

If only I could record her and play it back to her when she starts the same behaviors. Maybe Brad will be lucky with Jazzy, maybe she won't be such a challenge. When Ivy became a teenager, I called my mom and apologized for having to put up with me when I was a teenager. It's hard to believe what kids put their parents through daily. Maybe that's why my parents left me alone so much and why I didn't mind Ivy staying at a friend's house all the time—it was easier than dealing with someone who wasn't there.

"I guess you'll cross that bridge when you come to it," I say.

"What bridge?"

I laugh. "It's just a figure of speech. It means you'll deal with it when the time comes."

"Oh, okay. Are you going to be here when I cross that bridge?"

"I don't know. But I will always be in your heart. So even if you can't see me or hear me, I'll be with you."

"I don't want you to go. I want to be able to talk to you all the time."

"I'm here now, so let's make the best of it."

"How about we play a game?" Jazzy asks.

"Sure, I'd love that."

Jazzy sets up the Game of Life, and I sit with her on the floor. I never did this when she was alive, and now I feel I've missed out on so much. I was so busy *doing* that I wasn't *being*.

I was too worried about the future rather than focusing on the present.

We play and laugh. Jazzy has to move my car around and spin the wheel and take care of the money, but we're having fun.

"Hey, kiddo, what are you up to?" Brad asks as he enters the family room and sees the game on the floor. "Playing a game all by yourself?"

"Nope. I'm playing Life with Mommy, and I'm beating her."

Brad's face reddens, and his once relaxed hands dig into his thighs. He grabs the game board, shakes off the pieces, and folds it.

"Daddy what are you doing? No! Stop!" Jazzy tries to capture some of the pieces off the floor before Brad does. He puts the board in the box and throws the rest of the pieces in after it.

"Jasmine, you need to stop this nonsense. No more talk about Mom being here. Do you understand?" His vehement voice bounces off the walls.

"I hate you!" she yells as tears flood her poor little face. My chest aches for her, and once again, there's nothing I can do. Brad doesn't see me. Well, let's be honest here—he's Brad, and if the one thing he was looking for were right in front of his face, he probably wouldn't spot that either.

Jazzy rushes up the stairs and into her room. A door slams and her muffled cries travel through the ceiling. Brad sits in the wingback chair and takes a few calming breaths. He gazes out the window; his face hangs as though every muscle has ceased working.

"This has to stop," he says.

Because of Jazzy's age, it's hard for anyone to believe her.

It's not a common occurrence for a dead parent to come back as, well, whatever I am. But it's also hard to instantly disappear from Jazzy's sight, and I want to be here for her. I want to fill in the blanks I've left behind.

"I'm here, Brad," I say.

Brad's eyes skitter across the room before he shakes his head.

"I need to get a grip," he says. He rises and retrieves the keys from the counter before walking to the stairs. "I'm running out for a little bit," he shouts and waits for a response. "If anyone cares." Without a reply, he trudges out the door.

I should follow him, but if I appear to him in the car, it might cause an accident and make things worse than they already are. Staying home with the kids is the better option. Brad can take care of himself, but I worry the kids can't. They all seem to be self-destructing.

—

I STAND OUTSIDE Ivy's room. Through her closed door I hear her talking to someone, her voice shaky and desperate. One of the benefits of being in this state is my ability to walk through doors, walls, or any obstacle. They're not in this limbo world I'm somehow trapped in. Although I still reach for the door handle and feel a need to knock, even if no one would hear me. I'm still a creature of habit.

"Ivy," I call through the door. Ivy stops talking. "Ivy, can I come in?" No response. "Please, Ivy, can I talk to you?"

Ivy's door opens a crack, and all I can see is one eye and half a nose. Ivy won't speak to me, and her eye focuses on something behind me. Jazzy's looking at me from her door.

"See, I knew it. She *can* see you," Jazzy says.

"She just needs some time," I say. "And some privacy." Jazzy purses her lips before closing her door.

I pass through Ivy's closed door. She sits on her bed with her iPad propped on her lap.

"What are you doing here? Please leave," Ivy says.

"I want to see how you're doing."

"Why? Why now? All of a sudden you care?"

"I've always cared, Ivy."

Ivy lets out a sarcastic laugh. "Seriously, you need to leave."

"I'm sorry if I wasn't there for you like you needed me to be. I thought I was, but now I see how little attention I gave you. You were always so easy. I should've known."

"Well, you didn't. Not much you can do about that now, huh?"

"I can't change the past, but I'm here. Isn't that worth something?"

Ivy twists an elastic hair tie tightly around two of her fingers until they turn purple and then releases them. She does it a few more times, avoiding eye contact with me.

"You can't pop in as some ghost and fix things." Ivy's blue eyes pierce through me. "What are you, anyway? God! This is so—" Ivy takes a breath and lowers her voice. "Please, leave."

I rise, consumed with an urge to embrace her and apologize a million times, but she would never feel the warmth of my love, of my heart beating with understanding and regret. That opportunity has passed.

"I'll be around if you change your mind," I say before disappearing through the door.

Brad's return is announced with the slam of a car door. His arms are loaded with groceries as he maneuvers into the kitchen. He actually went to the store. I almost need to confirm with

Jazzy if what I'm seeing is real or if this is part of an illusionary event playing out in my world. He puts the bags on the kitchen island and then goes back out to get more. When he's finally done unloading the car, he puts the groceries away. In addition to the staples, he bought different cuts of meat, fruit, and veggies. He bought veggies.

Brad pulls out a box of powdered sugar donuts.

"Jazzy," he yells up the stairs.

"What?" she shouts back, still sounding upset.

"Got you something from the store."

"I'm not interested."

"You're going to like it."

Jazzy doesn't hold out long before she's down the stairs and facing Brad in the kitchen with her hands on her hips.

"What?"

"Look." Brad picks up the box of donuts and hands it to her.

"Donuts? My favorite." She takes the box from Brad's hands and opens it before pulling the milk out of the fridge.

Brad's smug face makes him look like he's pulled off this century's biggest heist. He retrieves a glass from the cabinet and hands it to Jazzy.

"Thanks, Daddy."

"I'm sorry I yelled at you earlier. I shouldn't have done that."

"It's okay. I know it's hard for you. I wish you could see Mommy like I can."

"Me too, sweet bug." He kisses her on the top of her head. "Can you forgive me?"

"Yep." She pours herself some milk and then puts the container back in the fridge.

She plucks the first donut from the box, tears it in half, and dunks one of the pieces in the milk until it's soggy. With milk dripping from the donut, she takes a bite. White powdered sugar coats her lips as the milk leaks from the spongy goodness and streams down her chin. She wipes the milk with the back of her hand. If I were alive, my mouth would water at the anticipation of the soft, sweet cake squishing and melting in my mouth. I loved powdered sugar donuts as much as Jazzy does.

"Mmmm," Jazzy says.

"Good?" Brad asks and Jazzy nods. "Are *we* good?"

"Really good," Jazzy says and takes another bite.

And there it is, as simple as a favorite food to an accepted apology. Why didn't I ever try this type of coercion? This Brad guy is pretty darn smart. He may survive this nightmare after all. He takes one of the donuts and soaks it as well before taking a bite and sharing a laugh with Jazzy.

Chapter Fourteen

"Get out, Dad! I'm not going to school today!" Ivy says as Brad tries to get her out of bed.

I had a feeling Ivy would pull this, considering what went down at Ashley's on Friday night. I can't blame Ivy one bit for not wanting to go; I wouldn't want to face school either.

"Ivy, you need to get up and get ready. You're not going to be late anymore," he says.

"I don't want to," she says, sounding more like Jazzy.

"Ivy, sweetheart, everything's going to be fine," I say.

"Get up. Let's go." Brad barks like a drill sergeant.

Ivy waits until Brad walks down the stairs and then sits up and looks at me. "And you know this because . . .?"

"Because everyone was beyond drunk at that party. No one's going to remember a thing."

"Really? For a ghost, you're kinda dense." She rolls on her side, away from me. "I've been ghosted, do you know what that means? I'm like you now, I no longer exist." Ivy's voice quivers. "I can't do this. I feel like I'm going to puke."

"I don't think your dad's going to let you stay home if he doesn't know what happened. But if you tell him—"

"No way!" Ivy rolls out of bed and drags her feet to the bathroom.

"Do you want me to come to school with you today?" I ask through the now closed door.

"NO!" she says and then lowers her voice. "I don't want you stalking me. It's creepy and totally not normal. I'll deal with it. I'm fine. I'm fine." Her voice lacks its usual confidence.

I want to go and make sure she's okay, but there would be no way I could go without her seeing me. All I can do is hope today won't be as bad as Ivy thinks it's going to be and to be here for her when she returns.

"I can't find my shoes," Jazzy says after Edward and Ivy are already out the door. Her heavy backpack bounces up and down as she rushes through the house checking all her usual spots.

"Hall bath," I say.

"Oh yeah." Jazzy retrieves her shoes and dashes out the door with them in her hands. "Bye, Daddy. Bye, Mommy," she says, before getting into the car and disappearing down the driveway.

—

THE DOOR SPRINGS open at 3:37. Ivy runs up to her room while Edward yells after her.

"I told you he was no good. You didn't listen. Why can't you ever listen to me?" He disappears up the stairs, taking them two at a time and a moment later, his door slams. Loud, thumping music penetrates the thick wood door and fills the hallway.

"Ivy, can I come in?" I peek in. Ivy's crying on her bed.

"Go away. I don't want to talk about it."

I enter Ivy's room before she can shoo me away and sit on the foot of her bed. Mascara-smudged eyes and wet blotchy cheeks face me.

"He told everyone," she says, barely audible.

"About Friday night?"

"Yeah, but he completely changed the story."

Ivy plucks a tissue from the box beside her bed and blows her nose. Her sad, steel blue eyes peer at me. There's not an ounce of hope within them.

"He told them I came on to *him*, that I did things to him that . . . Oh God, he said horrible things!" She cries again but continues to talk. "He told all my friends I said they were losers and sluts. He told them he had sex with me because I begged him. He told so many lies, and they all believe him. Why would he do this?"

I place my hand on her outstretched leg, but I can't feel her and she can't feel me. My chest feels as though someone's hand is wrapped around my heart and squeezing. I don't know how to make this all better.

"He's a desperate person who's decided to use you to get what he wants."

"What does he want, Mom? What does he want?"

It is the first time Ivy's called me Mom since I appeared to her at the party. It's a good sign, one I won't take for granted.

"I suppose the biggest way to get to someone is through those they love."

"You think he's hurting me to get to Edward? That's so messed up."

I sense someone on the other side of the door. From the beat of his heart, I know it's Edward. I lower my voice.

"Some people aren't happy unless they can enjoy someone else's misery. I think Zane likes to see people hurt. It seems like it's what makes him happy."

"What am I going to do? I don't want to go back to school."

"You have to. You have to show him, no matter what he does, he can't get to you, just like Edward does." I'm not entirely convinced of this myself. I wouldn't put it past Zane to stomp on a litter of helpless puppies just to hear their painful cries. Proving something to him might not be the correct answer.

"I sat alone at lunch today. No one would sit with me. No one would talk to me except for Ashley, telling me what a pathetic bitch I am."

"The truth always comes out. And when it does, Ashley will see the mistake she's made taking Zane's word over yours."

"But I don't think I could ever respect her as a friend anymore. I shouldn't have to prove myself to her. She should believe me, not him."

"Trust is a hard thing to earn back. For now, show them you don't need them to be happy."

"How? I did everything with them."

"Make some new friends? Rekindle some old friendships? It's going to be tough for a while, but you're strong, you always have been. Remember, high school is just a teeny tiny part of life."

Ivy blows her nose and then looks searchingly into my eyes. "Mom, why do you think you're here?"

"I don't have an exact answer, but I'm beginning to think it's because you all need me."

"Whatever the reason is, I'm glad," she says. A small warm smile I haven't seen since Ivy turned fourteen appears on her swollen, tear-encrusted face. The one that says *this is for real* rather than the fake ones she's learned to plaster on her face since she started high school.

"I'm glad to be here for you. I just wish I knew how long I have."

"I wish I could hug you. I didn't hug you before you died," Ivy says. There's a slight waver in her voice.

"This smile, this beautiful, genuine smile you're wearing right now is like getting a million hugs all at the same time," I say.

"I'm sorry about everything." Ivy looks at the blanket on her lap and picks off some of Buddy's long hairs.

"You're almost sixteen. I think I'd rather jump out of a plane without a parachute than go through that age again."

"That sounds extreme."

"But it's direct. And I bet the scenery on the way down is to die for."

We sit in silence, enjoying what we've missed for so many years. The fog that's hovered between us is dissipating, leaving a clear view of each other. There's a closeness between us that had never existed before today. It feels like a cool, calming breeze on a hot summer day; a welcome relief. I glance around Ivy's room, worried the white light will now appear and tell me it's time to go. I still have so much to accomplish. I still need to connect with Brad and Edward and make sure my family is safe from Zane.

"What are you doing?" Ivy asks.

"Just looking for . . ." I stop. Ivy's eyes beg me to continue, but there's no reason to worry her with the idea of me leaving, not when we've made such significant progress in our relationship. "Thinking this room could use some fresh, bright paint, don't you think?"

"Maybe. Like you said, change can be a good thing."

"In this case, a very good thing."

"Don't tell Jazzy I can see you yet. I'm just not ready for another 'I told you so' today. Plus, I'm still not convinced this is real."

"Just don't take too long. She could use someone on her side right now."

—

THE KIDS EAT randomly at dinnertime. Edward sneaks down and nabs a loaf of bread and some ham from the fridge and disappears back into his room to play more of his mind-numbing video games. It's not hard to imagine what the remainder of the ham will look like in a few days when it doesn't make its way back to the fridge. The ants will love it. Jazzy comes downstairs and sees me sitting at the kitchen table.

"Hi, Mommy."

"Hi, Jazzmatazz. Hungry?"

"Starving. I called Daddy, but he said it will be another hour before he's home."

"What are you hungry for?"

"A cheese quesadilla."

"I can show you how to make one. It's easy."

"Daddy told me not to use the stove without an adult."

"Well, I'm an adult."

"He says you don't count." She cups her hand around her mouth and whispers, "Because he doesn't think you exist."

"I don't want to get you in trouble. Why don't you pick something that doesn't require cooking."

Ivy enters the kitchen and looks in the pantry.

"Ivy, do you think you could make your sister a quesadilla?" I ask and immediately regret my question. I forgot Ivy didn't want Jazzy to know she can see me. Ivy doesn't respond.

"Why don't you ask her if she could make you one?" I say to Jazzy.

"No way! She hates me."

Ivy pulls her head out of the pantry, eyes Jazzy, and sighs.

"Who hates you?" Ivy asks.

"You do."

"I don't hate you. You're a little annoying, that's all," Ivy says. "What are you having for dinner?"

"I want quesadillas. Mommy was going to show me how to make them, but Daddy told me I can't use the stove without an adult."

"Quesadillas sound pretty good. Why don't we make them together?"

"Sure." Jazzy's blue eyes grow wide with shock and excitement. "I'll get the tortillas and cheese if you get the pan out."

"Okay. Do you know how long we have to cook them for?" Ivy asks.

Jazzy glances at me and I whisper, "Until they turn a golden brown, and then you flip them."

"I think you cook them until they turn brown, and then you flip it," she says to Ivy and smiles back at me.

Ivy grins while she puts the pan on the stove and heats it.

"Do you think I'm using the right pan?" Ivy asks.

Again, Jazzy looks at me, and I nod.

"Yeah, I've seen Mommy use that pan before to make quesadillas."

"I wonder if we have to butter the tortillas first," Ivy says.

I shake my head.

"I don't think so. Mommy never buttered them first."

"Alrighty then, let's try this." Ivy places the tortilla onto the hot pan. "Do you want to sprinkle the cheese on?" she asks Jazzy.

"Yeah." Jazzy runs over and snatches the bag off the countertop and opens it. She sticks her hand in and pulls out a fistful of grated cheddar cheese and dumps it on the tortilla. She adds two more mounds of cheese before Ivy puts another tortilla on the top and then checks the bottom to see if it's golden brown.

"Not quite yet," Ivy says.

"Thanks for making dinner, Ivy." Jazzy beams at her sister. "I like cooking with you."

"It's kinda fun, isn't it?"

"Yeah, it's fun."

"Time to flip it."

"Be careful," Jazzy says.

As I view from the kitchen table, I know I've been given the privilege of seeing love in its rawest form. The kind of love that runs in their blood, so thick and yet so fluid it flows even when everything else stops. This was the gift I gave my children. I'd hoped as siblings, something I never had, they would be close, and they would always have each other no matter what happens in their lives.

I had no idea I would have three kids who would dislike each other so much, be cruel to each other, and who wished their siblings away. It always pained me to watch them fight or completely ignore one another. I often examined what I'd done wrong, beating myself up over it as "friends" on Facebook posted all the great things their kids did together, showing how wonderfully they got along, and how much they laughed at home. I couldn't help but think how lucky they were. But now I see a spark of sibling love, the melting of icicles at the end of a long, cold winter. Maybe this is the beginning of a strong sisterly relationship, the one I longed for—not for me, but for them.

Brad arrives home rather late. Not like this is unusual for him, but considering I'm no longer here in body, he should be home earlier to see what the kids are up to. He can't possibly think they're going to raise themselves. Sure, the transition is tough, but at some point, he needs to realize some things have to change whether he wants them to or not.

Ivy greets Brad as he enters the kitchen. "Well, it's about time."

"You sound just like your mother," he says, setting his computer bag on the floor and flipping his keys on the countertop. "Great to see you too."

Did I really sound like that? There were too many nights Brad came home late, missing the kids before they went to bed. I'd wanted him to come home at 5:30, so we'd all have dinner as a family like the sitcoms of the fifties. But, over time, I grew accustomed to his lengthy workdays and accepted the truth that my family would never be like the Cleavers.

"Hi, Daddy! Me and Ivy are making quesadillas for dinner. Ivy is a really good cook!"

"Well, that's great." Brad opens the fridge and stares into it.

"Do you want us to make you one?" Jazzy asks.

"Thanks, but I'll pass," he says.

Ivy and Jazzy appear disappointed, but they finish the second quesadilla and cut them up on their plates.

"Let's watch *Dance Moms* together, Ivy," Jazzy says as she shuffles to the couch.

"Um, yeah, sure."

Ivy sits on the couch next to Jazzy, and Jazzy scoots closer to her so that their legs touch.

"This is nice. I wish we could do this all the time," Jazzy says.

"Let's watch this episode." Ivy tousles her sister's brown curls.

And there they are, sisters and sworn enemies, sitting together watching one of the worst shows on television. The fact that they're together and not fighting proves that miracles do happen, even in my house.

Before bed, I spend time with Jazzy playing Barbies in her cluttered, disorganized room. Stuffed animals have multiplied and taken over her bed and floor. Little plates filled with plastic food mingle with crayons and papers on her play table. Unplayed games and a mix of clean and dirty clothes litter the floor. Her dresser drawers remain partially open, and her shirts and pants drape over the side as though trying to escape. It's a miracle her shoes seem to be one of the few things she can't find in the morning.

"This room could use a cleaning, don't you think?" I say while Jazzy dresses her Barbie for a trip to the beach.

"Nah, it's fine," she says, sticking out her tongue in concentration as she struggles to put on the doll's shoes.

"Remember when we would play the clean-up game?"

"Mom, that's when I was little," she says as though the clean-up game ended years ago instead of a short six months prior.

"Seems like yesterday to me."

"Not to me."

Jazzy's always been disorganized. Even as a baby, she had an affinity for putting her pacifiers in odd places or taking off her socks in different rooms. As she got older, she'd leave a trail of clothes in her path, too busy to bother with putting them where they belonged. It was a joke in the house, the fact that if we couldn't find Jazzy, all we needed to do was follow the path of her things.

"Why don't we start with your shoes?" I say. Jazzy pulls her eyes from her Barbie and stares at me like she doesn't understand.

"What's wrong with my shoes?"

"Wouldn't it be great if you knew where they were every morning?"

"I do, but someone always moves them."

"Why don't we put them on the stairs and see if anyone moves them?"

Jazzy's quiet for a moment, and then her eyes widen and her mouth pops open. "I know. We can put them on the stairs and record it. Then I can see who's moving them."

"Great idea."

Before Jazzy goes to bed, she finds her pink shoes hiding under the coffee table and places them on the bottom stair near the front door. I'm happy Brad's allowed her to continue wearing her pink shoes to school and so far, the school hasn't pushed back. The principal must have received Brad's not-so-subtle message.

Jazzy sets up her iPad and presses the record button. "As you can see, my school shoes are on the stairs. If they are not there in the morning, I'll know who moved them. So, whoever is moving them—I'll catch you!"

Chapter Fifteen

"Can I tag along with you to school today?" I ask Ivy on Tuesday morning.

"Mom, I really don't want you there. It's weird." Ivy puts on far less makeup than last week. She stands in front of the bathroom mirror and combs her golden locks until they shine and hang midway down her back.

"I won't follow you around. I just want to check some things out at the school."

Ivy pauses her makeup application and gazes at the sink in obvious contemplation. She takes a deep breath, lets it out, and then looks back into the mirror and resumes.

"Fine. But I better not see you in my classes or near me at lunch. I don't even want you looking at me."

"Deal. I'll stay away. Thanks."

At first, Jazzy's face brightens when she notices her shoes on the stairs exactly where she had placed them last night, but then her face drops. Her shoulders and head slump forward as she lumbers to her iPad and turns it off.

"Maybe you'll catch them tonight," I say. "At least you found your shoes."

"Yeah," she says, her lips twisted, her voice quiet.

Both Jazzy and Ivy are aware of my presence when I enter the car, but Edward still doesn't see me. The ride is quiet except for the pulsing music escaping the speakers. Edward pulls up to Jazzy's school and helps her take her hefty backpack out of the car.

"See you after school," he says.

"Have a fantabulous day!" I say to her before Edward shuts the door. Jazzy turns and waves, and I wave back.

If I had a tongue, I'd have to bite it to not say anything to Ivy. Ivy doesn't want me to say anything when others are around. But I want Ivy to ask Edward what's going on. He seems on edge as he tenses his jaw and grinds his teeth, a sound I can hear thanks to my supersonic ears. His heartbeat increases the closer we get to school.

Edward parks, but this time Ivy doesn't rush getting out of the car. She hoists her backpack out of the trunk and onto her back and waits for him. I follow them as they trek into the school courtyard together. This might be the first time Edward and Ivy have ever walked in together. I get the sense Ivy feels safer with Edward at her side.

After we enter the school gates, Edward and Ivy part ways, but not before looking at each other and giving the slightest gesture of a nod. I stick with Edward. In a way, I'm glad he can't hear or see me because I need to know what he's up to. Edward arrives at his locker and exchanges some books before heading to his first period.

I sit through Honors Calculus. If I were capable of it, I'd fall asleep. Math is not an appealing subject to me, and this teacher does nothing to change my mind. I sucked at it when I was alive, and I still suck at it now that I'm dead. I keep my sight on Edward though. He checks his phone under his desk at least six times. His restless legs bounce during the entire class period. He takes some notes and at the end of class, writes down his homework before closing his notebook and shoving it into his backpack. I'm right at his side as he strolls down the hall and out the door. The students are heading to the gymnasium for an assembly.

"Well, if it isn't Edweirdo," Zane says, strutting toward Edward. Edward takes a deep breath while his eyes try to avoid Zane's glare. "Just the homo I wanted to see," Zane says as he locks onto Edward's arm and pulls him to a secluded area between two buildings.

"Zane, stop." Zane towers over Edward's five-ten frame.

"That's what your bitch of a sister said too, the little slut."

"What the hell are you talking about?" Edward says, his voice raised.

"You mean she didn't tell you? Friday night? Her and me." Zane makes a circle with his thumb and pointer and puts his other pointer in and out of the hole.

"No way, that's a lie."

"How would you know? You weren't there, you fucking loser. She put up a good fight, but I still nailed her."

Edward's face turns an alarming red. He takes a step toward Zane, but before Edward can show any threat of an attack, Zane punches him in the stomach. Edward doubles over and falls to his knees. Zane kicks him in the back, forcing a grunt out of Edward. Somehow Edward gets upright on his feet, but he's shaking. His eyes gloss over, his hands turn into fists, and his body takes on a life of its own as he reaches for Zane and grips his shirt. With his other hand, he punches Zane in the face. Zane's head whips to the side from the force, and when it returns to its original position, Edward slugs him again.

"Don't you ever touch my sister again, or so help me, I'll *kill* you!" he says and drops Zane to the floor.

I'm incredibly proud of Edward for sticking up for his sister. I never knew he could fight like this or that he was physically strong enough to take on Zane's more muscular frame. If I hadn't seen it, I wouldn't have believed Zane's bloody face was Edward's doing.

"What's going on here?" a middle-aged teacher with wire-rimmed glasses and a severely crooked nose says.

"Mr. Berg, thank God!" Zane makes the sign of the cross. "This bully pulled me here and beat me up." Zane wipes his bloody face on his shirt.

"Is that right?" Mr. Berg asks Edward.

"No, he pulled *me* here. He started it." Edward rubs the spot where Zane kicked him.

"You heard him. He said he was going to kill me," Zane says.

I recognize Mr. Berg. He's an assistant coach of the football team, the same team Zane is star quarterback for. Mr. Berg gives Zane's face a quick study and then glances at Edward with narrowing eyes. "Both of you, come with me. Now"

Edward and Zane trail Mr. Berg to the dean's office. He instructs them to sit on the mocha leather couch in the administration lobby. Zane leers at Edward with a shit-eating grin on his swollen, bloody face.

"You can kiss this school goodbye, Edweirdo. No one's going to believe you."

Edward stares straight ahead at the wall.

Zane's called into Dean Livingston's office. I go with him and sit in the empty seat.

"What happened, Zane?" the dean asks, scratching his black, groomed beard while the light from the window behind him bounces off his shiny, bald head.

"I was walking to the assembly when Edward pulled me aside and said he wanted to talk to me, so I went. Then he started yelling at me about some girl he liked that I supposedly took away from him. Then, he grabs my shirt and starts hitting me in the face, BAM, BAM, BAM," he says punching his fists in the air. "I thought that was going to be the end of me, man. I saw stars. And then he threw me to the ground and told me he was going to kill me. That's when, thank God, Mr. Berg stopped him."

"Did you do anything to cause him to hit you?" Dean Livingston asks.

"Of course not. In fact, I told him I was sorry if he thought I was stealing his candy, ya know what I mean? He just completely flipped out."

"From now on, stay away from him, understand? You've got a big game coming up, and *we* can't afford any problems. Now, go to the nurse and get your face cleaned up."

"Sure." Zane slowly rises from the chair and lets out a small grunt before leaving the room. I've got to hand it to him, that kid could bluff anyone at a poker game. But right now, he holds a bigger card than Edward, the state football championship. There's no card higher than that.

Dean Livingston ushers Edward into his office and closes the door behind him. Wearing a defeated face, Edward sits in the chair next to me.

"So, let me get your side of the story, Edward," he asks, sitting upright with his forearms on his desk and his hands clasped.

Edward recounts the entire confrontation, being precise and factual. He doesn't leave anything out, except for the specifics of what Zane said about Ivy. Dean Livingston shakes his head slowly as he looks at his desk and then up at Edward.

"That's not what Zane said. It appears your stories are going in completely opposite directions. I have to be honest with you, Edward. Zane has come into my office a few times in the last couple of weeks complaining about you harassing him. He's written complaints."

Edward scoots up in his chair. His face is a mix of shock and confusion.

"What do you mean? I haven't done anything to him. I try to avoid him. It's Zane who's always coming after me. Ask my mom," he says. He covers his mouth with his hand and tears break free from his eyes.

"Look, Edward, your behavior's creating an unsafe environment. I just can't have it anymore," he says with a tone of regret that contradicts his hardened face.

"But, I'm not the one starting it, Zane is."

"Then why haven't you come to me to report it? Zane did, but not you. He has paperwork to back his story, what do you have?"

"I . . . I." Edward throws his hands in the air and then lets them drop like dead weights onto his thighs.

Dean Livingston pulls up something on his computer screen and then picks up his phone and dials.

"Mr. Blackwell? This is Dean Livingston. Yes, I'm sorry to bother you, but there's been an incident, a pretty serious one here at school between Edward and another student. I need you to come to the school now so we can discuss it." I can hear Brad's heavy sighs through the phone.

"I'll be there in about thirty," Brad says.

"Thank you," Dean Livingston says and hangs up the phone.

With his forearms resting on his thighs, Edward lowers his body and places his face in his hands.

"It's going to be alright, Edward," I say.

Edward looks up and around and then puts his face back in his hands.

"Your dad will be here in about thirty minutes. You can wait out there on the couch until he arrives," the dean says as he motions for Edward to leave the office.

Edward did what he was supposed to. He tried to avoid the confrontation and told the truth, and it still got him into trouble, serious trouble. It's obvious Zane's been planning this for a while, and Edward fell right into his trap, making Zane look like the ultimate victim. Zane must have known that if the timing were just right, he could ruin Edward. I completely underestimated Zane's intelligence.

—

I SIT NEXT to Edward in the lobby desperately wanting to take his hand in mine, to let him know I'm here. Parked at her L-shaped desk, Ms. Becket fills out pink slips for more erroneous students to pay a visit to the dean. Edward stands and paces the length of the eleven-foot space.

"Edward, please take a seat," Ms. Becket says, looking over her black-rimmed glasses.

But Edward continues the back and forth motion, picking up speed with each pass. His flushed face and fisted hands worry me.

"Edward Blackwell, if you don't take a seat, I'm going to call security to contain you," Ms. Becket says.

Edward doesn't listen, and Ms. Becket picks up the phone.

"Edward, sweetheart, calm down. It's going to be okay," I say.

Edward stops. He spins in my direction but looks right past me. Slowly, he rotates his body all the way around while his eyes scan the room.

"You can hear me, can't you?" I say. He whips around and examines the exact spot where I'm standing but disappointment fills his face. "Have a seat, Edward. Dad will be here soon, and he'll fix all of this."

Edward's hands relax. He reluctantly takes a seat on the couch, but his eyes dart around the room, and his heart races. Why can he hear me but not see me? He must think he's going mad. Who wouldn't when they hear the voice of their dead mother while they're in trouble at school? Especially when I'm trying to console rather than scold. He continues to shift his eyes from one corner of the room to another and then shakes his head as though he can rid the thoughts and sounds with the quick movement. He leans back on the couch and crosses his arms in front of him, becoming calmer with each passing minute until his eyes close.

"Edward." Brad lightly kicks Edward's feet, which are stretched in front of him. Edward's eyes jolt open. "What the hell is this all about?"

"You wouldn't understand," Edward says as though he's lost everything.

"Well, try me. I need to know what happened before I go into the dean's office."

Edward recounts the details to Brad, again not leaving much out except for what exactly was said about Ivy. His determination to protect his sister is admirable. Brad asks a few questions before turning to Ms. Becket.

"Please tell Dean Livingston that Mr. Blackwell is here to see him," Brad says.

Ms. Becket picks up her phone and calls.

"Dean Livingston is ready to see you," she says and guides them to the door.

"Mr. Blackwell, thank you for coming," Dean Livingston says, stretching his hand over his paper-ridden desk as both Brad and Edward walk into his office. Brad shakes it and has a seat.

Brad changes his position in the black, thin-cushioned chair multiple times, eventually settling for both feet on the floor, and elbows on the armrests. He straightens his back and paints on a serious, businesslike face making him appear confident.

"So, Mr. Blackwell, there was an incident between your son and Zane Goodman today," Dean Livingston says.

"Is that so?"

"Fortunately, Mr. Berg was there to stop the fight before it got out of control. Seems like Edward's been bullying Zane again."

Edward's eyes shoot open, and his hands grasp the arms of his chair. "What?"

"Again? What do you mean *again*?" Brad asks.

"Zane's filled out multiple written complaints against Edward, three just this year, and we aren't even halfway through the school year."

"Why haven't we been notified of these reports against Edward?" Brad asks.

"You have. I spoke with your wife."

"My wife . . ." Brad peers at the floor. His face pales like all the oxygen has evaporated from his lungs.

"Yes. I'm quite certain I've spoken with her several times. Did she not discuss this with you?"

"Several times?" I shout, knowing he's full up to his eyeballs in bullshit. I glance at Brad. He looks at me, a puzzled expression contorts his face. I wave, and he shakes his head. He focuses back to the dean.

"No, my wife never mentioned these conversations," Brad says.

"He's full of shit, Brad. Tell him he's full of dirty, rotten, stinky shit!" I say.

"Is that really you?" Brad asks. He rubs his eyes and stares at me again.

"Mr. Blackwell, I don't quite understand your question."

"Yes, it's me, and he's lying about the whole thing," I say. Edward glances in my direction and then at Brad, his mouth open wide enough to accommodate a Big Mac.

"How can this be?" Brad says to me.

Dean Livingston begins to talk of the incident at the same time I do, but Brad puts up his hand to the dean to stop him and continues to look at me.

Brad stands. "Excuse me for a moment. I need to get some air," he says and walks out before waiting for a response from the dean. I follow him as he exits the lobby and pushes his way through the double doors leading outside. He bends over, resting his hands on his knees, and gulps air into his lungs.

"Brad?" I say.

He freezes. Only his eyes move, glancing in my direction. He blinks a few times, before peering back at me. "Shit."

"You can see me?"

"This isn't possible."

"I know it's a lot to digest. So, let's pretend I'm not really here but helping you pull some information from your brain, okay?"

"Sure, that makes total sense," Brad says, straightening and rubbing his face.

"Everything Edward told you is true." I continue talking while Brad walks in a large circle with his hands on his hips and his head down, occasionally eyeing me before looking back at the ground. "Zane instigated everything. He pulled Edward away from sight and told him horrible things about Ivy and then punched him in the stomach before Edward hit back. Check his stomach, I'm sure he has a bruise or something. And I was only contacted once by Dean Livingston regarding Edward. I'm sorry I didn't tell you, but it wasn't a big deal, and I didn't want to upset you."

I'm not sure he's listening as he continues his dizzying circular steps.

"I don't know why Livingston is throwing this on Edward except that the football state championship is coming up. Losing Zane now would be a bigger loss to the school than Edward."

"That's insane. And why do you think they're going to get rid of Edward?"

"Because he told Zane he'd kill him, and one of the teachers heard it."

Brad leans his head back and smacks his palm to his forehead. "Oh, for Christ sake! Of all the things he could say."

"Yeah, well Zane asked for it."

Brad looks at his watch and lets out a frustrated growl. I follow him back into the building.

"Edward needs you to fight for him, Brad," I say before we enter the dean's office. Brad pulls the chair closer to the desk. After he sits, he leans his forearms on the dark oak desk and clasps his hands, mirroring the dean's intimidating posture.

"I apologize for stepping out. This is all just a little upsetting."

"I can imagine. This is a difficult situation I wish we, Edward, could have avoided."

Brad glares at the dean with a determination I imagine he uses at work to get what he wants. "I believe my son. He's not the problem, and I think, deep down, you know this. What you're feeding me is a load of bullshit."

Edward, who had remained in the room when Brad stepped out, straightens in his chair and watches Brad like he just slapped a pile of malodorous shit on the dean's desk.

"Mr. Blackwell, that language will not be—"

"Don't talk to me like I'm one of your students. I pay your fucking salary, and I'll speak the way I wish."

If I were alive, I'd probably be a little turned on at Brad's ferocity. I can't remember ever seeing him this way, but ooh, this is some good stuff. It's a relief to know he's got it because he's going to need more of this to raise our kids on his own. I want a set of pom-poms to give him a *rah-rah,* but it could take him out of the "I'm going to kick your ass" zone.

"Blaming this on Edward is unacceptable. He's a great kid, an exceptional student. None of this adds up."

Dean Livingston opens his desk file cabinet and pulls out a couple of forms. He writes a few things on one of them and hands it to Brad.

"I see where Edward gets his volatility."

Brad's eyes scan the expulsion form before he stands. He places his palms on the desk and leans over, closing the distance between him and Dean Livingston. "If I didn't see it for myself, I never would've believed it. It's all about sports, isn't it? Turn a blind eye to the athletes because we need to be the champions."

"Edward threatened to kill a student, Mr. Blackwell. We have zero tolerance for that type of behavior." Dean Livingston hands Brad another paper. "Here's a list of alternative schools in the area. You'll want to contact them as soon as possible."

Edward deflates in his chair.

"Show him Edward's stomach," I say. Both Brad's and Edward's heads whip in my direction. Edward shakes his head and looks at the floor.

"His stomach?" Brad says.

"Excuse me?" the dean says.

"Where Zane punched him. I think he kicked him in the back too," I say.

Edward won't look at me, but his heart pumps wildly.

"Edward, stand and lift your shirt," Brad says.

"No way."

"Yes. I need to see something."

Edward reluctantly rises from his chair and lifts his shirt exposing bright red areas on his stomach and back. The beginning of bruises makes them look exceptionally painful.

"How did you get these?" Brad asks Edward. "Did Zane do that?"

Edward nods.

"So, what happens to Zane for hitting Edward?" Brad asks.

"I believe he hit Edward in self-defense," Dean Livingston says.

"You believe?"

Brad picks up the expulsion form, balls it up and throws it on the dean's desk.

"This is not over. Consider yourself warned," Brad says.

"Mr. Blackwell, are you threatening me?"

"With a lawsuit, you bet I am." Brad puts his arm around Edward's shoulder. "Come on, Edward. Let's get the hell out of here," he says leading him out of the office.

I follow them, not sure if Brad even wants to acknowledge I'm here. As soon as we get outside, I say, "That was amazing. *You* were amazing."

Brad turns and stares at me. "Please, whatever this is, stop."

"I'm sorry, Dad."

"No, not you. Didn't you just hear her? Don't you see her?"

"Who?" Edward looks around, his eyes skipping over me before returning to Brad.

"Your mom. You were looking right at her in the office."

"Dad, are you feeling okay?"

"I know he at least heard me when he was waiting for you," I say.

"There! Didn't you hear that?"

"I need to get my car. I'll see you at home," Edward says.

Brad's eyes are on me "Are you for real, Claire?"

"As real as I can be while I'm dead," I say and laugh, but he's not laughing.

"You've been talking to Jazzy this whole time?"

"Yes."

"Who else? Who else can hear or see you?"

"Just Jazzy, Ivy, you, and Edward."

"You have to at least hear her, Edward."

"Nope, nothing," Edward says, quickly looking away as if something in the distance has caught his attention.

Strange. Why would Edward dismiss my presence so quickly? I know he can hear and see me, it's obvious.

Brad checks his watch. "Shit. I'm late for a meeting. Edward, pick up Ivy and Jazzy from school, and I'll see you at home at seven. We'll discuss *all* of this tonight." He looks at Edward and then back at me. "You are a figment of my delirious imagination."

It doesn't surprise me that Brad would question my presence; he's an engineer—one who uses science to prove the validity of things. But his heartbeat tells me he's at least hopeful that what he's hearing and seeing is real. Even the struggle on his face, his tense jaw, and his searching, anguished eyes tell me he wants to believe.

"Your donut apology was impressive. Wish I would have thought of that one. And what you did in there, fighting for Edward? Father of the Year for sure," I say.

Brad tilts his head back and looks to the sky "This is—"

"Crazy, I know."

"I have to go." He reaches to touch me, but his hand falls through me. His eyes shift to his hand and then back at me, perhaps wondering *what* I am.

He turns and walks to his car. In the faintest whisper I would have never heard if I were alive, he says, "Great, I'm having a mental breakdown."

"No. It's just your engineer brain getting in the way," I say. "Believe me, some things can't be explained with science."

He studies me one last time before getting in the car and driving away.

—

I ASSUME Edward can still see me, but I remain quiet as I accompany him to the student parking lot. He doesn't acknowledge me as I join him in the car.

"So, you can't hear me or see me, huh?" I ask and wait for his response.

Edward cranks his music so loud I'm surprised the windows don't explode. He pounds his hand on the steering wheel to the beat of the music and bobs his head up and down. This must be my answer. He can hear me but refuses to acknowledge me.

It's still morning as Edward heads home. He's quiet on the drive, not saying anything to me and keeping a careful eye on the road, another obvious sign he knows I'm here. My presence in the car appears to make him nervous. I would nearly dig my fingernails into the seat riding with him when I was alive, worried he wasn't going to stop in time before hitting the car in front of him but, miraculously, he's never been in an accident or received a ticket.

Edward makes a beeline to the top of the stairs when we arrive home. He stops and looks back before he disappears into his room leaving me with an entire day to wait until the rest of the family comes home—again.

Chapter Sixteen

When Brad arrives home, I let Buddy greet him at the door first.

"How was your meeting?" I ask after he crouches to pet Buddy. Brad loses his footing and nearly falls backward. He slaps his hand to his chest and sucks in a noisy breath. I want to say, "Geez, you look like you've just seen a ghost," but I don't. He probably wouldn't appreciate that comment right now.

"Holy shit!" He says, with his hand still on his chest as Buddy squirms around him, his tail wagging with complete fanfare.

"Sorry, I didn't mean to scare you." I try not to laugh at the erratic pump of his heart and his contorted face. I move aside allowing him to enter without walking through me. "How did your meeting go?"

Brad studies me for a moment. "Alright, fine. Let's play this game. Why the hell not?" he says. "The meeting went swimmingly, albeit, I was late and a little out of my fucking mind."

"Well, that's understandable."

"Is it? It doesn't even make any sense. But then I think, if Jazzy and Ivy can see you, then I can't be crazy right?"

"You're not crazy, sweetheart. I know it's an impossible concept to accept, let alone understand, but I'm really here."

He waves his hand. "This, all this is just weird. I keep thinking I'm going to wake up and find this was all a dream."

"Yeah, me too." If the accident was only a bad dream; one of those "this is your life" moments teaching me never to take what I have for granted, then waking up renewed with a sense of purpose. "But it's not."

"No, it's a nightmare." Brad deflates onto one of the kitchen chairs and rests his head in his hands. "How can this be? You died. We buried you. You're *gone,* Claire." His voice wavers and his eyes grow wet.

"I'm gone, but I'm here. I've been here since the day you let me go."

"How? Why?"

"I'm not entirely sure, but there has to be a reason. Maybe because you all need me."

The silence between us stretches for minutes.

"You said you've been here since . . . since you died?" Brad asks.

"Yes, and before that. I was watching you all in the hospital. I'm so sorry you had to go through all of that. I know it must have been difficult."

"Difficult? It was fucking impossible." Tears drip down his face. "You have no clue. No clue! I had to decide to let you go, and when I signed the paperwork, I felt like I was ordering your murder."

"You did the right thing. I was never going to be able to come back."

"Did you try? Did you even try to come back to us?" he asks, hurt thick in his voice.

"Of course I did. I didn't want to leave you or the kids."

"You have no idea what it's like, Claire. My heart was ripped from my chest that day. It weakened me."

"I'm sorry."

"You're *sorry*? All our lives are changed forever, and all you can say is you're sorry? Should we talk about how this all happened because I sure as hell could use some answers."

"You're upset. Why don't we wait until you're calm."

"Damn straight I'm upset. Having a conversation with my dead wife has me questioning my sanity."

He rises from the chair and peers out the picture window, overlooking the tired backyard. His heartbeat slows, and his shoulders relax.

"Did you do it on purpose?" he asks, his eyes still focused past the window.

"What do you mean?"

"You were unhappy. I knew it and, for whatever reason, I ignored it. The morning of the accident, when I kissed you goodbye, it felt different."

"Different? You think I was saying goodbye-*goodbye*? You think I tried to kill myself?"

"It has crossed my mind a few times, yes."

"I was texting and driving, Brad. I was stupid, not suicidal."

Is this what everyone thinks, that I purposely drove into the intersection to end my life? How absurd! If I'd wanted to kill myself, I certainly wouldn't have put anyone else in danger. And I'd have prepared for my departure in advance, leaving a binder filled with detailed information Brad and the kids would need in my absence. How could he think I'd leave without advanced preparation?

"I'm sorry you were unhappy. I should have done something

to help you. Why didn't you tell me about the job? If it had meant so much to you, we could've made it work."

I move next to him, wanting to place his hands in my own to offer additional reassurance.

"Until I died, I didn't know how to live. I was so consumed with filling the void I felt within me that I missed the only ingredient I ever needed—my family."

"I wish we could go back and change the outcome of that day. I would have done things differently," Brad says.

"But we can't change what happened. Honestly, without the lessons we've been forced to learn from the accident, I think the morning would have gone the exact same way. We must move forward. *You* must move forward and focus on what you can change. Focus on our kids," I say.

"It's kind of hard when I work all day. I'm doing the best I can."

"I know you are. Sticking up for Edward today was a great start."

"What choice did I have? You pop up out of the blue, and I think I'm going insane." He sinks his hands into his front pants pockets and shrugs.

"Well, Edward needs someone in his corner. Zane Goodman's cooking up all kinds of lies to get Edward in trouble. I saw a note in his room from Zane calling him a 'homo' and 'Edweirdo.'"

"What? Why would he do that?" Brad asks.

"Remember back in fourth grade when he was always making fun of Edward?"

"That was ages ago."

"I know, but remember what happened after I got his parents involved? His mom didn't do anything, so I called his dad. I made a big mistake that day."

"We don't know if that's what caused his injury," Brad says.

All I wanted was for Zane's dad, Steve, to tell Zane to stop being so mean to Edward, something I would have done if the roles had been reversed. Zane made fun of Edward's tics, a continual hard blink and a persistent sniffing of his nose. He also made fun of Edward when they were on the same football team—not something Edward excelled in, but we encouraged him to try all sports.

The mean little digs from Zane became more frequent and more severe until Edward broke down at home one day and refused to go back to school. That's when I decided to call Zane's parents. It was a dumb move on my part, but I had no idea it would create such a ripple effect. Steve told me the kids should work out their own problems and that I was setting Edward up to be a sissy by getting involved. But the day after I spoke with him, Zane didn't come to school and was out for a week. When he returned, he had a cast on his left arm and a large green bruise on his face. He told everyone he fell, but it seemed too coincidental.

After that incident, Zane's aggression increased, and he started to physically hurt Edward in addition to the verbal abuse he threw at him. The school was of no help, so at the end of the school year, we pulled Edward out and enrolled him in a different school.

"No, we don't know for sure, but this is all starting to add up," I say.

"But why would Zane go after Edward now?"

"A way of deflecting abuse from home?"

"I have a hard time believing Steve's abusing Zane," Brad says. It's been years since Brad and Steve coached the boys' Little League team together—so much has changed since then.

"I don't."

"Well, what if he is? I still don't see why he would take it out on Edward."

"He sees Edward as weak, an easy target, and they have a history. Zane already knows how to get to him."

"So, what do we do?" My heart warms to hear him use the word "we." He's acknowledging I'm here.

"*We* keep a close eye on the kids and on Zane. It's only a matter of time before he slips up."

"What about Edward?" Brad asks.

"You need to take this issue up with the school. Find that letter and show it to them."

"You really think the school's going to back Edward? There's so much already stacked against him."

"All false. All fabricated. We can't let this . . . *them* destroy Edward."

"I'll see what I can do." Brad sounds exhausted, and he looks like he's carrying an entire house on his back.

"There's something else. I saw Edward sell his meds to a kid at school," I say.

"Why the hell would he do that?"

"For money, I'm guessing. But I don't know what the money's for."

"God, what else?" he asks, but I know he doesn't want an answer to that question.

I want to tell him about Ivy, but not now. There's so much he's forced to deal with already.

"We need to have a family meeting and figure out how to handle you being here," he says.

"That's a good idea. Why don't you round up the kids, and we can discuss the ghost in the room." I crack a smile, proud of my little joke, but Brad looks as though I've stabbed him with a dull kitchen knife. "Sorry."

—

WITHIN TEN MINUTES, the entire family convenes in the living room. Ivy and Jazzy crowd together on the cream, slip-covered couch while Edward and Brad sit opposite of each other on dated, sea-foam green, wingback armchairs. I'm on the piano bench, a little offset from the rest of the family.

Jazzy waves. "Hi, Mommy!" she says and then looks at Brad, waiting for her punishment.

"All right, we're all here," Brad says and clears his throat. "We need to discuss the fact that Mom is . . . well, she's with us."

"You can see her too?" Jazzy asks, her face lit with hope.

"Yes, I believe we all can. Isn't that right, Ivy and Edward?"

Ivy nods.

"No, I can't see her. You're all hallucinating," Edward says, his arms crossed in front of his chest.

"Edward, you at least heard her at school today," Brad says.

"No, I didn't."

"You can't hear me, Edward?" I ask.

Edward's gaze moves to his feet, but his quickening heartbeat gives him away.

"You didn't just hear Mom talk to you?" Brad asks.

"He did. He's just not ready to admit to it. Let's move on," I say.

Brad continues. "Okay, we need to have some rules."

"Rules? I don't like rules," Jazzy says.

"What kind of rules?" Ivy asks.

"We need to establish some boundaries with Mom here."

"Why? What does that even mean?" Jazzy asks.

"We don't want everyone thinking we've all lost our minds. Not every family has a ghost living in their home that can talk to them," Brad says. "So, we need to make sure we know when we can and can't talk to her."

"Yeah, like you at school, Jazz. Didn't all the kids make fun of you for talking to Mom? You don't want that to happen again, do you?" Ivy says.

"You made fun of me, too. See, I'm not a freak."

"I'm sorry I didn't believe you, and I'm sorry for calling you a freak."

"Apology accepted." Jazzy offers her hand, and Ivy shakes it. "Daddy, I want Mommy to come back to school with me so I can show her how smart I am."

"I already know how smart you are," I say and wink at her.

"I think it's best if Mom stays here at home. Having her go places with us could cause people to wonder." There's a tinge of regret in Brad's voice. "And it would be nice if you somehow warn us of your presence and respect everyone's privacy, just like if you were here physically."

I understand his logic, but I'm disappointed I can't be with the children when they're away from home. What would've happened if I hadn't gone with Ivy to that party or with Edward when Zane attacked him? How can I protect them if I'm not with them?

"I understand," I say. Brad and I have always been a united front with the kids, even when we don't see eye to eye. We never wanted the kids to feel there was a way to penetrate our parental decisions. This was one of those moments when I had to stand firm with Brad. After all, he's the only one who can physically enforce the rules.

"But can't she come to school with me on special days? Like on awards day or when we have our Christmas play?" Jazzy asks with a slight whine.

"Let's take it one day at a time, okay?" Brad says.

"Okay." Jazzy's face is solemn.

What if the roles were reversed, if I were alive and Brad came back? I wouldn't believe it and probably wouldn't want him following me around either. I'd have no privacy, and it *would* be disturbing. But I don't know how much time I have here, and waiting for Brad and the kids at home every day is an enormous waste of precious time with them.

"It's only to protect all of you," Brad says.

"Protect us from what?" Jazzy asks.

"From others thinking we're crazy," Ivy says.

"Oh, yeah. They probably already think I'm crazy, but I don't care," Jazzy says.

"And, one more thing. Even though Mom's here, I make the decisions. You must ask me, not Mom. I need to know where you are and what you're up to."

"Well, I think that's a little nonsensical. I'm perfectly capable of making decisions when it comes to the kids. That's the way it's always been."

"Forgive me for being blunt, but you're dead. I'm in charge, and I need to have the control now."

I want to argue with him. This is my domain, my job. Letting go of the control I've always possessed seems like an impossible task. He was right, though. He's the one left to physically raise the kids. Even if he gave me control, I'd never be able to physically enforce anything. They'd walk right through me if they so wished and I wouldn't be able to stop them. Brad *has* to be the one and only creator and enforcer of the rules.

"You're right. I agree," I say.

"Edward, do you understand?" Brad asks.

"I don't even see or hear her, so I don't know why I'm agreeing to this stupid thing, but sure, whatever you say."

"Ivy?"

"Yeah, okay," she says. She glances at me and shrugs.

"Jazzy?"

"Yep, you're the boss, Daddy. But can I ask Mommy for help on my homework?"

"Of course. Any more questions?"

Everyone shakes their head.

"Meeting is adjourned." The kids get up to leave. "Edward, we need to talk," Brad says before Edward can scurry up the stairs. "Have a seat." Brad motions to the chair Edward just vacated. "We need to set some ground rules. Until we find another school, you'll need to drive your sisters to school and pick them up. I'll be expecting you to pick up the slack around the house, getting groceries, running errands, that sort of thing."

"What about school?" Edward asks.

"I'm working on it. I think we should fight the school on your expulsion."

"No way. I don't want to go back there."

I don't even attempt to interject because I know Edward will ignore me anyway.

"If you didn't do those things—"

"I didn't! I try to avoid Zane at all costs. I even change the way I walk to some of my classes so I won't see him in the halls. Don't you believe me?"

"I *do* believe you. That's why we should fight these allegations. If we don't, it could hurt your chances of getting into college."

"You don't understand. Even if I go back, Zane will still mess with me, still try to get me kicked out."

"Mom mentioned something about a note Zane wrote to you. Do you still have it?"

"I don't know what you're talking about. I don't have any note." His knee bounces and he avoids eye contact with Brad.

"No note?" Brad asks.

"Nope, no note. Now, can I go?" Edward stands.

"I guess," Brad says, and in a few heartbeats, Edward disappears upstairs.

"He claims there's no note," Brad says, quick to dismiss its importance.

"I was here. I heard him," I say. My sarcasm's still very much intact. "So, you're going to believe him?"

"What choice do I have? He has to want the help, and he doesn't, so I need to drop it."

"You didn't ask him about the medicine."

"If he lied about the note, do you honestly believe he'll tell the truth about the medicine?"

"No, I guess you're right." Wait, did I admit he's right for the second time? What's happening to me? When I was alive, I never openly admitted such things.

While Brad disappears into his office, I retreat to the backyard. The garden does nothing to ease my worry that continues to grow like a menacing storm cloud. Something doesn't feel right. I can't place the feeling, but it's a heavy, uncomfortable, foreboding.

Chapter Seventeen

It's the Wednesday morning before Thanksgiving, but there's no evidence of a holiday within the walls of the house. Every year our entire home had been decorated for Christmas before the turkey made its way into the oven on Thanksgiving morning. I'd spend days before Thanksgiving hauling the tree and boxes of decorations out of the attic and moving from room to room, adorning the walls and tables with years of collected angels, snowmen, nativity scenes, and Santas. I set up the tree, leaving it bare, and on Thanksgiving night, after our stomachs were stuffed beyond full, we'd open the ornament boxes and place each memory on the tree. It's my favorite day of the year. But it looks like this year the holidays might pass by without its usual celebration.

The kids need to get up for school, and now I'm able to help Brad with the chaotic routine and encourage them to get out the door. I can't make breakfast or lunches, but I can make sure they get out of bed, Jazzy and Ivy at least. Edward still isn't acknowledging I exist in my ghostly form. Jazzy had put her shoes on the stairs last night without me reminding her or recording them all night, making the morning routine less hectic.

"Have a fantastic day, Jazzmatazz," I say as she heads out

the door with shoes on her feet and a smile on her face.

"Thanks, Mommy. I'll miss you." She blows me a kiss. I catch it and blow her one back.

"Have a great day, Ivy."

"I'd rather be near death with rabies than go, but thanks."

"What's rabies?" Jazzy asks.

Ivy pushes Jazzy out the door. "Why must you know everything? Let's go, hurry it."

"Bye, Edward. Drive safely," I say. There's no acknowledgment from Edward; I didn't expect there to be, but I'm not giving up on reaching him.

I stroll around the house, giving Buddy a little exercise since he's always following me. He finally tires and sits by the glass front door, probably hoping to spy a rabbit hopping across the front lawn. He perks up when Edward pulls into the driveway and greets him at the door.

Edward pets Buddy. "Were you waiting for me?"

He walks to the kitchen and scans the room before he opens the drawer and pulls out his medicine bottle. He pours almost half of the pills into his hand, retrieves a baggie, and places them inside. After he slides them into the front pocket of his jeans, he picks up his phone and sends a text. His phone chimes and he glances at it, then places his phone in his back pocket and heads for the door.

"What are you doing, Edward? What's going on?" I ask.

Edward hesitates, and his heartbeat surges.

"I'll be back in a little bit, big boy," he says, scratching Buddy behind his ears before leaving.

As much as I want to jump in the car, I promised Brad I'd stay home, respect boundaries, let him parent, blah, blah, blah. Watching Edward walk out that door is like him being too close to the cliffs and me too far away to catch him from falling. Oh hell, screw promises! I move toward the car, but Edward's eyes shoot in my direction and he punches the gas. In an instant, he's out of my reach and out of the driveway. I've got to be the slowest ghost this side of Heaven.

"Dear Lord, don't let him do anything stupid," I say, before going back into the house.

Edward returns home hours later, his hair slicked back and his gray tank top almost completely wet with what I'm guessing is sweat. His tired, bloodshot eyes stare right through me before he turns and climbs the stairs. Moments later, his door clicks closed, and silence once again fills the house.

At 2:30, Edward's alarm blares. Despite how it begs to be turned off, it continues its high-pitched beep. It's not unusual for Edward to sleep through his alarm; he could probably sleep through a catastrophic earthquake if he were tired enough, which is why I usually had to wake him up for school in the morning. But something's not right this time. His eyes were different, he was different when he came home. I glance at the clock; it's 2:38. Jazzy will be out of school in twenty-two minutes, and her school is twenty minutes away.

Poised at the bottom of the stairs, I check the decorative brass clock on the fireplace mantle every minute. This is maddening. If I were alive, I'd march right up there and yell at him to get out of bed. Actually, if I were alive, I'd be the one picking up Jazzy. I ascend the stairs slowly, giving him more time to wake on his own, but when I reach his closed door, the alarm continues, unanswered.

"Knock, knock," I say. "Edward?" My chest tightens. I pass through the door to his bed. His comforter covers his head, and without being able to physically pull it off, I can't force him to look at me. "Edward?" I say louder, but I don't get a piddly grunt or any movement from under the covers.

The sound of his breath and heartbeat offers me some relief. At least he's alive.

"The girls need to be picked up. Please, wake up. Please show me you're okay." Again, he doesn't respond.

Jazzy will be waiting in the pickup line, watching each car enter and exit and wondering where her ride is. Her heart will sink with each passing car. And Ivy will be stuck on campus with Zane looming and ready to attack.

All I can do is wait at the foot of his bed for him to wake. I need to know what's going on with him, why he's selling his meds, why he's so out of it. Is he drunk? Is it drugs? It's such a helpless feeling, like watching a car accident before impact, each car traveling toward the other, neither suspecting what *I* know lies ahead.

Edward's phone rings. It's 3:15. The phone continues to ring, and Edward sleeps right through it. There is a slight pause before the phone rings again, but he still doesn't wake. Then the house phone rings four times before being directed to voice mail, which no one ever checks.

—

CAR DOORS SLAM outside at around 4:30. I leave Edward and make my way downstairs.

"Jazzy, please stop crying. I'm sure there's a good explanation." Brad's voice is full of frustration.

"I waited and waited, and then I thought that something bad happened to him like Mommy," Jazzy says.

She runs past me and up the stairs and pounds on Edward's door.

"Edward? Edward?" she says, pounding again.

The door opens, and Edward peers out, his eyes half open, his hair disheveled.

"What? Why are you banging on my door?"

"You forgot to pick me up."

"Sorry, I was taking a nap."

"Are you sick?" Jazzy asks, her anger now replaced with concern.

Edward rubs his eyes. "I'm not sick." He lets out a sigh and leans to Jazzy's eye level. "I'm sorry, Jazz. I won't do that again."

"Pinky swear?" Jazzy holds up her hand and extends her little finger.

Edward clasps his much larger pinky around hers and then shakes. "Pinky swear."

While Jazzy and Edward conclude their make-up session, I find Brad rummaging through his laptop bag at the kitchen table. Ivy stands in front of the open refrigerator.

"Something's going on with Edward," I say to Brad. "He left for a while today. Took a bunch of his ADD meds, put them in a baggy. When he came home, he looked like he was on something or like he'd been crying. I'm not sure."

Ivy closes the refrigerator door. "Mom, Edward wouldn't do drugs."

"I'm not saying he's doing drugs, but it looks that way."

"Ivy, can you give us some privacy?" Brad asks.

"Fine. But if there's one thing I know about Edward, this is it. He doesn't even take his meds. He's not a druggie," Ivy says before popping a baby carrot in her mouth and heading to her room.

"You think he's doing drugs?" Brad asks once Ivy's gone.

"According to Ivy, he's not. But he's doing something."

"Huh," is all Brad says before he marches up the stairs. I hear him rap on Edward's door.

"What do you want?" Edward says.

"We need to talk."

"Not now."

"You don't exactly have a choice. Open the door."

"Not right now. I'm tired."

"You missed picking up the girls today. I had to leave work to get them."

"Sorry, it won't happen again."

"You bet your sweet ass it won't. If it does, there'll be major consequences." Brad returns to the kitchen.

"You're going to walk away?" I ask.

"What else can I do? I've tried to talk to him, but I can't."

"Brad, something serious is going on with him. You can't ignore it."

"Look . . . Claire, I don't need you meddling. I'm the parent here. I don't need you to get in the way of that."

"So, that's it? You let him do whatever he's doing?"

"I can't be here to watch him every minute of every day, so yeah, for now, I have to assume he overslept and missed the pickup. He's been through a lot lately, getting kicked out of school, his mother dying. He doesn't need me in his grill right now."

Brad never wanted to be the "bad guy" when it came to the kids. Spending so much time at work made him overly understanding and indulgent with all three of them when he was home. Even though we'd always had a united front when it came to difficult matters, I was ultimately the enforcer.

I understood his motivation for avoiding conflict and confrontation, given the lack of time he had with the kids, but now that he insists on being the enforcer, he needs to gain some control. What Edward's doing is dangerous, life-altering, and probably illegal and Brad's refusal to address it places me in a helpless state. When I was alive and felt helpless, I did something about it—took action. But now, my hands are tied; I have no pull here anymore, and the pain that comes with it is nearly unbearable. What's it going to take for Brad to assume full control? I hope it doesn't come too late.

Chapter Eighteen

Peace fills the house once again, as though Edward not picking up the girls earlier has been forgiven and forgotten, at least by everyone but me. Getting Brad to see what I see before it's too late has proven to be next to impossible. My tenacious husband has been a hard one to influence since the day we met nearly twenty-five years ago. If he doesn't witness it, it can't be true. Only a couple of things, like God and dinosaurs, does he give exception to.

I check on the kids. Jazzy's sound asleep, Pink Kitty in a choke hold in the crook of her arm. Little sounds of air puff from her relaxed lips. Edward and Ivy are also sleeping. It's amazing how young and innocent they look when they're in dreamland. Flashes of their baby faces remind me of how far they've come, how much time has passed since they were infants.

Brad's calm heartbeat and soft snore pulls me to our bedroom. He's conked out and fully dressed on top of the navy and white striped nautical comforter of our king-sized bed. He looks so vulnerable resting on his side, his strong hands fisted under his chin like a child. And the snore I once found completely annoying is now music to my ears; a familiar, comforting sound like the hum of the refrigerator or the swish of a tree under a summer breeze.

I have no need for sleep or a desire to be entertained during these peaceful nights. When I was alive, idle time was my enemy, allowing my mind to wander into treacherous waters of yearning for more—for better. What if I'd never stopped teaching? What if Edward didn't have ADD? What if I'd nurtured Ivy more when she was younger? What if I'd never had Jazzy? These questions would often keep me up at night in tossing fits of regret. Yet, every day, I'd bury myself in mundane tasks, keeping my mind and body busy, always needing more hours in the day. Now, the idle hours I wait to spend time with my family seem infinite.

All those hours I'd wasted on meaningless chores appear just that, wasted. The kids never cared if the house was spotless or if their beds were made. So many of those things that consumed my days took me away from the most important part of my life—my family. I want to start over, but I can't. The past has been written in indelible ink. Yet, the acceptance of knowing the past can't be changed is a relief, like I can stop doggy paddling to a shore I can no longer see.

A warm glow illuminates the living room. It intensifies until the contents of the room disappear along with all my worries and fears, my regrets and sorrow, leaving me with the most glorious sense of peace and lightness. A figure, hazy at first, appears and as it comes closer, I can see it's a human form. It moves toward me, and the moment I recognize the figure, joy floods me.

I reach for the figure. "Gammy, is that you?"

"Oh Claire, my sweet Claire," Gammy says. Gammy takes hold of my hands. The touch, startling at first, makes me pull back for a moment. I've been starved of touch for so long it almost hurts for an instant, like connecting with a hot stove.

But then, the feel of Gammy fills me with such comfort—much stronger than any I'd felt in the physical world.

Gammy is brilliant, like she's made from a million twinkling stars.

"Gammy, what are you doing here?"

"I've come to take you home. It's time to go, Claire."

It's as though Gammy has her own gravity that pulls me to her. I can't resist.

"I don't understand. I looked for the light Mom talked about and couldn't find it. I looked everywhere."

"Oh Darlin', I think you may have gotten a little lost."

I laugh. "Wouldn't be the first time."

"No, I'm a witness to that." Gammy smiles. "I remember the time after Ivy was born when you took me to the airport to fly back to Florida and got all turned around. I think we drove down every street in San Diego before you finally stopped for directions."

"I made you miss your flight," I say, unable to hold back my smile.

The truth is, I didn't want Gammy to go. I didn't get lost on purpose, but having Gammy with us an extra day was hardly a disappointment. She had been my partner in crime and, if we were not born decades apart, my twin.

"What's it like, Gammy?"

"Heaven? Oh, I could tell you, but then I'd have to kill you," she says with her wide, crooked-toothed grin.

"Apparently, you haven't lost your sense of humor. Is Pop there with you?"

"Oh yes, and Uncle Frankie and Aunt Bess and . . ." She stops for a moment and looks into my eyes, hers radiating truth and wisdom. "We're all connected, Claire. Our souls are all connected.

That's how we find each other. How I found you."

"But, what about—"

"Jazzy? The souls I never met when I was alive?" she asks. I'm amazed at Gammy's ability to read me, like she knows my thoughts before I speak. "Still connected. I know Jazzy as well as I know you and Brad and Edward and Ivy. There's no limit to our connection with others whether by blood or by association."

"It all sounds wonderful," I say.

"It is. Come, Claire. Come see." The pull increases like a riptide tugging me from shore. Gammy looks exactly as I remember, with piercing pool blue eyes, white cotton hair, rosy pink wrinkled cheeks, and a lopsided smile, warm and full. I've missed her so much.

"I can't." I yank my hands away from Gammy's soft touch and turn to avoid seeing her disappointment.

"Of course you can. Your time here is over."

I turn and look at Gammy. "Over? No, I can't accept that. There's a reason I'm still here."

"Sometimes, when the soul is conflicted, it gets a little lost, that's all. You didn't feel fulfilled, you feared you took too much for granted, you questioned whether you were a good enough mother." Gammy takes my hand and pats it, "Which we all do, dear. But tonight, your soul came to terms with it. You finally let it go."

"But they still need me."

"Do they *really* need you or do *you* need them?"

And there it is, the question I was too afraid to ask myself. What is it that's keeping me here? Is it for them or is it for my own peace of mind?

"Edward's struggling. He's up to something, and I need to help Brad figure it out. And Ivy's finally communicating with me—we're becoming close. And my little Jazzy needs her mother. She's so young, and there's still so much I need to teach her." I ramble at a speed I'm not sure Gammy can follow.

"They'll figure it out, sweetheart."

"Gammy, you don't understand. I need to protect them."

"Protect them from what?"

"I don't know." I shake my head. "I just don't know."

"You have no pull here, Claire. There's nothing you can change."

"There *are* things I can change. I already have. I saved Ivy from Zane that night at the party."

"Ivy saved herself. You just happened to witness it."

"And Edward. I was able to tell Brad what really happened at school with Zane—I helped him see what we couldn't before."

"Again, my darling, you were merely a witness. He would have seen that without you. You can no longer take the credit or the fall for their actions. You did the best you could for them, but you need to allow them to fight their own battles now."

I'm deflated and yet proud at the same time if that's possible. I've always fought the kids' battles for them, protected them, and worried I'd never given them the tools to fight on their own. But according to Gammy, they're doing it without me. Maybe my grandmother's right—they don't need me anymore, and the feeling to stay is because *I* still need them.

"I need more time," I say.

"I can see your soul is again, conflicted. I thought I could help you resolve your apprehension, but you've always been a little on the stubborn side." Gammy gives me a conciliatory smile. "You won't have much time. I'll be back soon, and when I return you must come with me. Find your peace, Claire." Gammy caresses my face like she did when I was a child. No words were ever needed with that one gesture that said, *I believe in you.* "But, if you choose to stay here now, there's a price."

"A price?"

"Yes. Even in Heaven, you can't get something for nothing."

"What kind of price? Like selling my soul to the Devil?"

Gammy lets out a childlike giggle. "Oh heavens no. God would never make you do that."

"Then what is it?"

"I can't tell you. Only you can decide if the unknown price is worth the risk."

She said risk. What am I risking? What could I possibly have to risk if my soul is safe?

"Gammy, is it worth it?"

"I don't know, Claire. Is it?" Her words fade, and with them, the light.

My family is worth everything.

"How long?" I ask as the light recedes, like Gammy's closing the door to the sun and stars, to Heaven. "How long, Gammy?" I shout, but there's no response—only the absence of Gammy, the light, and an answer to the one question that holds so much weight.

Have I bought myself a day? A week? Months? Did I make a big mistake? What do I plan to accomplish if, like Gammy said, I have no influence here? And now, I've risked something without knowing what it is, without knowing what my price will be for staying.

Chapter Nineteen

I t's Thanksgiving. The Southern California sun, still strong and warm, always promises the weather will never be too unbearable while turkeys roast and Christmas decorations go up. Growing up in the temperamental weather of the Midwest left me more than grateful to live in the predictably mild weather, free from shoveling snow or worse, driving in it. I appreciated the amiable rays on my skin, the sway of the palm trees, and the scent of citrus, eucalyptus, and fresh cut grass during the winter months. And, today I'm thankful I've been given, what I believe is one last holiday with my family.

"Good morning," I say to Brad as he exits the bedroom, showered and dressed yet looking anything but rested. His glassy, glazed eyes hold bags under red rims. But when he sees me, his mouth turns upward, his eyes come alive, and his heart beats hard and fast.

"You're still here," he says and lets out a relieved exhale. "I had a dream you left."

"Yes, something to be thankful for . . . on Thanksgiving."

Brad puts his hands on the top of his head. "I forgot to get the turkey. I was going to stop on the way home from work yesterday."

"You've had a lot on your plate, sweetheart."

"That's no excuse. Jazzy kept reminding me, and it totally slipped my mind." He rubs his temples. "The kids are counting on me to keep it together."

"You can't expect for everything to work like it did before."

"I know, but it's Thanksgiving, for God's sake!"

"Don't panic." I glance at the clock; it's a few minutes after eight in the morning. "The grocery store is open. Let's get a list, and you can run out now."

Brad's shoulders relax. Normally, my parents would be celebrating this holiday with us. Their yearly pilgrimage to our home has been a tradition for years. My mom and I would plan the meal, set the table, and prepare the turkey and all the trimmings. Once dinner was over, we would make our way to the Christmas tree in the living room, its outstretched branches waiting to be adorned with all the ornaments we've collected throughout the years.

With each ornament holding a special memory, we'd recount its significance as we placed it on the tree. My mom would bring out the eggnog and insist we sing carols as we put on the finishing touches while my dad would sleep off his turkey coma. It was the one day of the year when I didn't worry about a hectic schedule or what lay ahead or behind. It was the one day of the year I made myself live in the moment and truly find gratitude for all I had.

But this year, my parents aren't coming. They told Brad they would be here, but he insisted they not make the trek this year, especially since it was so soon after the funeral. "It would be too hard for you," he had said to them. Even though Brad made it seem as though he didn't want them to endure the emotional holiday, I know, for him, it was an act of self-preservation. My parents are hard enough to deal with in normal situations with their bickering and my father's tirades that put everyone in a bad mood. Having them here when Brad has no energy to engage could turn into a catastrophic blowout.

Brad opens the junk drawer, the same drawer he dug through the day he invited Bridget into our house. It's now organized, and new pens and a pad of paper are easy to find. His face lights up with delight and there's a little pang in my chest. I didn't cause that delight, Bridget did. But I wonder if he would have noticed this small thing if I were still here, if so much change hadn't happened. I wonder if he, like me, notices more of the little things he took for granted before everything changed.

"What do I need to get?" he asks, with a fresh pen and the pad of paper in front of him.

"Well, you need a turkey."

"Obviously." Brad writes it down and then looks back at me like an eager student. I give him a list of ingredients, which includes stuffing mix, potatoes, the have-to-get-it-but-no-one-eats-it cranberry sauce along with the fixings for our traditional corn casserole, and kid's champagne. "Oh, and don't forget an apple pie. Don't get pumpkin, the kids won't eat it. And get eggnog."

He looks over his long list. "Anything else?"

"That about covers it, but you might need a little patience. It's a madhouse there on Thanksgiving."

"Got it. Be back in a bit." He leaves as though he's at the starting line of a race and the gun has gone off.

"Where's Daddy?" Jazzy asks as she hops down the stairs with Pink Kitty in her grasp, dangling by its ear. Her disheveled hair is mashed down with a paper Indian headband. Three colorful feathers stick up in the back and writing adorns the sides.

"He went to the store. He'll be back soon. I love your headband."

"Thanks. I made it at school yesterday," she says with pride. She takes it off her head. "I decorated it myself. Do you like my Indian name?"

"'Brave Butterfly.' It's perfect."

"My teacher said the butterfly means joy and change. I was just going to write 'Butterfly,' but Bella told me I should put 'Brave' in the name because she thinks I'm brave."

"I think you're brave too. Why does Bella think you're brave?"

"Because sometimes, when I'm sad and I want to cry, I don't, and she thinks that's brave."

"That *is* brave. But, sometimes it's okay to cry if you're sad or hurt. There's nothing wrong with crying if you feel like it."

"I know, but I'm a big girl now, and I don't want anyone thinking I'm a crybaby anymore."

It's sad that Jazzy feels she needs to grow up so fast, to hide her feelings to protect herself. She's still so young, and her deep emotions are one of the things that make her incredibly unique. The way she feels and empathizes with others is the core of who she is. Of the three kids, she connects the best with others and their needs.

"Jazz, don't change who you are because you're afraid of what others think," I say, thinking of all Ivy gave up for the same reason.

"Mommy, I have to grow up sometime."

"Of course you do. I'm not telling you to not grow up, silly. But, growing up doesn't mean you have to change. You'll just be an older version of who you are right now. Do you understand?"

Jazzy gives me a tentative nod.

"Hey, want to help me?"

Jazzy's eyebrows pinch together, and she cocks her head to one side. "With what?"

"I'd like to set the table for Thanksgiving, but I need working hands. Could you be my hands for me?"

Jazzy's face brightens. "Yes! That sounds like fun."

She sets the table with my guidance. First the tablecloth, then the dishes. I tell her about the history of our china and silverware, passed down from Gammy when Brad and I married, as Jazzy carefully places them on the table.

"Only four settings. Grandma and Grandpa won't be here this year," I say, trying to avoid any sadness in my voice.

"No, we need five." Jazzy pulls out one more plate from the china cabinet. "You need a plate too."

"That's sweet, but I think we should skip mine this year." At some point, Jazzy's going to have to understand I won't be here forever. Gammy will be coming back for me.

"Nope, you need a plate. You're going to sit right here, next to me." She takes the plate and with gentle reverence, places it on the table.

"I guess that would be nice. Thank you."

—

AS JAZZY PROUDLY finishes preparing the table, Brad enters the house, loaded down with bags of groceries.

"You have to be on a suicide mission to go to the store on Thanksgiving," he says slightly out of breath. He deposits the heavy bags on the counter and leaves to retrieve more.

"What's all this for?" Ivy asks, entering the kitchen in her pink sleep shorts and black concert T-shirt of a band I've never heard of.

"It's Thanksgiving," Jazzy says. "Happy Thanksgiving, Ivy."

"It's just a day," Ivy says without an ounce of enthusiasm while pulling open the fridge and grabbing the orange juice from the door.

"Oh hey, Ivy. Happy Thanksgiving," Brad says, carrying in the last two bags and plunking them on the kitchen island. "That's what I call a strenuous workout."

"Ivy, we could use your help in the kitchen today," I say, looking at Brad for backup.

"Yes, *we* could," Brad says, putting the groceries away.

Ivy fills a glass from the cabinet and downs half of the orange liquid before filling the glass back up and returning the container to the fridge.

"You know what they say, the more the merrier," Brad says. He raises his eyebrows in Ivy's direction, waiting for a response.

Ivy makes an audible, I-can't-be-bothered-with-this groan. "More like, too many cooks spoil the broth."

"Where'd you hear that?" Brad asks.

"My English teacher says it all the time. She can't stand group projects. Stuff always goes wrong when too many people work together."

"Well, I don't agree. And today, we all need to roll up our sleeves and learn how this is done from the expert," he says.

"Expert at your service," I say with a laugh and a bow.

Ivy tries but can't hold back a smile. "Fine. I wouldn't want you two to burn down the house."

Brad clunks the turkey on the countertop. His lips jut out as he stares at it.

"Sounds like a block of ice," I say.

"It *is* a block of ice. They only had frozen ones left," Brad says. "Can we defrost it in the microwave?"

"Daddy, I don't think it's gonna fit in the microwave."

"I suppose you're right, Jazz. Claire, suggestions?"

"I've never cooked a frozen one. Run it under warm water?"

"Alrighty then, warm water it is." He moves the turkey to the sink.

Ivy reads the tag tied to the packaging. "It says we need to thaw it in the fridge."

"That'll take days and we only have hours. I think the warm water will work," Brad says, a hint of doubt behind his cheerful voice.

He turns on the oven and gets to work on the turkey while I teach Ivy how to make the stuffing and Jazzy how to peel potatoes. Once Ivy is done with the instant stuffing, I coach her on how to make the corn casserole and then work out the timing on when it needs to go in the oven as well as the rolls. Jazzy insists on making Great Grandma Blackwell's famous carrot and pineapple Jell-O mold, and once it's in the fridge, the girls look over to Brad who has the turkey in the pan.

"It's defrosted already?" I ask.

"It's good enough. It'll thaw the rest of the way in the oven. I'll just turn up the temp a little," he says turning the oven dial.

"Hmmm, I don't know about that," I say.

"It's fine, Claire." There is a distinct edge to his voice.

"Well, then it's time to put the stuffing in the bird." I give the girls an encouraging smile. "Girls, take handfuls of the stuffing and put it inside the turkey."

"Ewww, I'm not sticking my hand inside the turkey," Jazzy says.

Ivy rolls her eyes. "Fine, I'll do it."

When Ivy finishes, I have Brad butter and season the turkey and then put it in the oven. I feel like I've instructed a blind person to cross a busy road successfully.

"All right, now we wait," Brad says. "What's next?"

"I know, let's get out the Christmas decorations," Jazzy says.

Brad turns away from the girls and stares out the window above the sink. His heart thumps faster. "Maybe we could wait on those, Jazz."

He doesn't want to explain or discuss; he wants to avoid like so many of our arguments. He always needed time to think it through before hashing it out. It's obviously too soon for him to deal with another holiday while this one seems to be turning into a physical and emotional challenge. *Put on a good face for the kids* is what's most likely playing inside his head. He turns back around and looks at Jazzy, who has disappointment etched in her face. A single tear threatens to spill down her heated, rosy cheek.

"Oh Jazz, don't do this," he says.

"But we *always* have the decorations out before we eat the turkey." Jazzy's chin quivers and the corners of her mouth pull down.

"Dad," Ivy says, looking at Brad with pleading eyes. "Please."

Brad glances at me, but I can't read him and don't know if he wants my input. Where is my place in all of this? I don't want to push him, but it's important to the girls.

"Girls, maybe you should give Dad a little more time," I say.

"I'm sorry. I can't, I just . . ." Brad rushes out of the kitchen and into the bedroom, closing the door behind him. Both girls unleash tears.

"Hey, hey, it's okay," I say. It's so difficult to not be able to wrap my arms around them and kiss their tears away.

"But now Daddy's mad," Jazzy says.

"No, he's a little sad that's all," I say.

"Are we ever going to be okay, Mom? Is *Dad* ever going to be okay?" Ivy asks, wiping her nose on her sleeve.

"Holidays sometimes make us sad when we think of those who aren't here to celebrate with us anymore. Remember how sad we were that first Christmas without Gammy? It wasn't the same without her. But we learned to adjust, right? We found ways to celebrate her and include her with all our stories. It takes time. Daddy needs some time."

"But you're still *here*," Jazzy says.

"Yes . . . and no. My spirit's here, but my body isn't. I can't do anything physical like I used to. Jazz, my . . ." I stop. Telling Jazzy my time here is limited will only make this harder.

"What?" she asks.

"I just wish everyone could see through your eyes."

"What does that mean?"

I raise my hand and caress Jazzy's cheek, as though I'm touching its soft curves. "If everyone saw the way you see things, me being here would be so much easier for everyone."

Ivy puts her arm around Jazzy's shoulder and leans over to look at her. "Why don't we go upstairs and decorate our rooms, and when Dad's ready, we can decorate the rest of the house?"

Once the girls leave, I enter the bedroom without knocking. Brad's on the edge of the bed, his arms wrapped tightly around my pillow, his striking blue eyes bloodshot, his heart's pace erratic.

"I'm sorry," he says.

"Sorry?" I sit next to him. He buries his nose in my pillow and inhales.

"For losing it in the kitchen. I shouldn't have done that in front of the kids."

"They understand."

"I'm supposed to be the strong one."

"Who says? You're entitled to feel however you need to feel."

"Not in front of the kids," he says.

"It wouldn't hurt for you to share your grief with them. Be human in front of them. They need to know they're not alone."

"I don't know if I can do that."

There's so much to say, but how? I don't have all the answers; I don't have any answers for him, navigating through this new life he's forced to live. I'm as lost as he is.

"I'm so confused. You're here, but you're not. I can hear you and see you, but I can't touch you . . . *physically* love you." He squeezes the pillow harder into his chest. "I want you, ache for you."

"I wish I could give that to you."

"I feel like an addict, forced to sit in front of the temptation with my hands tied behind my back," he says. "Sex, Claire. I miss sex . . . with you."

"We always miss what we can't have."

"Don't you miss it? Doesn't it bother you that we'll never be together like that again?"

"I do miss it, but probably not the way you do. I don't have that physical urge like when I was alive. But I do miss your touch, the warmth and smell of your skin, your strong arms holding me."

"Every time I catch a whiff of you, from your clothes or . . . this pillow, I feel like you're not really gone and then . . . reality crashes down and suffocates me."

His heart picks up its pace, but the only way I can comfort him is with my words, and they would fall short.

"And when I hear your voice? It awakens me and taunts me and reminds me over and over what I will never have again."

"What do you want me to do? Do you want me to leave?" I ask, not out of anger, but out of concern and love for him.

"Do you realize we'll have to go through losing you all over again? Maybe Edward's the smart one in all this."

"I think about it all the time. I'm still not sure if being here is a gift or a curse." I'm afraid to ask again, but I need to know. "Do you want me to leave?"

"No," he shouts, and then in a whisper, "I don't know."

I search for some sign in his eyes; the truth. "Just say the word."

"Not today." He places the pillow down at the head of the bed and stands. "We have a holiday to celebrate."

"They can wait . . . until you're ready."

"If there's anything I've learned from all of this, it's that life's too short to waste time waiting," he says flashing me a determined grin.

—

BRAD UNLOADS THE Christmas bins from the attic as the girls place their contents around the house. While they're not as detail-oriented in their decorating as I had been, they take on the task with the spirit of Christmas in their hearts, each pumping with an excited rhythm. Brad is much faster, more efficient at putting up the nine-foot artificial tree. His strong arms and height have the tree assembled in twenty minutes.

Decorating looks easier when more than one person does all the work. All those years I insisted on doing it myself so it would be perfect, and yet, it all looks perfect now, and I didn't touch one thing. I should've learned to let go of this control years ago. Watching my family, with the exception of Edward, who's still sleeping, decorate with such enthusiasm is really what this season is all about; sharing the love and spirit of the holiday.

"Mom," Ivy says. "I can't smell the turkey yet. Shouldn't we be able to smell it by now?"

"Hmmm. There's always pizza," I say.

The doorbell chimes and Buddy's ferocious bark echoes down the hall.

"I'll get it!" Jazzy says and skips to the front door.

"Hi, Mrs. Radcliff," Jazzy says.

"Hi, Jazzy. Happy Thanksgiving. I brought a few things for your meal."

"Okay. We're all in the family room. We're decorating."

Bridget follows Jazzy into the family room carrying two large grocery bags. Brad looks up from the Christmas bin he's digging into and his face brightens. He rushes to Bridget and collects the bags from her arms.

"Bridget! What a nice surprise. You didn't need to do all this," he says carrying the bags to the kitchen and placing them on the counter. He doesn't glance in my direction.

"I didn't know if you'd planned to cook so I thought I'd make some Thanksgiving fixings for y'all." She peers into the oven. "Looks like you got this under control. My husband . . . ex-husband, couldn't even boil water without nearly burning the house down. I'm impressed."

"Well, I can't take all the credit for this," Brad says.

"Yeah, Mommy's helping us," Jazzy says.

Everyone's eyes dart in different directions; Brad's to Jazzy, then to Bridget, Ivy's to Jazzy, then to me, Bridget's to Jazzy, then to Brad.

Brad laughs. "What she means is, we're trying to follow Claire's recipes."

Bridget slaps a hand on her bare chest above her low cut,

Pepto-Bismol inspired sweater and lets out a nervous snort. She clears her throat while brushing her long, ebony hair behind her ear. "Can I be of some assistance?"

Brad finally looks at me.

"It would be nice if it was just the five of us," I say. "Plus, it might get a little complicated."

"Yeah. I think Mommy's right," Jazzy says.

Bridget's eyes narrow.

"We were recently debating on an ingredient on one of Claire's recipe cards. I thought it seemed like too much . . ." Brad says.

"Sage?" I say

"Yes, sage, that's it. But Jazzy's probably correct to follow what Claire wrote down."

Brad gives Jazzy a subtle head shake while sweat glistens on his forehead.

"A little sage goes a long way." Bridget unloads her bags on the cluttered counter. "I brought you a homemade pumpkin pie, and thought I would whip up my Nana's famous sweet potato pie. It's to die for," she says.

"Maybe that's what happened to Mom. She was in such a rush to eat your pie that she died on the way," Ivy says, her words bathed in sarcasm.

Brad glares at her. "Ivy."

"Oh, shoot! I'm so sorry. I shouldn't have said that. Those silly idioms pop out before my brain can stop them."

"Dad," Ivy says, raising her eyebrows and nodding.

"I'll whip up this pie, lickety-split."

"Lickety-split?" Jazzy says, laughing.

"What? You've never heard of lickety-split? How about Heaven's to Betsy? I know, cattywampus?"

"Nope."

"If you're around me long enough, you'll hear them all."

Oh, good gravy, I certainly hope not.

The girls retreat upstairs while I keep a close eye on Brad and his uninvited guest. She appears harmless, but I don't trust her. Especially with those tatas looking like they need their own postal code.

"This is all so thoughtful, Bridget, but—"

"I just love cooking. Without the boys to cook for, I don't know what to do with myself. I'll skedaddle as soon as I get this in the oven."

"Where are the boys?" Brad asks.

"They're with Gregory. He gets them for Thanksgiving this year."

"That must be incredibly difficult," Brad says.

Bridget plucks a white apron, decorated with red cherries and ruffles, from her purse. She puts it on and ties it around her narrow waist before retrieving a mixing bowl from the bottom cabinet next to the sink and a large spoon from the utensil drawer. It's as if she's cooked in my kitchen a million times, but I never kept the bowls in that cabinet. Now I'm annoyed at how she rearranged *my* cabinets when she cleaned *my* kitchen. "It's our new normal. Not what I would have wanted, but we don't always get a choice, do we?"

"No, we certainly don't. Why don't you stay and join us for dinner," Brad says.

"Goodness gracious, you're too kind. But I couldn't intrude more than I already have."

I'm relieved Bridget's bowing out of our family time. It's not that I don't feel sorry for her, I do. But she doesn't belong here. She'll never belong here.

"Don't be silly. Stay. I insist." Brad's eyes pan to me before offering a slight shrug. I flash him back my what-the-hell face I perfected when I was alive, but all he does is give me a half smile and another shrug before turning back to Bridget.

"Are you sure?" she asks.

"Absolutely."

"Brad," I say capturing his attention. "Let's chat."

I exit the kitchen. Brad follows me into the hall bathroom around the corner and closes the door.

"I thought we agreed it'd be better if she left," I say.

"How can I send her away when she doesn't have anyone to go home to?"

"I bet we're not her only option for Thanksgiving. Plus, what about the kids? They can't talk to me if Bridget's here."

"This is so unlike you. You're always the one inviting people to our celebrations because you feel sorry for them."

"That's different."

"I completely disagree." Brad stares at me with his hands on his hips, inviting me to challenge him. "Wait a minute. This is all about Bridget, isn't it? What's really going on?"

"Nothing."

"Even as a ghost, you're a terrible liar."

There's a light rap on the door. "Brad, everything okay in there?" Bridget asks.

Brad gives me Ivy's exaggerated eyeroll. "Yeah. Damn phone's got a mind of its own. Be out shortly."

"This is the way the whole night's going to be if she stays," I say.

Brad reduces his voice to a whisper. "I can't exactly take back my invitation, can I?"

We stare at each other. I know he's right. It'd be rude to rescind his offer, but I'm disappointed. Footsteps clunk down the stairs followed by laughter.

"Last one to the kitchen washes the dishes!" Ivy says.

"Not fair! You have longer legs than me."

"At least the girls sound happy," I say before we both exit the bathroom.

—

WHEN BRAD AND I return to the kitchen, Jazzy's dressed in one of Ivy's old fancy Christmas dresses. It has a deep red, sparkly bodice and a full red, green, and navy plaid skirt. Jazzy's newly braided hair has scarlet bows tied to the ends. She's anything but a street urchin now. Ivy's wearing a dress too, the one I purchased for her and was left to hang in her closet for months, untouched. It's more conservative than the bandage dress I'd spotted on her floor. It's an off-white, flowy chiffon with the three-quarter length sleeves that billow when she walks, making her look like an angel. Her curled golden hair sways down her back with each move of her head. How beautiful they both look.

With less than an hour left on the turkey, Brad slides the corn casserole in the oven while the girls boil the potatoes. I continue to instruct them, but with Bridget in the kitchen, Brad, Jazzy and Ivy don't directly acknowledge me. Instead, I get a nod or a "got it" as though they're talking to each other. I'm nearly invisible to them, and when Bridget uses her sweet, southern charm to suggest adding a different ingredient or show them an "easier" way of doing something I've already told them, they act like she's some kind of cooking marvel.

Brad opens a bottle of wine while Bridget assembles a small charcuterie plate of meats, cheeses and nuts. Ivy and Jazzy drain the potatoes and put them in the mixer, adding copious amounts of butter followed by milk and a few dashes of salt. Pride grows on their faces as they look at the bowl full of fluffiness. I want to taste them, to enjoy the buttery silkiness again.

More footsteps pound down the stairs, and moments later, Edward enters the kitchen.

"Well, hey. Look who's graced us with his presence," Brad says, looking up from the turkey he pulled from the oven. "Happy Thanksgiving, son."

"What time is it?" Edward asks, squinting at the microwave clock.

"It's time for our Thanksgiving dinner, that's what time it is, Sleeping Beauty. You remember Ms. Radcliff?" Brad says gesturing to Bridget.

"Nice to see you, Edward," Bridget says.

Edward gives her a small nod. "Hi."

"You're just in time to help carve the turkey," Brad says.

"You can do it."

"No way, I insist you do it. It's tradition for the Blackwell men to carve the turkey. It's time for me to pass the knife."

"Seriously, Dad. I don't want to."

"Sometimes you have to do what you don't want to do."

"Fine, whatever."

"I'll go check the table," Bridget says, smartly dismissing herself from the growing tension in the kitchen.

The girls put the rolls in the oven and then watch Brad explain to Edward where to cut while motioning with his hand. Edward looks on with crossed arms while his right foot taps on the chipped tile.

"Here, you try it." Brad hands Edward the electric knife. A loud exhale escapes Edward's mouth before turning on the knife and bringing it down on the meat.

Jazzy dips her finger into the mashed potatoes and takes a sample bite. "Oh man, this is good."

"Jazz, don't do that. That's gross," Ivy says, but then dips her own finger in and takes a taste. They share a giggle.

"Dad, it's not cutting all the way," Edward says.

"You're probably hitting bone. Cut at a different angle and give it a little muscle," Brad says.

"I'm telling you, it's not cutting." Edward forces the words through his teeth while pushing down on the knife embedded in the turkey.

"Edward, it's not that hard. Seriously, just cut the damn thing."

"I'm cutting the *fucking* turkey, see?" Edward yanks the knife out of the turkey, lifts it high in the air and brings it back down on the beast with brute force. He repeats the karate chopping; turkey bits fly into the air before landing on the counter and floor. Buddy's at Edward's feet feasting on the scraps. "It's still frozen."

"Stop. Edward, Stop!" Brad says.

"This is so fucking ridiculous." Edward yanks the cord from the wall and throws the knife to the floor, cracking the plastic base and chipping another tile. "You all act as though everything's okay. Well, news flash, Mom's dead, and I don't want to fucking celebrate anything."

Brad stares at Edward with his mouth half open and his eyes wider than the gaping hole in the turkey. The girls take a few steps back and cower like scared dogs. It's the first time Edward's exploded or shown any significant emotion since my accident. Although the girl's faces reflect horror, his outburst could be a needed breakthrough.

"Mommy *is* here," Jazzy squeaks.

"Really? Then why is this meal such a fucking mess?" he says. Jazzy covers her ears and leans into Ivy for protection.

"Stop with the language, Edward," Brad says.

"What's the point? Let's stop pretending that this is like every other Thanksgiving. You want to believe Mom's here? Then leave me the fuck out of it." He kicks the broken knife across the floor before storming out of the kitchen and back to his room.

"Daddy!" Jazzy points to the oven. Black smoke billows out of it, and moments later, the smoke alarm blares while Buddy barks at the ensuing chaos.

"Shit, shit, shit!" Brad says.

Bridget rushes into the kitchen as Brad opens the oven door and reaches in with both hands for the tray of rolls.

"Fuck!" He pulls his hands back and quickly moves to the sink, forcing his bright red hands under the running water. Bridget joins Brad at the sink and looks at his hands.

"Make sure that's cold water," I say.

"I know. I'm not stupid."

"What? I didn't say you were stupid," Bridget says.

Brad grinds his teeth. "I was talking to myself."

"It's an honest mistake. I've burned myself plenty of times," Bridget says holding his hands under the water.

"Turn off the oven," I tell Ivy. "Get the hot pads and take the tray out."

Ivy pulls the tray out. The rolls are completely black. She reaches back into the oven, takes out the corn casserole, and places it on the oven top. It's dark brown and not how it's supposed to look.

"See, too many cooks," Ivy says.

Chapter Twenty

"This is a disaster. A complete disaster," Brad says. "Edward's right," he adds in a whisper.

Bridget pulls his hands from the stream of water and he winces as she pats them dry. He walks to the pantry, snags the broom, and smashes the smoke alarm with its handle multiple times until its pieces fall to the floor, and the blaring stops.

Bridget hasn't moved from her spot near the sink, her face frozen in a permanent state of bewilderment.

Brad's eyes focus on the mess littering the floor when the doorbell rings.

"Who the hell could that be?" he says, his voice tight and clipped.

"I'll . . . get it," Jazzy says, shock still painted on her freckled face. She slogs to the front door, but when she looks through the window, her eyes light up. She opens the door and runs.

"Grandma! Grandpa! I thought you weren't coming."

"Oh, we couldn't stay away," my mom says, embracing Jazzy's head into her soft midsection.

"It's a good thing you're here. Dinner's not going too well."

As they walk in, my dad fans the air in front of him. "What the hell's burning?"

"The rolls . . . and the casserole," Jazzy says.

"Well, at least we have turkey," my dad says.

"Nope, it didn't cook. Edward tried to karate chop it with the knife, but it won't cut," Jazzy says with such a matter-of-fact presentation it almost sounds like she's joking.

My dad pats the top of her head. "Funny. You're a funny kid."

When they enter the kitchen, my mom takes in a loud breath and places her hand on her chest. "Oh, dear," she says, surveying the carnage. Then her eyes rest on Bridget who's, once again, tending to Brad's burned hands. "Oh, dear."

He pulls his hands from Bridget's grasp. "Dot, Frank. You said you weren't coming. I wasn't expecting you."

"Well, that's quite obvious," my mom says.

"You remember Bridget, Claire's friend? She's been a great help to us these past few weeks."

"I'm sure she has."

"It's nice to see you again," Bridget says folding the towel she used to dry Brad's hands.

"Yes, dear. Very nice . . . to see you." My mom looks around the kitchen again. "What in God's name happened here?"

"Just a few timing problems," Brad says.

"Huh. It's a good thing I listened. Claire must have sent me some kind of message from heaven because, early this morning, I got this little pang in my chest, and I told Frank, 'Frank, we have to go to them.' Well, he didn't know what I was talking about. So I went online and found some last-minute airfare—"

"Expensive as hell," my dad says, his gaze cemented in Bridget's direction.

"Frank." My mom gives him the stop-right-there eye. "We packed our bags and headed to the airport within the hour."

"I told her not to—that you insisted, Brad, but she didn't listen. God that woman never listens."

"I'm glad you're here. It wouldn't be Thanksgiving without you," Brad says.

"It's still not going to be the same without Claire," my mother says.

"But she's here," Jazzy says taking another finger dip into the potatoes.

"Yes, of course she is," my mom says. "Now, all of you, out of the kitchen. I have some work to do." Ivy and my dad leave the room while Jazzy, Brad and Bridget stay. My mom looks down to roll up her sleeves and sees Brad's hands. She grabs his wrists to take a closer look. "These look bad. They're blistering. Take some Advil and go sit down. I got this."

"Thanks, Dot," Brad says. "This didn't go the way I had hoped."

"Few things ever do."

"Let me help you, Dot," Bridget says.

"I appreciate the offer, but I'll take it from here."

After Brad and Bridget vacate the kitchen, Jazzy plops down on a chair and watches my mom.

"Did you really hear Mommy calling for you?" Jazzy asks my mom and then looks at me as though she's asking me the question.

"Well, I got a little bump in my heart. You know that feeling when your heart beats a little harder than usual?" she says.

"Maybe you were having a heart attack. Besides, Mommy couldn't be talking to you 'cause she's been here the whole time."

My mom turns toward Jazzy and studies her face. Her own, full of understanding.

"She has, *has* she?"

"Yep. She helped us with dinner, but we all kinda messed it up." Jazzy looks at me and then to my mom. "She's right here if you want to say 'hi,'" Jazzy says, pointing to me.

My mom looks to where Jazzy's pointing, but there's no recognition on her face as she shakes her head. "I don't see her."

"Most people don't. Only me, Daddy, and Ivy can see her. We think Edward can see her, but he won't say that he does."

"Hi, Claire," my mom says.

"Hi, Mom."

"She said, 'Hi, Mom,'" Jazzy says.

"Did she really?"

"Yep, she really did."

My mom gazes at where I am, and a smile forms on her face. "I can't see you, darling, but I've always been able to feel you. I love you."

"I love you too, Mom."

"She says she loves you too, Grandma."

My mom stares for a bit as though, at any moment, I'll appear to her. As though, if she concentrates long enough and prays hard enough, God will grant her one last look. She makes her way to the hacked-up turkey.

"Looks like we have some work to do," she says to no one in particular. "Good thing I believe in miracles."

My mom cuts off what she can from the half-frozen turkey and cooks it in the microwave while she salvages some of the corn casserole and whips up some biscuits from scratch. The one thing my mom could always do was make something out of nothing, especially when it came to food. Jazzy is in the dining room, adding extra place settings.

The sound of my dad's snores from the couch cause my mom to sigh loudly.

"Some things never change, Claire." She takes the hot biscuits out of the oven and places them in the breadbasket. "And yet, other things change so much it makes your heart ache."

My mom, the savior of Thanksgiving, brings the hot dishes to the table and stops her gaze on the plate with my name card right next to Jazzy's. A tear travels down her soft, wrinkled face. She pauses for a moment before she yells, "Dinner's ready. Come and eat."

—

"WHERE'S EDWARD?" MY mom asks as everyone takes their seat. I had Jazzy place Bridget's plate at the opposite end of the table from Brad.

Brad blows out a breath. "Hold on." He rises from the table and heads upstairs. From my seat, I hear Brad knock on Edward's door. "Dinner's ready."

"Not hungry," Edward says.

"Grandma and Grandpa are here. They want to see you."

"Maybe later."

My dad's eyes are once again hooked on Bridget while we wait for Brad to return to the table.

"Look, I get it. This is all overwhelming and—"

"No, you don't get it. You'll never get it," Edward says.

"Maybe you're right. I don't get much of anything these days. But we're family, and we need to stick together. Just come down for dinner."

"I don't want to."

"Then do it for me, for your sisters." Brad's request is almost a whisper, but I hear it as though I'm standing right next to him.

"Fine," Edward says.

When Edward and Brad approach the table, my mom scurries over to Edward and gives him a hug and kiss. "You look taller than just a few weeks ago," she says. Edward gives her a small smile, and when everyone finally takes a seat at the table, Jazzy leads the family in grace.

"Amen," she says. "Now, everyone needs to say what they're thankful for."

Ivy and Edward groan.

"I'll start," my mom says, perking up Jazzy's waning smile. "I'm thankful Grandpa and I could be here this year. I missed all of you too much to stay away. Frank?"

"Yes, me too, I'm thankful to be here," he says and looks to Edward to speak next. "Your turn."

"Pass," Edward says, his eyes cast downward at his empty plate. Brad flashes him a disappointed look but doesn't say anything.

"I'm thankful you two didn't listen to me," Brad says. "This would have been a total disaster without you. I'm also glad Bridget could join us." He nods at Ivy.

"Same. I'm thankful Grandma and Grandpa are here and that the house didn't burn down," Ivy says.

"Bridget, would you like to say anything?" Brad asks.

"Yes. I'm so humbled you invited me to spend this important day with y'all."

I want to roll my eyes. She basically invited herself, showing up with bags of groceries and a sob story about being without her boys.

"My turn," Jazzy says. "I'm thankful for Grandma and Grandpa too. And that Mommy's here with us." My dad's lips pull to one side and his bushy gray brows furrow while Edward lets out a big, impatient grumble. Bridget also has a confused look on her flushed face. "And for the Pilgrims and the Indians, and the turkey who died for us, and the corn—"

"Okay, enough already," Edward says.

Jazzy shoots angry eyes at Edward. "And the corn, and the farmer who grew the corn. And . . . that's all."

"That was very nice, Jazzy. I think it's important to thank the farmer for the corn. They don't get thanked enough," my mom says. She picks up a dish and hands it to my dad.

"Yes, that was so sweet of you, Jazzy," Bridget says.

"What was that about your mom being here?" my dad asks, the dish now in his hands. Brad shakes his head at Jazzy.

"She's here. Right here, actually." Jazzy points to my chair next to her. She scoops up some potatoes and plops them on my plate.

"What are you doing?" Edward asks.

"I don't want Mommy to feel left out."

"You're wasting food," Edward says.

"So?"

"Let's not argue," Brad says. "Pass me the potatoes, Jazz."

She nearly drops the dish as she adjusts her headband on her head.

"What's with the Indian hat?" my dad asks.

Oh Lord, not this again. I'd have warned Jazzy about the headband if I'd known my parents were coming to dinner.

"I made it in school. See my name?" Jazzy proudly points to the side of the brown construction paper band.

"What the hell are they teaching kids these days? Damn Indians."

"Frank!" my mom says, scolding him like a child.

"The Indians taught the Pilgrims how to plant, Grandpa. Without them, the Pilgrims would have starved," Jazzy says, her voice meek and hesitant. She takes a bite of mashed potatoes and stares at her plate.

"You should be wearing a pilgrim hat, not some damn Indian hat," my dad says.

Brad glances at me, worry on his face. He knows where this conversation is headed. My dad's strong views of history have often been an instigator of family arguments, especially at the dinner table after he's chased down a couple strong martinis.

Bridget eats like a bird, wiping her face with her napkin after every tiny bite.

"In my day, we didn't celebrate the Indians," he says.

"No offense, Grandpa, but in your day, life was a little politically incorrect," Edward says.

"Politically incorrect? Is that what they're teaching nowadays? Since when was honesty called being politically incorrect?" My dad's voice rises with each word. His fork clanks loudly on Gammy's white and platinum china.

"Frank, please. Let's just drop this," Brad says.

"Yes, Frank. It's Thanksgiving," my mom says. She throws him a warning look while she grabs his forearm and squeezes.

My dad scans the table like he's hunting down everyone with his eyes before focusing on his plate. "Damn schools," he mutters before taking a bite of dry turkey.

"This certainly has an interesting taste," my mom says pointing her fork at Bridget's sweet potato pie on her plate. "Is that Brandy?"

"Just a little. It's my Nana's southern recipe."

"You southern women are very sneaky, aren't you?"

"It's delicious, Bridget," Brad says.

My dad holds out his plate. "If it's got Brandy in it, I'll take another piece."

Bridget stands and cuts another wedge and places it on my dad's plate while he stares at her cleavage as it pops out of her pink sweater. Those puppies are going to fall out and roll across the table if she leans over any further. I swear he just moved his plate slightly out of her reach.

"So, you were a friend of Claire's?" My mom asks.

"Yes, we served on quite a few committees together. Your daughter was a wonderful woman," Bridget says.

"Funny, I don't remember her mentioning your name." My mom waves her hand. "It must be that early dementia setting in. Did you already have dinner with your family?"

"I had a small dinner with my boys last week. Their dad has them this week. We're divorced."

My dad's face lights up as though he's woken from a long, restful slumber.

"Oh, those poor boys," my mom says. Yet I can't help but think of how lucky they are to at least have both parents, even if not at the same time.

"Divorced, huh? He must be a total ass. This brandy pie alone would keep me from leaving," my dad says stuffing a large bite into his mouth.

"Yes, we know dear, it doesn't take much to keep you polishing my derriere."

"What's a derriere?" Jazzy asks.

"What a lovely party dress you have on, Jazzy," Bridget says.

"*Party!* I almost forgot." Jazzy hops out of her seat and heads for the stairs.

Brad stops her before she reaches the landing. "Jazzy, say thank you."

"Thanks," she says. "Be right back."

Moments later, Jazzy bounces down the stairs with a card

in her hand. "Grace Lee invited me to her birthday party next week." She waves the card in front of Brad.

"How nice." Brad takes the card and reads it. "This Wednesday afternoon? Who has a party on a Wednesday afternoon on a school week?"

"It's at Freedom Park. She's going to have a jumpy and a magician." Jazzy hops up and down, her voice an octave higher than usual.

"I don't know. It's awfully late notice. I have a meeting that afternoon and a work dinner. Edward, can you pick her up from the party? It's over at 5:30."

"Can't. I have a meeting with a . . . someone at five."

"Dot, how long are you and Frank going to be here? Maybe you could pick her up?" Brad asks.

"I wish we could, but we're out of here first thing tomorrow morning. We have a cruise to catch on Sunday— can't miss it. Non-refundable. I'm sorry," my mom says.

"I don't think it's going to work, sweetheart," Brad says.

"I knew it. I knew there'd be a reason I couldn't go. I told Grace, but she didn't believe me." Jazzy falls onto her chair and slumps forward.

"I can pick her up," Bridget says.

"Oh no, that's not necessary, Bridget," Brad says.

"Really, it's no problem."

"Perhaps one of Jazzy's *friends* could pick her up?" my mom says.

"I don't have the boys next week. You'd be doing me a favor by giving me something to do," Bridget says. "I don't mind at all."

Jazzy perks up. "Yeah, Daddy, she doesn't mind. Please?"

Brad takes a moment, obviously contemplating his options.

Say no to Jazzy and disappoint her or say yes to Bridget and place his trust in someone other than family. He looks to me, and I want to shake my head "no," but Jazzy's excited face reminds me how hard it has always been to deny her. Besides, Brad made it clear he's the one making the decisions from now on. I don't even know why he's looking at me, perhaps out of habit. I shrug. If it were up to me, I'd say no and find some other solution to the problem. But this is all on Brad, it's his call.

"Are you sure?" he asks Bridget.

"Totally. It's settled, then? I'll get her on Wednesday at 5:30 from Freedom Park?"

"Sounds good. Thanks so much," Brad says.

Jazzy jumps out of her seat, runs to Bridget, and gives her a big hug. My chest pulses with a growing ache. It's pure torment to watch another woman, a beautiful, successful woman, comforting my family.

"Thank you, Mrs. Radcliff. Thank you, thank you, thank you!" Jazzy says. "I'm going to Grace's birthday party, I'm going to Grace's birthday party."

"You're welcome. Why don't you call me Ms. Bridget?"

"Okay, Ms. Bridget. You're the best."

"Let me put it on my calendar." Bridget pulls her phone out of her purse. "I have a couple missed calls. Excuse me for a moment," she says and walks down the hall toward the kitchen. "What's the temp?" I hear her ask. "Okay, I'll be there in fifteen minutes," she says before she hangs up and returns to the table.

"Looks like I need to run. My poor little one's come down with a fever."

"Oh, no. It's no fun to be sick during the holidays," Brad says.

"Grayson kept calling for his mommy. He always needs his mommy when he's sick. Daddy just won't do." She places her hand over her mouth. "Oh, gosh, I'm so sorry. How insensitive of me."

My mom opens her mouth, but Brad quickly raises his hand. "It's okay. No need to be sorry," he says. Again, I want to smack him over the head. She *should* be sorry.

"Thank you for inviting me to join you for dinner. Happy Thanksgiving to all of you. I'll see you on Wednesday, Jazzy."

"It was nice of you to *drop* by," my mom says, her voice dripping with sarcasm.

"Yeah, the pie was delicious," my dad says, eyeing Bridget's back view as she walks to the door. My mom slaps him lightly on the back of the head.

"Grab some plates and follow me," my mom says through her teeth to my dad.

He follows her into the kitchen. I hear him whisper. "Did you see the rack on her? You think those are real?"

"Frank. Honestly."

"Hey, I may be old, but I'm not dead."

"Don't tempt me," my mom says.

"Thanks for stopping by," Brad says, following Bridget to the door.

Bridget turns to face Brad and flashes her illuminating smile.

"Thanks for inviting me in." Her eyes linger on his face a little too long for my liking before she leaves.

He watches her walk to her car before he closes the front door and turns, making his way back to the table. He looks at me.

"What?" he asks.

"What do you mean *what*?" I say.

"You were glaring at me. Yes, I'm pretty sure you were glaring at me."

"No, I wasn't glaring. I was concentrating on the cross above the door, trying to get it to fall off and hit you on the head."

Chapter Twenty-one

A fter a short holiday weekend, a new week is about to begin. Everyone goes to bed while I sit on the couch in the living room. Jazzy's shoes rest on the stairs, ready for school tomorrow. Buddy's sprawled at my feet since no one bothers to keep him in the back room anymore. The white carpet is now dingy from his dirty paws and it doesn't bother me a bit.

I gaze out the window, into the night with only a sliver of a moon to light the sky. The creaks of the house, the hum of appliances, the variations in the howls of coyotes, or the scurry of a rat just outside the door are all noises I either couldn't hear or didn't pay attention to while I was alive but are now very prominent.

In the distance, there's the slam of a car door. Who would be up after one in the morning with school and work only a handful of hours away? Buddy doesn't stir at the sound—Brad should probably get his hearing checked. There's nothing but darkness outside the door as I peer through the beveled glass. If I pass through the door, I might set off the alarm and wake the family which is not an option after everything they've already been through. More than a few minutes pass before a car door slams again, but this time it drives away.

The long, hidden driveway and the darkness keep me from seeing the street. I continue to survey the area outside the door, but it's silent now, except for the coyotes who must have found their dinner in the distant canyon as they howl and bark their announcement.

I wait in anticipation for morning to arrive. What once was a time I dreaded is now one of my favorite times of the day. I get to rouse Ivy and Jazzy from their beds and get them out the door for school. They still yell at me, but I don't mind; I love hearing their voices and seeing their faces. If I could, I'd even enjoy their morning breath.

Brad's alarm blares. He stirs, presses the snooze button, and the house is silent again. I ascend the stairs and begin the routine.

Ivy and Jazzy wake much faster these days, coming down for breakfast so they can chat with me.

"Okay, Jazzy, pour the oatmeal into the bowl," I say. "Now pour the hot water in a little at a time and stir. Be careful not to burn yourself. That's it."

"Thanks, Mommy, you make the best oatmeal."

"What do you have up for today, Ivy?" I ask.

Ivy sits at the table with her bagel and a glass of milk. She runs her finger through the cream cheese and then pops her finger into her mouth. "Nothing. My social life is over, remember?"

The quiet manner in Ivy's voice means something's up. Something's bothering her, but she's not offering any information right now. I don't want to press her. She'll tell me when she's ready—I hope.

Brad walks into the kitchen and makes his cup of coffee.

"Good morning," I say. "You look tired."

"Didn't sleep well last night—heard a noise and couldn't fall back to sleep for a good hour after."

"I heard something too, but I didn't see anything," I say.

"Probably one of the neighbors forgetting that the rest of us sleep at night," Brad says.

Edward enters the kitchen and pours himself a glass of milk. He stands at the island and looks right through me.

"Edward, you'll need to get Jazzy and Ivy after school today. Also, here's a list of things I need you to do today."

Brad hands Edward the list, and as Edward reads it, his eyes narrow and his mouth drops open. "I have to do all of this?"

"Yep, you're not going to sit around all day and do nothing. I need help with the house," Brad says.

"I'm not Mom, Dad. I shouldn't have to do her jobs."

Brad lifts his hands into the air like a preacher giving the gospel. "I need help, Edward. I can't do this all on my own."

"Do I get paid?"

"Yeah, you get three meals a day and a bed to sleep in, how's that?"

Edward shakes his head, crumples up the paper, and shoves it in his pocket.

"Come on, Edward. We're going to be late," Ivy says, heading to the front door with her backpack over her shoulder.

"Fine." He flashes Brad a pissed-off look before following Ivy and Jazzy out the front door.

—

ONCE THE KIDS are gone, I ask Brad the usual questions, "What do you have up for today? What time do you think you'll be home?" A horrific scream comes from outside. Brad and I run out to the driveway to find Jazzy and Ivy screaming as they stare at the tree to the right of the house. Two rabbits hang from their back feet on the tree's lowest branches. Blood stains their brown fur; their throats slit, heads dangling in the breeze.

"Brad, grab Jazzy," I say. Jazzy continues to stare at the rabbits and scream.

Brad pulls Jazzy into his chest to shield her from what she's already seen. There will be no erasing this from her mind. We usher the kids inside, and Brad retrieves a box cutter from the kitchen drawer before marching back outside and cutting the rabbits down from the tree.

"Who would do that, Mommy? It's so horrible," Jazzy's says.

"I don't know, sweetheart," I say, but I have a hunch.

"They're all down. You can head out now. I'll call both schools and let them know you'll be a little late," Brad says.

"What did you do with them?" Jazzy asks.

"I put them in the trash can."

"No! You can't do that. We need to bury them."

"Jazzy, you need to get to school," Brad says.

"I'm not going until you agree to bury them."

"Fine, I'll take care of them." Brad rubs his temples. "Now, get going."

Edward and Ivy don't say a word through the whole ordeal. There are so many things that could be going through their heads, and from the look on Ivy's face, she's scared. She's probably thinking the same thing I am. Zane Goodman.

Brad and I watch the kids pull out of the driveway. Jazzy turns and waves, and I wave back. Brad goes back into the house.

"Aren't you going to bury the rabbits?" I ask him as he grabs his laptop bag and his keys.

"I don't have time to bury the damn rabbits. I'm already late for my first meeting of the day."

"You can't make a promise like that and not follow through, especially with Jazzy."

"I didn't really promise her I'd do it. I'll just move around the dirt out back, and she'll never know."

"Shouldn't we call the police and file a report?"

"We? You act as though you're completely capable of picking up that phone and talking to someone. By all means, go right ahead."

"I'm only trying to help."

"You can help by staying out of it. I'm in charge here, remember?"

Brad's body shakes. He covers his face with his hands and a sob escapes. He moves to the living room, and I sit next to him on the couch.

"This is all too much. It's as though I can't seem to catch my breath before something else happens." He curls his hands into fists.

"It'll get better."

"How do you know? Do you have some crystal ball? A direct line to God?"

"I have faith it'll all work itself out."

"Faith? Like the faith I had that you'd be okay after the accident? That kind of faith?"

"I know it's hard to see it now, but—"

"But what? Faith, I've learned, is a futile thing, so forgive me if I can't see it the way you do."

Brad holds his head in his hands and stares at the dirty carpet. How can I possibly preach to him about faith when he feels like everything around him is falling apart?

"I don't know how you did it, Claire. Somehow you always managed to keep it all together. I had no idea how much you did when I was at work."

There's a ping in my chest. That's all I ever wanted really, for him to acknowledge all I did. I wasn't lounging while he was in the office all day. I took care of the things he didn't even know needed to be taken care of.

"Thank you."

"For what?"

"For understanding. It means a lot to me."

"I'm sorry if you didn't . . ."

"No apologies. Let's move forward. We've both fallen short at times, but we moved forward," I say.

"But we can never truly move forward, can we?"

"Not in a physical way. But we can accept what was and what wasn't, and both of us can move on."

"But, not together."

"Not together."

Brad nods, a slight smile forms on the right side of his face and then fades. "We were supposed to grow old together."

"We never were very good at planning."

"Now what?"

"I need you to forgive me. I don't want you angry at me for leaving."

Brad looks at me and lifts his hand to my face. His eyes follow his finger as he traces its shape, starting at my temple and slowly moving to my jaw and chin and then up the other side. His eyes then stare into mine, the pain and anger turning to acceptance.

"I forgive you, Claire. I'm sorry if you think I blame you because I don't. I'm just angry it happened. I'm angry at every-thing—at things I don't even understand. Yesterday I yelled like a lunatic at the gas pump because it wouldn't take my damn credit card, and last week I ranted at the woman down the street with the psycho Dalmatian to stop allowing her dog to shit on our lawn. I waffle between being utterly sad and uncontrollably angry."

"It's going to take time. I remember Luke's wife going through the same things. Now she's remarried and happy again. Cut yourself some slack. You're going to be fine."

His heartbeat slows, and his shoulders lower until they're no longer perched by his ears. His forgiveness makes me feel lighter, and for a moment, I'm worried Gammy's going to appear before I can help Brad fix this threat to our family.

"Not now, Gammy. Not now," I say in the faintest whisper.

"What?" Brad asks.

"Who do you think is behind the rabbits?" I ask.

"Probably Zane. Can't think of anyone else who'd do something so twisted."

"Zane's handy work. What are you going to do about it?"

"What *can* I do about it? I don't have any proof. Damn it. I should've gotten up when I heard that noise outside."

"If it's Zane, he's taking this way too far. I'm getting scared for the kids' safety."

"I just don't know what to do," Brad says.

"Filing a police report is the first step. You need documentation. Serial killers often hurt animals before they start killing people."

"I don't think Zane would kill *people*," Brad says.

"Maybe not, but let's cover all our bases."

"Fine, I'll call the police and have them write up a report. Then I need to get to work."

"What do you need me to do?" I ask, feeling useless.

"Be here for the kids when they get home. Just be their mom."

"Edward still acts as though he can't hear or see me, but I'm pretty sure he can."

"He's a tough nut to crack. I think he's reinforced his shell since the accident. Can't blame him for protecting himself."

When the police arrive, Brad meets with them outside. He gestures to the tree and then takes them to the trash can at the side of the house. Jazzy's not going to be happy if she sees the rabbits there when she gets home.

One of the cops takes pictures while the other writes on a small notepad. It doesn't take them long to fill out the report. Brad signs something and waves to the cops as they disappear down the driveway.

Brad enters the house with the police report in his hand. He raises it up like an offering of evidence. "That's all done. I need to run. They didn't think the rabbits were killed here."

"Did you give them Zane's name?"

"Yes. They're going to question him."

"Is that a good idea? Do you think he'll do something worse if he knows you suspect him?"

"I don't know, but it's out of our hands now."

Brad packs up his things and heads to the door. He turns and looks at me.

"It's . . . nice having you here, Claire. See you tonight?"

I nod slightly, unable to give him a straight answer to his question. "Brad?"

"Yeah?"

"I love you."

"I will always love you," he says and walks out the door.

Chapter Twenty-two

E dward returns home two hours after dropping off his sisters. A list of potential places he could have gone runs through my mind, my chest heavy with each option.

Confident he can hear me, I grow frustrated. He's ignoring me when, in my opinion, he could use me to talk to. It's not like I can punish him or anything, and I wouldn't share anything with Brad unless I thought Edward was in danger. I want to connect with him before my time runs out, have the chance to let him know how much I love him like I've been able to do with the girls.

The rabbits remain in the trash. I'm quite certain Jazzy will check to see if Brad buried them when she gets home. I don't want Jazzy to lose her trust in him, she needs him. I follow Edward into the kitchen and watch him fix himself a bowl of Captain Crunch cereal.

"Edward, do you think you could bury those rabbits before Jazzy gets home?" I ask. He doesn't even blink at the sound of my voice, but his heartbeat speeds up. "Jazzy will be crushed if she sees them in the trash when she gets home. You know how sensitive she is."

Still, no response. He stares straight ahead, focusing on a tree right outside the kitchen window, crunching on his cereal.

"I know you love her. I see how good you are to her. You're a wonderful big brother."

Edward doesn't say anything, but after he finishes his cereal, he goes into the garage and grabs a shovel. He walks to the side yard and digs a deep hole among the ferns and overgrown ivy. After a few minutes, he stops and wipes his forehead and looks up at the cloudless sky. If only I could read his mind right now. Better yet, if only he would say something, talk to me, yell at me, anything other than silence.

He thrusts his shovel back into the dirt again. A thud and clank stop him. He leans over into the hole and tugs at a football-sized rock until it comes loose. For the first time, I notice how grown up he looks. He's turned into a man with newly defined muscles on his arms and chest, his shoulders broader. Edward was a thin boy, bony even. I had to buy him slim jeans because regulars would fall right off his narrow waist. But now his body is full and strong.

After the hole is dug, he walks over to the large trash can and opens the lid. He scrunches his face and turns his head away while lowering the can on its side. Using the shovel, he scoops out the rabbits and carries them to the hole, dumps them in, then covers them with dirt. He cleans up the area and puts the shovel back into the garage before retrieving two pieces of scrap wood from the storage closet. With the hammer and a few nails he joins them together to form a cross. With permanent marker, he writes, "RIP."

Edward returns to the grave and pounds the cross into the soil. He steps back and eyes his work, leans back in and straightens the cross. I stand next to him, admiring his work and honored to be in this moment with him. He has a heart bigger than most, and right now, I couldn't be prouder.

—

AS I PREDICTED, the minute Jazzy gets home she runs to the trash can and lifts the lid.

"They're not in there," Edward says and gestures for her to follow him. "They're right here." He points to the fresh grave.

"Did you do this?" Jazzy asks. Ivy, with a messy ponytail and tired eyes, walks up behind her. Edward nods.

"You buried them?" Ivy says like she doesn't quite believe what she sees.

"Thanks, Edward, you're the best." Jazzy bounces over to Edward and wraps her little arms around his waist. "We should say a little prayer." She lets go of Edward and folds her hands. She glances at Ivy and Edward, and gestures for them to do the same. They reluctantly follow.

"Dear God, please take care of these poor little rabbits, Pancake and Peaches. I know they must be hopping in Heaven right now. Take care of them and give them lots and lots of carrots. Amen."

"Awesome," Ivy says. The sarcasm in her voice is quickly followed with an affectionate rub to the top of Jazzy's head. "Pancake and Peaches?"

"I was kinda hungry," Jazzy says, shrugging. She sees me standing near the garage door. "Hi, Mommy. Edward buried the rabbits. Now they can go to Heaven," she says, and then looks confused. "How come you didn't go to Heaven when we buried you?"

"I'm not quite sure, sweetheart. I guess God has other plans for me right now."

"What kind of plans?"

"Not sure of that either. It's one of those mysteries we'll hopefully find the answer to."

"I like mysteries." There's a slight pause, and then her face brightens. "Guess what? I get to sing part of a song all by myself at the Christmas program." She skips to the door.

"That's fantastic. Will you sing it for me?" I ask.

"Not yet, I need to practice first. Maybe you can come to my Christmas program. I want you to be there."

But I don't feel Christmas. It's a strange, indescribable feeling, like looking down the road and only being able to see so far before the road fades away. Why didn't Gammy tell me how long I have? How can I prepare my family when I don't even know? I'm afraid of what leaving again will do to all of them, especially Jazzy.

"We'll need to see what Daddy says," I say, knowing Brad may not be the reason I won't be able to be there. "You know, I'm not sure how long I'll be here." I lead Jazzy to the couch in the living room, and we both take a seat.

"What do you mean? You'll always be here." Her voice is confident, as though she has proof to back up her statement.

"I'll always be here." I put my hand near Jazzy's heart. "But you might not be able to hear me or see me."

I don't know why I feel I need to tell Jazzy this, but not preparing her for my final exit would most certainly set Jazzy up for a big fall. I know, if given a choice between being here or in Heaven, I'd choose Heaven. I love being with my family, but this limbo state is like watching the world go by behind the bars of a jail cell. This place is made for the living. I don't belong here.

Jazzy's mouth trembles. "But I don't want to lose you *again*."

"You won't lose me. I'll always be with you. But I want to meet Jesus. You understand that, right?"

"I'd like to meet Jesus someday too." She wipes away the tears with her palms.

"You're such an amazing girl." I reach for Jazzy's face, wanting to brush the warm, salty tears away. "You're so smart and kind and loving. Just know I'll always be proud of you."

"If you're still here, I want you to come see me sing."

"I'd like that."

"I need to go practice now." Jazzy retreats up the stairs with a slow, somber walk. Halfway up she stops and pulls off her shoes. She walks to the bottom of the stairs and places her shoes on the first step. Noticing Ivy's shoes on the floor, she picks them up and places them on the step above hers. Jazzy looks at me, and I give her a thumbs up before she runs up to her room.

—

IVY AND EDWARD are already in their rooms, their doors closed. Music escapes from Edward's room and faint crying from Ivy's. I go to Ivy's door.

"Ivy, are you okay?"

"I'm fine."

"You don't sound fine. Want to talk?"

There's no answer, but I wait for a response. Her door opens.

"I don't know what to do, Mom," she says and bursts into tears.

I follow Ivy to her bed and sit.

"Ever since Zane spread all those rumors about me, my friends won't even look at me. And when I see him in the hall, he looks at me like, well, I don't know. It's creepy," Her hands shake.

"What do you mean by creepy?"

"Like he's got something planned. He has this sick smile on his face, and his eyes follow me. It just feels . . . wrong."

"Have you told a teacher or the school?"

"What am I going to say? 'He's looking at me weird?' or 'I don't like the way he looks at me?' What would they possibly do if I say that?"

"Is there anything else he's doing? Is he saying anything to you?"

Ivy stares at her hands and slowly shakes her head but then stops.

"I've been getting typed letters stuffed into my locker."

"From Zane?"

"They're not signed, and I obviously have more enemies than friends right now, but . . . yeah, they're probably from him."

"Do you have them?"

She trudges to her backpack like she's wading in tar with a hundred-pound weight attached to her back. She pulls out six sheets of paper and unfolds them.

"I don't remember what order I got them in exactly, but this was the first one I received." She lays it on her bed for me to see.

> *To the Cock-Teasing Slut,*
> *I knew you were a loser just like your brother. No one*
> *fucks around with me and gets away with it. Be*
> *prepared to lose everything that means anything to*
> *you. I will destroy you. By the way, your light was on*
> *late last night—you obviously aren't getting enough*
> *beauty sleep.*

Some of the notes give information no one would know

unless they were watching her, listing what she wore to bed or when she turned off her light at night. He has a vendetta against her so large he's stalking her.

"Ivy, you need to show these to Dad. He has to get the school and possibly the police involved. This is serious."

"No! It'll make it worse. No one will do anything about it, and then he'll retaliate even more. I'm scared, Mom."

"At least show Dad. He needs to get you out of that school."

"That won't stop him. You read them. He *watches* our house." Her voice quavers and her eyes are wide and full of fear.

"Did you tell Edward?"

"I showed him the first one, but not the others," she says. "He got angry and told me to stay away from Zane. I'm afraid Edward's going to do something to him."

"Why do you think that?"

"I can't explain it, but he had that look like he had something important he needed to do."

"Tell Dad and see what he wants to do, okay?"

"Mom?"

"Yes?"

"Do you think Dad will be mad at me?"

"Why would he be mad at you?"

"Because of the party?"

"I didn't tell him about the party. It's up to you to tell him what you want him to know. He's probably going to need some information, but he doesn't have to know all the details. He loves you and will only want to protect you."

"I've really messed things up, haven't I?"

"This is life. We make mistakes, big and small. But that's what makes us human and what allows us to learn and grow." I wait for Ivy to look at me. Her red eyes meet my worried ones, regret written on her face. "But what he's doing? It's not right. It's not normal and it's *not* your fault."

"Why won't he just leave us alone?"

"I wish I knew."

I scan Ivy's room and notice it's not nearly as messy as usual. Most of her clothes are off her floor, and only two cups sit on her desk. She's spent some time getting organized.

"Your room looks pretty good," I say.

"It's a work in progress." Ivy allows a small laugh to escape while wiping her wet cheeks. It was what I would always say when her room was in a disastrous state.

"Well, the process seems to be much more efficient."

"I'm figuring it out."

"Are you okay now?" I ask.

"Yeah, better. Thanks, Mom. I'm really glad you're here."

"Me too."

Chapter Twenty-three

I head downstairs and follow the sound of giggles emanating from the kitchen.

"Do the next problem, and we'll see if you're still as smart as I think you are," Edward says.

Edward's at the table with Jazzy helping her with her homework. There's a bowl of Jelly Bellies in front of them, and Jazzy reaches in to grab some.

"Uh-uh. Not till you solve that problem correctly, and then you can make me some other disgusting concoction."

"I'm going to make it the worst yet," Jazzy says.

"I'm sure you will." Edward laughs, and Jazzy giggles again before working on her math problem. She stops and looks up at Edward.

"You're a great teacher, Edward. You make boring math fun." Her eyes return to her homework paper and then she raises her pencil as if she has a question and whispers, "Don't tell Mom, but I think you're smarter at math than she is."

Edward grins but doesn't say anything. He points back to the paper to get her to finish the problem.

"There, and I know it's right," she says with confidence, tapping the eraser end of the pencil on the glass table.

"Oh man, now I have to eat your jelly bean creation," he says.

Jazzy sticks her hand in the jar and pulls out a handful of jelly beans and puts them on the table. "Okay, I'm going to go with piña colada, popcorn, and hot cinnamon," she says.

"That sounds putrid."

"What does putrid mean?"

"Go get the dictionary and look it up."

Jazzy rolls her eyes but gets up and retrieves the pocket dictionary from the homework bin.

"P, P, P. Oh, here's P. Pu, Pu," she continues. "How do you spell it?"

Edward tells her, and she finds the word.

"Here it is, 'putrid: very un… plea… sant, re… pul… sive.' Huh. You don't think you're going to like it?" she says with a big belly laugh. "Here you go. Delicious."

Edward puts the jelly beans in his mouth and exaggerates his displeasure with drawn lips, raised eyebrows, and a head shake as Jazzy falls to the floor in laughter.

"That was indeed putrid. All right, looks like your homework's done. You have some time to chill before dinner."

Jazzy stuffs her books in her backpack and zips it closed. She runs to Edward, still sitting in the chair, and puts her arms around him, placing a kiss on his cheek.

"Thanks, Edward."

"You're welcome."

I've witnessed another miracle. The transformation of Edward the boy to Edward the man; from a typical selfish teen to a caring and concerned young adult. Pride swims within me, creating waves of gratitude for my family.

—

BRAD ARRIVES LATE, so before he gets home, I put Jazzy to bed, listening to her read a chapter from a *Magic Tree House* book. Her eyes tire, and she falls asleep in record time. I lie next to her and soak in her sweetness while Buddy pants loudly on the floor. Jazzy seems happy, yet I worry about her safety— everyone's safety while Zane plans his next attack.

I enter the kitchen. Brad reaches for a wine glass as I greet him. The glass falls to the tile floor and shatters into what looks like a million pieces.

"Shit, Claire. You can't just appear and scare the crap out of me. That's a good way to leave the kids orphans." He leans down and picks up the larger pieces of glass.

"Sorry." Sometimes I forget I make no sound when I move. "How was your day?" I ask like this is an ordinary day in the Blackwell household.

"It started out pretty shitty with rabbits hanging from the magnolia tree, but it got better, thank God." He pulls the broom and dustpan from the pantry and sweeps the glass into a pile.

"What's wrong?"

"Nothing." Brad stops sweeping. He rests his hands on the top of the broomstick and locks his eyes on the ceiling as though an answer is going to drop from it.

"I'm afraid."

"Afraid of what?"

"Afraid that one day you're not going to be here when I come home. This morning I felt like we were part of a team again, like things were back to normal. I don't want to go back to you not being here."

"I'm sorry," I say in almost a whisper. "But I'll have to leave, eventually."

"Today I was excited to leave work, anxious to see you. For a moment, I even anticipated the taste of your soft lips and the warmth and smell of your body as I embraced you. But beyond the disappointment of not being able to physically love you, I feared you'd be gone. I'm so confused. I can't move on with you here, and yet I can't breathe if you're not."

I hadn't completely considered how hard me being here would be on my family, especially Brad. I thought he'd be thrilled to have me here, to be able to talk to me and have me help with the kids. But the physicality of it, the lack of touch and smell, the lack of intimacy that reminds us we belong to each other, has to be both painful and confusing.

"How can I make this easier for you? I want you to be happy again. I don't want to cause you any more pain."

"I need to know when I get to heal. When will I feel like I'm not going to fall apart? I'm not a crier and tears leak from my eyes, sometimes without any warning, multiple times a day." He shakes his head. "Truth is, you're more beautiful than any memory I have of you. Every time I see you, I want more. I want all of you."

"I never knew you loved me that much," I say, wishing I'd have known the depth of his love when I was alive.

"I did . . . I do. I'll always love you." He sweeps the shattered glass into the dustpan. "Kind of symbolic isn't it? Sweeping up the shattered pieces?"

"I wish I could help you sweep it all up and put it back together," I say.

"Me too."

"Maybe it's best if I keep my distance. I want you to heal."

"No." Brad stops sweeping and straightens his tall, lanky frame. "I can't be afraid to feel pain. I can't go through the rest of my life regretting pushing you away. I'll cherish this time we have. I don't think I would ever forgive myself if I didn't take the risk, if I didn't embrace this . . . gift."

If I were capable of tears, they would create pools at my feet.

—

ONCE BRAD FINISHES cleaning the broken glass, he retrieves two wine glasses and pours the deep burgundy liquid into them before carrying both out to the fire pit. I follow, and we chat like old times.

"I think you need to talk to Ivy," I say, not wanting to be the one to tell him what has been happening with her.

"Why?"

"I can't say. It's up to her to tell you."

"Then shouldn't I wait until she comes to me? She's a teen you know. Nothing good comes from prying," he says.

"I'm worried, by the time she does, it'll be too late."

"Too late for what?"

"You'll have to get all of that from her."

"Okay, I'll check on her later." He takes a drink of his wine. "Got Edward into Valley High. He'll start there next Monday."

"That's good, but how are the girls going to get to school?"

"Crap. I didn't even think about that. See, you were always the one that thought everything through."

"Not always. Remember when the kids colored eggs for Easter one year, and I didn't think anything of letting them put their hands in the cups?"

"They were the most colorful kids at church that Sunday," Brad says.

"Or the time I scheduled a charity event at our house on the same day as Ivy's dance recital? Or the time—"

"You went out of your way to bring my favorite meal to the office because you knew how stressed I was?" He leans in closer to me, his face mere inches from my own. "You were what held us together, Claire. Even though I didn't say it nearly enough, I appreciated everything you did for me and our family."

"We were a good team."

"Yes, we were." He raises his glass and toasts my full glass perched on the table next to my chair. "Well, guess I'm on driving duty for a while."

"Or you could get Zane kicked out of the school for good," I say.

"I don't know how that's going to happen. He seems to have Dean Livingston wrapped around his little finger."

"Yes, he does. But I think I may know a way."

Chapter Twenty-four

I t's Tuesday morning, and the girls are difficult to wake. I get them moving, making sure they don't crawl back into bed. I wonder if they'd get up on their own if I didn't prod them.

Jazzy's frantic morning quests for her shoes is a thing of the past as she retrieves them from the bottom step and puts them on her small feet. Ivy plucks her shoes from the second step. She glances at Jazzy while she bites her lower lip and wrinkles her forehead.

"Ivy, I'm coming with you to school today," I say while Ivy sits next to Jazzy and puts on her shoes.

"What? Why? I thought Dad didn't want you leaving the house."

"Dad agreed to this. We want to see what Zane's up to. I'm going to follow him home. Jazzy, that means I probably won't be home tonight."

"You have to come home, Mommy. Who will tuck me in and wake me up tomorrow?"

"I think Daddy would love to tuck you in."

"Just don't follow me around, okay, Mom?" Ivy says, tightening her laces.

"I won't. I promise."

We drop Jazzy off at school before heading to the high school. Edward pulls into the circular drive, and Ivy and I get out. We wave at Edward as he exits the school grounds, but he doesn't wave back.

"Be careful, Ivy. I don't trust Zane," I say to my daughter as she looks straight ahead and nods. "I'll see you tomorrow at school."

I search the halls for Zane and oddly, enjoy the sounds of high school. Again, I'm the fly on the wall, able to watch what happens when no one thinks anyone's looking. There are certainly some teachers I wouldn't mind following, especially Mr. Colbert who many of the girls nicknamed Mr. Hands. But I need to find Zane and see what he's up to.

With Zane's inflated popularity, he's bound to be in one of the gathered crowds. I spot him in a thick mob of students outside the entrance to one of the school buildings. Once I reach him, I memorize his heartbeat so I can find him if I can't see him. We head to his first class, American Government. He lounges at the back of the room, surrounded by giggling girls, and I catch myself doing the Ivy eye roll. These girls act like hungry puppies circling a food dish. I think back to those days when I was in high school—did I do that? It's embarrassing to the female population. Logan fist-bumps Zane as he takes a seat.

"Dude, what's up for today?" Logan asks Zane. Zane must be his social coordinator.

"Whatever we want," Zane says with a sick, cocky smile.

"Rich is having a party Friday, you going?" Logan asks.

"Yeah, maybe. Depends on who my date's gonna be." His voice and eyebrows rise as he eyes the gaggle of girls.

"I'm free," says one of the girls with straight, mousy brown hair, green eyes, and few poppable zits on her chin.

"Umm, naw, not my type," Zane says and laughs, giving another fist-bump to Logan. The girl's face reddens, and she swivels away from him in her seat.

At this point, I want to smash their heads together. Is this typical behavior for boys?

"I was thinking of asking Ashley," Zane says.

"Dude, you know I have dibs on her," Logan says. "She's my girl."

"Yeah, but you owe me, remember? Time to pay up."

"Shit, Zane, that's low, even for you."

"Hey, when I need payment, I need payment. It's business, you understand?"

Logan's face falls, and light pink patches sprout on his neck. He sinks in his chair while focusing on the front of the room as the teacher talks. Logan must be rethinking this friendship thing he has with Zane right about now.

As I trail Zane throughout his day, I now know, without a doubt, he's a bad seed. He doesn't seem to have any concern for those around him; taking a girlfriend from his best friend, tripping unsuspecting students in the halls while getting high off their terror, and spreading rumors with one text or tweet. He appears to get a kick out of everyone else's misery; even his friends, who, quite frankly, should be questioning why they even associate with him.

When the bell rings at 2:30, I stick close to Zane so I don't lose him in the throng of students trying their best to get the hell off campus. He raises his hand to passersby like he's king and they're his people. My nonexistent stomach somehow feels sick. He's the type of kid who makes your skin crawl, yet everyone seems to worship him, or maybe they're afraid that if they don't, they'll be his next victim.

He enters the crowded locker room and gets suited up for football practice.

"Zane. My man," says one of the guys sitting on a bench, putting on his equipment.

"Hey. You guys ready to kill Benton this weekend?" Zane yells and then raises his fist in the air encouraging hoots and hollers from his teammates. Turning to one of the heftier players, he leans forward and gets in his face. "You better have my back, Debrowski. None of that weak sauce defense bullshit this time." He points his finger directly into Debrowski's face.

"Don't worry. I got your back," Debrowski says with a slight defensive head duck and an edge of fear in his voice.

"But that's just it, I do worry. It's my ass out there and you better protect it," Zane says with a threatening tone. Debrowski nods, never looking Zane in the eyes.

There are more shouts and the slamming of lockers as they finish suiting up and head to the field. From the sidelines, I view Zane's skill and leadership as he calls the plays and throws the ball over and over. He seems to own this team. He points and they follow.

After two hours of grueling practice, the boys, sweaty and filthy from top to bottom, head to the locker room.

"Goodman," Coach Payne calls and waves to Zane who jogs over. The coach puts his hand on Zane's shoulder.

"You looked good out there today."

"Thanks, Coach."

"Big game this weekend. It's what we've worked all year for— the championship. Make sure you get plenty of rest and keep that arm iced up. You want those recruiters to see your A-game."

"I'll be ready. Looking forward to it." Zane pats Coach Payne on the back. "See ya tomorrow, Coach."

—

AFTER ZANE CLEANS up, I follow him into his nearly new black BMW three series, with black leather seats and more buttons on the dash than a 747. This car beats anything I've ever driven except Brad's car that's now a heap of metal at the junkyard. He pulls out, not even caring that a car is directly behind him. There's a honk and he honks back. Rolling down his window, he yells, "Then get the hell out of the way, you pussy!" and gives the driver, a teammate, the finger.

He squeals out of the lot and speeds down the street. His arm is propped on the frame of the open window, his hand taking in the wind resistance, causing it to move up and down on its own. Music blares from the speakers, some fingers-down-the-chalkboard music that makes me want to cover my ears and cower in a corner.

Within fifteen minutes, Zane pulls into his driveway. His house looks like a small compound. The two-story modern block of concrete and windows faces the driveway that could host a full court basketball game, but it appears uninhabited. There are no potted plants or flowered wreaths adorning the entry, making it feel sterile and colorless. Zane hits the garage door button and pulls in his car.

I continue to be at his heels, just like Buddy is to me. He goes directly to the kitchen. From the fridge he grabs a Mountain Dew and then pokes into the pantry, coming out with two bags of Corn Nuts, three packages of Oreos, and a commercial-size bin of red licorice. With his arms full, he strolls to his room on the second level. His room's cleaner than Edward's. In fact, it's way too clean for a high school boy. How could this be? Zane seems like a loose cannon, a person who couldn't care less about how things look but rather, how they feel. I didn't expect to see such organization. It's just a hunch, but I'm guessing they have a diligent housekeeper.

He methodically unpacks his backpack. A psychology book, a Spanish book, and a few notebooks. It's what he pulls out next that catches my attention. In his hands are folded pieces of paper just like the notes Ivy had. There wasn't any question in my mind he was the one writing the notes, but now I have confirmation. He unfolds one of them and reads it, giving himself a smile.

"God, I'm good," he says as he opens each one and reads them with a smirk of satisfaction on his face. He reminds me of that Sid character in *Toy Story*, thinking up his next torture. Unfortunately, Zane has somehow inherited exceptionally good looks, which, despite how evil he is, makes him a magnet to three-quarters of the school population. While his built football physique and golden hair might woo the girls, there's something about his brilliant movie star smile that's sinister and that sends a chill through me.

"Ivy Blackwell, you'll regret you ever said no to me." Moving to his dresser, he opens the third drawer from the bottom and reaches in. His hand moves around, and there is the sound of something solid scraping the bottom of the wood drawer, hidden under some neatly folded clothes. He must have found what he's looking for because his face changes from happy to determined. If only I could see what he has his hand on. He slowly pulls his hand out from under the clothes, but I'm disappointed to find it empty. I want to know what's in that drawer. He fixes the clothes back into a neat pile and slides the drawer closed.

He organizes his books on his desk, setting up a scene that looks like he's been working. One of his books is open; a highlighter lies beside it, and a notebook is opened to a page of notes. Once that's set up, he walks over to his TV, turns it on, and gets his game controller. On the screen, a man with an automatic rifle appears, and Zane disappears into some fantasy shoot-'em-up game for hours while the rest of the house remains quiet.

Zane doesn't seem inspired to get any of his homework done tonight. Why bother when he's going to have a full-ride football scholarship handed to him? When his parents arrive home, the lack of conversation that plays between them and Zane makes me a little sad. Zane's mom brings home some boxed-up meal which Zane grabs and begins to take to his room.

"Homework done?" Zane's mom asks.

"Yep," he says.

"All right, I'll be in the study," she says and disappears down the hall.

His mom seems emotionally disconnected, never once looking Zane in the eyes when she talked to him. She disappears for the remainder of the evening while his dad never makes contact with Zane. Zane goes back to playing his game until almost three in the morning. I have no choice but to remain here since I can't float away like ghosts in the movies.

Chapter Twenty-five

I return to school with Zane, disappointed at how little I've learned about him or his plans, but two things are certain. His lack of interaction with his parents explains his need for attention, and he's not done with Ivy yet. He still has more letters to deliver to her locker, and he's hiding something in his room I couldn't see, but the sound it made in the drawer held some weight, like some kind of weapon, which is absolutely terrifying.

I exit Zane's car and spot Edward pulling up the circle drive to drop off Ivy. Part of me wants to stay at school and continue to follow Zane; the other wants to go home and be there for Jazzy when she comes back from her party. Edward and Ivy won't be home until late and neither will Brad. Seeing Edward in the endless line of vehicles entering the drive must be some form of divine intervention or something. I need to go home.

I get to Edward's car while Ivy reaches into the trunk to collect her backpack.

"Mom," Ivy says. Like a ventriloquist, her lips don't move, but her eyes express relief.

"How were things at home?" I ask.

"Fine." The golden teenage response.

"Come on, Ivy. Get your stuff and get moving," Edward calls from the car.

"I'm going home with Edward. I'll talk to you later tonight, okay?" I say. Ivy nods. "Let me get in the car before you close the trunk or I may miss my ride." Ivy waits until I'm in the car. The trunk slams shut and immediately, Edward drives away.

Buddy wags his tail furiously when I enter the house. Edward flies up the stairs, two at a time, and disappears into his room. Moments later, he's downstairs with a backpack slung over his shoulder. He plucks a bag of chips and a water bottle from the pantry; his keys dangle from the lanyard in his hands.

"Where are you going?" I ask. There's a pause and his heart beats faster, but he doesn't answer. "I wish you'd talk to me. Tell me what you need, Edward. Just tell me." His gaze falls to the floor. There's a flash of physical pain on his face, and then it relaxes as he walks away. "When you're ready, I'll be here," I say, following him to the front door and watching him leave. He's almost there, almost ready to acknowledge me.

———

IT'S BEEN A long day, waiting for everyone to come home. With Jazzy at a birthday party, I'm unsettled. Brad should be there with her, but he insisted he had to attend a meeting and business dinner. It's difficult to juggle all the kids while trying to accomplish your own list of commitments, but I don't like Jazzy being in an uncontained environment without someone keeping an eye solely on her. And worse, Bridget's picking her up.

It's 5:32. Jazzy should be home soon, and then I can relax and hear all about the party. Before my death, when Jazzy would recount her day, I would sometimes respond with, "uh-huh, yes, I see," all while thinking of other things I deemed more important. I would think about what to make for dinner, what was on my schedule for later, who I needed to call for this or that. A constant flurry of thoughts would run through my head and keep me from tuning into what Jazzy was saying. Sometimes Jazzy would catch me by asking a question I wouldn't answer appropriately. "Mom," she'd say. "Didn't you hear what I said?" I'd feel bad and try to concentrate on what she had to say while hoping I wouldn't forget what I was working on in my mind. Now, I cherish every little detail of Jazzy's play-by-play accounts of whatever she's telling me. I hang on to every word as though each sentence is made of gleaming gold; beautiful, heavy, and precious.

Time passes slowly. I glance at the clock again. It's only been one minute, yet it seems like hours. There's a fluttering from within, full of nerves and keen anticipation; a feeling I don't like. It grates on me with each loud tick of the clock. *Tick tock, tick tock,* each one louder than the one before it.

The party ended an hour ago and Jazzy's still not home. Where is she? Isn't anyone concerned she's not home? And here I wait, unable to do anything about this situation. I can't pick up the phone and call Brad or Bridget or the police; I can't drive myself to the park to make sure Jazzy's okay. There's nothing I can do. My baby's not home and all I can do is wait. There must be a reason she's late. Maybe Bridget took her to dinner or spoke to Brad and told him she'd drop Jazzy off later. Maybe I'm overreacting. After all, they're adults, responsible adults, who would make sure Jazzy is taken care of. Of course, they are. I'm being silly. Silly, silly, silly.

The sun sets behind the tree-lined backyard, passing the baton to the darkness of early winter. Once the sun disappears during this time of the year, the air grows cold and crisp. Buddy sits at my feet as I peer out the window, waiting for a sign of Jazzy's arrival. Brad's car pulls into the driveway and relief floods me. I rush to the door leading to the garage and wait for Brad to open it, excited to hear all about Jazzy's party and Brad's day at work. The door opens, and Brad enters. I look behind him to catch a glimpse of my party girl, but she's not there.

"Where's Jazzy?" I ask.

"What do you mean? She's here, right?" he asks with a tinge of concern in his voice as he goes to the table and sets down his laptop bag.

"No, she's not here." I'm unable to hide the panic in my voice.

"Bridget was supposed to pick her up and bring her home after the party," he says with more concern and urgency.

"Brad, Jazzy never came home. Did Bridget call you?" I hope he just forgot, which he has been known to do.

"Call me? No. She was supposed to drop her off like we planned. She said she would stay until I got home." Brad's heart pumps fast and hard.

He checks his phone and shakes his head. He presses a button and then puts the phone to his ear. The phone rings four times and then goes to voicemail. "Hi, y'all, it's Bridget. Leave a message, and I'll ring you back as soon as I can. Have a great day." Brad waits for the beep.

"Bridget, it's Brad. It's almost eight. Where's Jazzy? Please call me as soon as you get this message. Please." Brad hangs up and looks at me with terror in his eyes.

"I don't know what to do." He puts his hands on his hips and taps his right foot on the tile, each contact with the floor pounds into me like a bass drum.

"What about Edward and Ivy? Could they have taken her somewhere? Maybe Bridget called them instead?" I'm trying to sound hopeful, trying to convince myself this is a possibility. Brad calls Edward first, but there's no answer. He leaves a message and then calls Ivy, who doesn't answer her phone either.

"They have those damn phones glued to them twenty-four hours a day, and they don't answer my call?" he says. "Damn it!" He goes to the refrigerator and removes the party invitation from under a magnet. "Maybe she went home with the Lees." His fingers shake as he punches the numbers into his phone.

"Hello?"

"Marjory, it's Brad Blackwell. Is Jazzy with you?" His voice is calm; professional. Marjory's voice travels through the phone, the words as crisp as the brisk outside air.

"No, she's not. She went home after the party. Bridget was supposed to pick her up, right? Hold on," she says. It sounds like she covered up the phone and is asking someone something, but I can't make out the muffled noise. There's a pause before she speaks to Brad. "I didn't see her leave. I thought Rich did, but he said he didn't either. But when we left, all the kids were gone. She's not home?" she asks.

"No. Are you certain all the kids were gone?"

"Yes. We scanned the area after we cleaned up. Made sure we didn't leave anything behind. The park was pretty empty. All the kids were picked up around the same time. It was a little chaotic, to be honest. Maybe she went home with one of the kids?"

"Could you call your list, please? I'm going to head to the park," Brad says, still holding it together, his voice strong and unwavering.

"Yes, of course. I'll send Rich to the park as well," she says. "Brad, I'm so sorry for this confusion. It was so crazy at pick-up time, so crazy and I—"

"Let's just find her. Please make those calls," Brad says.

"Yes, I'll do that right now. Call if you find her."

It's that one little word that carries so much weight, "If." *If* we find her.

"Shit!" Brad says, a little less composed as he grabs his keys from the table and runs to the door leading to the garage.

"I want to go with," I say.

"No. You need to stay here in case she comes home." His voice is shaky. He's unraveling, second by precious second.

"Brad, I can't stay and wait. Please, let me go with you. Please. If she's at the park, I can help you look for her."

Fear's etched in his face. "Okay." He jots a note, puts some tape on it, and attaches it to the front door. "Just in case Bridget or Jazzy shows up." There's no need to leave it unlocked since Bridget and Jazzy both know the garage door code.

I'm in the passenger seat as he speeds out of the driveway and down the street with his jaw firmly clenched, his heart racing, and tears trickling down his face.

"It's going to be okay, Brad." I try to reassure him; to reassure myself.

"You don't know that."

"No, I just have to believe that . . ." I'm at a loss for words. I'm as scared as Brad is. There's nothing else that would cause me more anguish than something tragic happening to my children. I would die a thousand painful deaths if I could spare them from harm's way. I know Brad feels the same.

"God, why did I do this?" Brad says, banging on the steering wheel with his fist.

"You didn't do anything wrong. This could all be a misunderstanding."

"I let her in. I opened myself up and let her in. Damn it!"

"You needed help, and she offered it. There's nothing wrong with that."

He needs to calm down before he gets into an accident. His phone rings and he answers it before the first ring ends.

"Hello?"

"Dad, I saw that you called. What's going on?" Edward asks.

"Is Jazzy with you?" Brad asks.

"No. I had that . . . meeting and then picked up Ivy after her group project meeting. What's going on?"

"Jazzy's missing. Bridget never brought her home. I'm on my way to the park now."

"We'll meet you there. Which park?" Edward says like a brave soldier ready to report for duty. He sounds just like Brad.

"Freedom Park."

"Be there in ten."

Brad pulls into the parking lot and barely gets the car in park before he flies out the door. He runs, his head whips from one direction to the next. "Jazzy? Jazzy?" His voice bounces off the tall trees only to be consumed by the chilled breeze that rustles leaves from above and underfoot. I break from him and go in the opposite direction, shouting Jazzy's name. It's dark, and even though I can't feel the air, the steam rising from the sewer grates tells me it's cold. I can't remember if Jazzy wore a jacket to school this morning. Edward's car pulls into the lot, and Ivy and Edward get out and run toward Brad. They exchange a few words and then branch out, their yells echo across the expansive park, one of the largest in the county. It boasts eight baseball fields, four playgrounds, six tennis courts, four basketball courts, and multiple picnic areas. With over one thousand acres of terrain and countless trails leading to a large reservoir, it would take days to comb every inch of it.

Another car pulls in; it's Rich, and he jogs toward Brad. He points to a location west of where they are and then runs to it. It must be where they had the party. Brad continues to walk north while Ivy heads south and Edward goes east. Their wild heartbeats pound, and even with their increased rate, I can differentiate between them. They each have their signature beat, like a fingerprint unique only to them.

I think about Jazzy's heartbeat and try to remember its signature sound with its gentle second thump. I would recognize it the moment I hear it. Trying to tune out the other beats, I listen for Jazzy's, but I can't hear it. Is she not here? Did it stop beating? Dear God, please let her be okay! She must be cold and scared.

Flashing lights approach. Three police cars enter the parking lot, and Brad meets with them. They point to different areas in the park and again, branch out. The magnitude of this situation hits me so hard I can't move. "Jazzy! Jazzy!" multiple voices yell, all coming from different directions. Brad's hoarse voice, almost a cry, cracks as he shouts her name. I force myself to keep looking, keep listening. "Jazz darling, where are you?" I call out, trying to stay calm and sound as though I'm playing a leisurely game of hide-and-seek.

I continue to move methodically past a large gazebo at the south end of the park. There's a heartbeat, but it's faint. Moving closer to the sound, I'm eager to find its source, eager to see Jazzy safe. The crackle of leaves and pine needles ahead propel me forward. "Jazzy?" I call out.

"Mom? Is that you?" a voice says, but it's not Jazzy. Sudden disappointment consumes me.

"Ivy?"

"I didn't know you were here, Mom."

"I thought I could help. For a minute, your heartbeat sounded like Jazzy's."

"There's a small building down this way, about two hundred feet. I'm going to check it out," Ivy says as she walks ahead of me.

It's easy for me to move through the large trees and brush, but Ivy must carefully navigate the dense area. As we get closer to the building, there's another heartbeat. Maybe Edward or Brad is already over here.

"Mom! Mom!" Ivy yells. "I found her!"

I pick up my pace and follow Ivy's voice and both heartbeats, each grows louder with my approach. The sound of the heartbeats together causes a sob to escape me. I find them through the brush. Ivy's arms are securely wrapped around Jazzy. Tears of joy and relief flow down Ivy's face as she kisses Jazzy's cheeks multiple times.

"Jazzy, you had us so worried. Thank God you're okay," Ivy says and kisses Jazzy some more. "We need to tell Dad. He's still looking for you." Ivy picks Jazzy up and holds her close.

"Jazzy, are you okay, sweetheart?" I ask. Her entire body trembles, and her bare arms are covered in goosebumps. She nods and then, like a dam unable to hold back the water, she cries.

"I . . . I . . . I was so, so scared," Jazzy says.

"I bet you were. But you're okay now. You're safe," I say as I trail behind Ivy who carries Jazzy out of the brush. All I want to do is reach over and pluck Jazzy out of Ivy's arms and hold her tight. How I long to hold Jazzy right now and make it all better, to inhale her sweet, warm scent and wipe the tears from her face.

"We got ya, Jazz. I wasn't going to give up until we found you." Ivy kisses her again like I would. Like a mother would.

Once we exit the brush into the open field, Ivy jogs with Jazzy still held tightly in her arms.

"I found her. I found her," Ivy says to whoever can hear her. Heads turn, and people run toward Ivy. Edward and Brad sprint across the field, causing me to worry that Brad's going to collapse due to his lack of a recent workout and increased stress level. As soon as Brad gets to Ivy, he plucks Jazzy from her arms and pulls her into him.

"Oh Jazzy, my baby girl." He buries his face in the crook of her neck and sobs. Edward puts his left arm around Brad and his right hand on Jazzy's back and rubs it while she cries with Brad. Ivy does the same on the other side, creating an impenetrable circle. Their hearts beat wildly while they comfort one another as I look on as an outsider, as though I'm intruding on a private moment.

"Daddy, are you mad at me?" Jazzy asks with a loud sniffle.

"No, sweetheart, I'm not mad. I was so worried about you. We all were worried," he says, wiping the tears from his eyes and then kissing the top of her head.

"We're glad you're okay," Edward says planting a kiss on her wet cheek while she's still nestled securely in Brad's embrace.

After giving Brad and the kids time to reunite, the cops ask some questions, and with Brad's encouragement, Jazzy answers them. She tells them she had gone to the bathroom toward the end of the party but didn't tell Mr. or Mrs. Lee because she was in a hurry. "I had the runs, Daddy. My tummy hurt," she says. "When I came out, everyone was gone. I waited for Ms. Bridget on the bench, but after a while, it got dark and I was cold. I tried to stay right there on the bench but . . ." She pauses and her heart beats faster as she wraps her arms tightly around Brad's neck and buries her face in his chest.

"But what, Jazzy? What happened?" Brad asks while the cops wait for her to continue.

"There was a man, walking by himself, and the closer he got, the scareder I got."

"Did he say anything to you? Do anything to you?" one of the cops asks.

Jazzy shakes her head. "No, but I was scared, so I ran." Her chin shakes, but she holds back her tears.

"Is that how you ended up by the little building?" the cop asks.

"I thought it would be safe there. He wouldn't be able to find me."

"Did he find you there?" the cop asks. Immediately I'm sick at the thought of a stranger touching Jazzy, hurting her. A surge of terror races through me.

"It's okay, Mommy. He didn't find me. I found a good hiding place," she says.

The cop looks confused but then looks down at his pad of paper.

"Okay, I think that's about it. Looks like we can close this up, and everyone can get back home," he says.

"Don't they need a description of the man?" I ask Brad.

"Do you need her to give you a description of the man?" Brad asks.

"That won't be necessary. He didn't touch her or harm her.

He didn't do anything criminal. Take care, Jazzy," he says. He looks at Brad. "I'm glad this one has a happy ending," he adds before heading to his car.

"Let's get you home and warmed up. How about a nice mug of hot chocolate?" Brad says.

"Yum," she says and and we all laugh as we make our way to the parking lot.

"I think you lived up to your Indian name today, Brave Butterfly," I say.

Jazzy smiles at me and squeezes Brad's neck tighter.

As the cop said, we're lucky this had a happy ending. God answered my prayers, but I can't deny that, for a short time, I wondered if it was going to end differently. Now, as for Bridget Radcliff, I'm not so sure she's going to be safe once Brad gets a hold of her.

—

IT'S LATE WHEN the kids finally settle down and head to bed. Brad hasn't let go of Jazzy since they arrived home. She's curled up on his lap while he relaxes on the worn leather couch and sips from a glass of red wine. He releases a relaxing breath as I take a seat next to him.

"You know, at some point, you're going to have to put her to bed," I say.

"I could have lost her today. I can't stop replaying it all in my mind. God, Claire, I've never been so scared in all my life." He takes another sip from the glass. "I took for granted what I had, never thinking I could lose it. But after losing you and nearly losing Jazz, I realize how precarious life really is—how it can be yanked away at any moment. I never thought any of this could happen to me. It always happens to someone else, not to me."

"No one ever thinks it's going to happen to them," I say, wanting to touch him, reassure him.

Brad's phone rings. He looks over to where it's perched on the arm of the couch, and immediately his heart rate increases.

"It's Bridget."

"Are you going to answer it?"

"I'm not sure I'm ready to hear some shallow excuse," he says, allowing it to ring again.

I'm furious with Bridget for not picking up Jazzy. But the crisis, as terrible as it was, pulled my family together. I'd never seen them be such a united force or show their love so openly as they did tonight. It was an amazing, miraculous sight.

I didn't care for Bridget, and for the life of me, I can't give a specific reason why, other than misguided envy, perhaps. Bridget's sparkling smile, her trim figure, her newly found writing success, all told my brain I was falling short of the invisible, unrealistic mark I'd set for myself. It was all me. Bridget had never done anything to hurt me. As far as I know, Bridget's never said a mean word about me and, to be honest, she was easy to work with on our various charity committees. Envy is such a destructive thing. But now I have a good reason to dislike her, beyond my insecurities.

"I think you should answer it," I say, pointing to the phone now in his hand.

He swipes the keypad.

"Hello?"

"Brad? Oh God, I just got your message. Is Jazzy okay?" Bridget asks.

"Yes, we found her."

"I'm so, so sorry. Please, forgive me," she says. Her voice shakes as she continues. "I forgot to put it on my calendar, and with all the stuff going on this week, it completely slipped my mind."

"Yes, I know how life can get busy," Brad says as though he's doing a dry, first read of a script. Bridget's small sniffles turn into a burst of sobs. Brad takes a cleansing breath then seems to go into full damage control mode. "It's okay, Bridget. Jazzy's okay. It was a mistake, no forgiveness needed. It's really on me, I should've double checked with you earlier today."

Bridget doesn't stop crying, and the sound of it makes my chest hurt. There's anguish in her cry.

"Something's not right. There's something wrong," I say. Brad's eyes question me, and then he speaks into the phone.

"Is everything okay?" he asks Bridget.

Bridget lets out an uneven breath. "Grayson's in the hospital . . . he's really sick."

"Oh Bridget, I'm sorry. What's wrong with him?"

"He has a severe respiratory infection. He seemed to be getting better over the weekend, but on Sunday night his fever spiked, and he was complaining that he was having trouble breathing. He couldn't stop coughing. In the middle of the night, he started wheezing, and his lips turned blue," she says as though she's living it over again. "Thank God, I was sleeping next to him or . . . or I might not have heard him. I called an ambulance, and he was rushed to Children's Hospital. They had to put a tube down his throat and sedate him."

"Is he okay?"

"He's better. They took the tube out today, but he's still pretty weak. They want to keep him here for a couple more days to continue breathing treatments and run some tests."

"Tests?" Brad asks.

"Just to rule out any larger problems. Well, that's what they're telling me."

"That makes sense."

"I was so scared. I thought I was going to lose him," she says. In that instant, even though I wanted to be angry at her, I could only feel compassion. All that envy and judgment fell off me. Bridget's fears are my fears. She's human.

"Is there anything I can do to help?" Brad asks.

"That's sweet of you to offer. I'm okay right now. My parents are here helping with Zach while Gregory and I take turns at the hospital."

"Let me know if you need anything. I mean it," Brad says.

"Thanks, I will. And Brad?" she says.

"Yeah?"

"Please tell Jazzy, I'm so, so sorry."

"I will. Take care Bridget," he says and ends their call.

"Looks like we've *all* been through a lot," I say.

"Things never are what they seem."

"No, they sure aren't."

Chapter Twenty-six

After the ordeal last night, I'm surprised Jazzy wants to go to school. When Brad asks her if she wants to stay home, she shakes her head. "I need my class to pray for Grayson."

Last night, Jazzy ceremoniously placed her shoes as well as the rest of the family's shoes on the stairs. This morning, they all remain on the stairs except for Edward's. I saw him retrieve them after everyone went to bed.

I go to school with Edward and Ivy, still hoping to learn more about Zane. I can't find him as I walk the halls and peek into classrooms. I listen for his name in the crowds and the sound of his heartbeat while the kids pass from class to class, but I still don't see him.

At break time, I search for Ivy, but when I don't see her in the common area where most of the kids hang out, I seek out the empty halls and outdoor crevices where students could hide. I find Ivy in a small alcove at the end of a long, vacant hall. The *thump, thump* of her heart is a perfect symphony in my ears.

"Had to follow the sound of your heart to find you," I say. Ivy looks up from a book she has nestled in her lap. "Studying?"

"Yeah, I know. A miracle, right?"

"No, just a glorious sight. But I don't like that you're alone."

"I've been shunned, Mom. If I sit in plain view, everyone can see what a loser I am. I think this is the better option."

"Maybe we can convince Dad to move you to a different school."

"I think I'd like that." Ivy's voice is one of surrender. "Strange how this used to be the one place I felt the most confident and happy. Now I hate it."

"Look at that. You really *are* crazy. Who are you talking to?" Zane says as he saunters toward Ivy. Ivy's heart picks up speed, each pump coming faster than the one before it.

"Just play it cool," I say. "I'm right here."

"Go away, Zane. I'm studying." Ivy points to her book.

"Is that what you're doing? Sounds more like you were having a conversation with the air," Zane says and laughs.

Ivy packs her bag while Zane moves so close to Ivy she can surely smell his breath.

"How's Edweirdo? Enjoying his expulsion?" he asks, but Ivy doesn't respond. He grinds his teeth, the muscle in his jaw pulses, and his heart pumps like a jackhammer, just like Ivy's.

"I'm talking to you, bitch!" He grips the front of her shirt and pulls her toward him. With his other hand, he yanks a few crumpled papers from his pants pocket. "So, why are you writing me notes and stalking me?"

"What are you talking about?" She tries to sound confident, but her voice cracks.

"These. Telling me you love me, you want to be with me, blah, blah, blah." He holds them up to her face.

"I didn't write you any notes. Who even writes notes,

anyway? Oh, wait, you do." Ivy pushes his hand away from her face and then tries to pry his other hand off her shirt. "Get your hands off me."

"Oh no, I'm not letting go until you admit what you've done."

Zane trembles, and beads of sweat form on his forehead. He slides the notes back into his pocket while still holding on to her shirt with the other. Ivy presses her lips together tightly. She cocks her head and squints her eyes. It's the look I've seen more times than I'd have liked. This is not good.

"You're a worthless pile of poisonous waste, Zane. I wouldn't give you the pleasure of writing stupid, childish love notes. And, if I did, I wouldn't misspell *handsome*, or mistake the word *then* for *than*. Have you learned anything in English class? You disgust me," she says through clenched teeth and then spits in his face. "Let go of me."

He doesn't. Instead, he slams her head into the wall behind her. Her eyes roll to the back of her head before coming forward and focusing back on him.

"And I thought your brother was an easy target," he says.

"Ivy, you need to yell," I say.

"Stop." Ivy's voice is barely audible as though she's out of breath.

"Why, are you scared?" he asks in a mocking voice.

"I'm not scared of you."

"Well, you should be."

"Fuck you!" she yells into his devilish face.

He tightens his grip on her shirt and slams her head against the wall again. Her knees buckle and she collapses to the floor. I want to scream for help, but no one will hear me. I want to punch the shit out of him, but I can't—I'm helpless, again.

"Ivy, you need to yell, please, sweetheart, yell."

"Help," Ivy says, but she's too quiet.

"You need to be louder so the teacher down the hall can hear you," I say.

"Help," she says again, but it's still not strong enough.

"I know you can scream. Now's the time to use it."

"Aww, seems to me you're scared," Zane says in a childlike voice. He grabs her hair, and yanks her head back, forcing her to look up at him. His eyes appear glassy, almost vacant.

"Someone help me!" Ivy reaches up and tries to pry his hand from her hair.

There's movement from down the hall. It's one of the teachers, walking slowly at first and then running.

"What's going on here?" the teacher asks. I recognize Ms. Bennett's dark red hair and funky, over-sized purple glasses. She was Edward's art teacher when he was a sophomore.

"He's hurting me, please," Ivy says.

"Let go of her, young man," Ms. Bennett says. Zane immediately releases his hold on Ivy.

"She started it," Zane says, backing away.

Ivy places her hand on the back of her head and winces.

"Are you all right?" Ms. Bennett asks Ivy. "Can you walk?"

"Yes," Ivy whispers.

"Let's get you to the nurse. Zane, you're coming with me to the dean's office."

"Great. First, she lures me here, and then she gets me in trouble. Ms. Bennett, this isn't my fault. And her head? She hit it against the wall all on her own."

"Dean Livingston will decide all of this," she says as she helps Ivy down the hall. Zane trails behind. He pulls the notes out of his pocket, looks at them, and smiles.

Ms. Bennett walks past the dean's office and gestures for Zane to enter.

"Go on, I'll be there shortly," she says and watches him disappear through the doors before she assists Ivy to the nurse's office.

I don't know whether to go with Ivy or stay behind and hear what tall tale Zane will be telling the dean. I decide to go with Zane.

He plops down on the couch outside the dean's office.

"Can I help you, Zane?" the secretary asks.

"Ms. Bennett told me to come here," he says like he's confused as to why he's here.

She picks up the phone and makes a call.

"Mr. Livingston? Looks like you have a visitor out here. Sure," she says and hangs up.

"You can go in."

Zane saunters into the office.

"Ahh, Zane. Have a seat," he gestures to one of the chairs, and Zane sits, stretching his legs out in front of him and crossing them as though he came for a casual chat. "So, what brings you to my office?"

"Ms. Bennett sent me."

"There has to be a reason why she sent you, so why don't you tell me."

Zane takes a dramatic breath and begins his speech.

"Okay, I know I should have come to you earlier, but I thought I could handle it by myself." He places the crumpled papers on the dean's desk. "Ivy Blackwell's been sending me these notes. I find them in my locker almost every day."

The dean picks up the papers and reads through them. His

facial expression doesn't give anything away. He'd be excellent at poker.

"Huh, and how long has this been going on?" the dean asks.

"For a few weeks. Honestly, I thought it was a little crush at first, but she started finding me in secluded places and tried to touch me, kiss me," Zane says and grimaces.

"This is serious, Zane. You should have come to me sooner."

I eye the thick paperweight on the dean's desk, wanting more than anything to hurl it at his brainless, bald head. It's like Zane has him in some trance. How could he be buying any of this? If Zane were Pinocchio, he'd be able to use his nose as a track and field vaulting pole.

"I know. I'm sorry," Zane says.

"So, where's Ivy?" the dean asks.

"Ms. Bennett took her to the nurse. She hit her head on the wall. I think she was trying to make it look like I hurt her, but I didn't. I would never do that."

"Well, let's hear from Ms. Bennett and Ivy. I need to get to the bottom of this."

"Fine with me."

A few minutes later, Ivy and Ms. Bennett enter. Ivy holds an ice pack to her head while she scans the room. Her body relaxes when she sees me.

"Ivy," I say, "he's using the letters to prove you're harassing him. He said you tried to touch him and kiss him and claims you hit your head on the wall to make it look like he hurt you. You need to be very convincing."

Zane looks at Ivy like the wolf looked at Little Red Riding Hood just before he ate her.

"So, Ivy, I'd like to hear your side of the story," the dean says.

Ivy tells the story, all the facts including calling for help. Zane tries to interrupt multiple times, but the dean stops him and allows Ivy to finish. I keep my eyes on the dean, trying to gauge a reaction, but again, his face gives nothing away.

"Ms. Bennett, do you have anything to add?" he asks.

"I didn't see the incident. I heard Ivy calling for help. When I got there, Zane was holding on to her—"

"She grabbed my hand and made it look that way!" Zane shouts.

"That's not true. God, Zane, for once in your life, tell the truth," Ivy says in an exhausted voice.

"I am!"

"Enough," the dean says. "The fact that Ms. Bennett saw your hands on her is cause for expulsion, Zane. We don't have any tolerance for this type of behavior. Both of you tell entirely different stories, and I don't know which one to believe. Because this is an assault, I'll need to call the police. Zane, as of now, you're suspended for a minimum of three days pending the police investigation."

"What? The police? Are you kidding me? I didn't do anything."

"I . . . I don't want to get the police involved, Mr. Livingston. I just want to go home," Ivy says.

"Ivy." I crouch in front of her so I can see her eyes. She's not thinking straight. "The best thing you can do is press charges. Zane's already being questioned about the rabbits, this will help prove he's the one behind all of this."

"No," Ivy says. "I can't." She looks at the dean. "Mr. Livingston, maybe I accidentally hit my head. I really can't remember."

"Are you changing your story, Ivy?" the dean asks.

"No, I'm just a little unsure of the facts. I really want to go home."

Dean Livingston studies her for a moment. "I'll still need to contact the police. I also think you need to get some medical attention. I'll contact your dad."

Zane pounds his hands on the end of the armrest. "So, I'm not suspended, right?"

"You're still suspended."

"That's ridiculous!" Zane stands and slaps some papers off the dean's desk.

"Do I need to call security?"

Zane calms and grows a let's-make-a-deal expression on his face.

"Look, Mr. Livingston, it's the championship game this weekend. Everyone's counting on me. You wouldn't want to let the school down, would you?"

"I'm not the one letting the school down. You're out of control, Zane."

"I'm not. I'm sorry. Please, let me at least play this weekend. Then I'll serve my suspension. Just let me play, I'm begging you."

Dean Livingston shakes his head. "I'll let the coach know you won't be participating."

"No! This wasn't even my fault."

"I don't know, Zane. You seem to be in my office a little too often for these problems to not be at least some of your fault. It's terribly unfortunate. The school was counting on you."

"This isn't fair. That bitch and her brother are out to ruin me!"

"Zane. That language will not be tolerated," the dean says, but Zane is an animal ready to pounce.

Dean Livingston fills out the bright yellow suspension form

while peering at Zane multiple times. He hands the form to Zane, who whips it out of the dean's hand with a growl. Ivy remains quiet and stoic in her chair. There's relief on her face.

"Both of you need to get your books and come back here. And no talking to one another. Got it?"

They both exit the office to retrieve their things. I follow Ivy.

"I'm going home with Zane. I don't like the way he's acting. Tell everyone I'll see them tomorrow," I say while we're alone in the hallway.

"But, Mom, if Zane's not coming back to school tomorrow, how are you going to get home?"

"Maybe Edward can pick me up?"

"He won't even admit you exist, so there's no way he's going to pick you up."

"Good point. What if you tell him you need him to take you somewhere and have him pass Zane's house? When you see me, have Edward pull over for something and I'll get in."

"That seems complicated, but we can try it."

"And make sure you have Edward take you to urgent care to have your head looked at. Have them document everything."

We settle on a time and return to the dean's office.

"Zane, your parents said to drive right home. I'll see you back in school on Tuesday."

Zane doesn't say anything as he stomps out of the office like a five-year-old.

"Ivy, Edward's picking you up. He'll be at the circle drive in twenty minutes."

"Thank you, Dean Livingston." She turns to leave but stops and looks back. "I didn't do any of what he says I did. I wish you'd see Zane the way he really is. He's mean and manipulative and seems to have something against Edward and me." She clears her throat and looks directly at the dean. "I'm actually happy to be going home. I'll feel much safer there," she says and walks away.

Chapter Twenty-seven

I can barely keep up with Zane and narrowly manage to jump into his car before he drives away. He spins his tires and smoke billows from the rear of the car. His turns are hard, and when he brakes, it's sudden and extreme. If I were alive, I'd be holding on to the car door to keep from sliding from one side to the other. I'd also worry about suffering severe whiplash. Who the hell gave him a driver's license?

"Go right home? Fuck that," he says as he drives randomly, obviously not having a destination in mind. He whips along the side streets, almost hitting a pedestrian before getting onto the freeway and pushing one hundred miles per hour. I experience a slight tinge of guilt wishing he'd crash and allow this to all be over. There's no way he'd survive a crash at this speed. Where are the cops when you really need them?

His phone chimes. He glances at the caller ID.

"Crap," he says and answers it. "Hi, Mom. Yeah, of course, I'm home. Okay, see you later tonight. Bye."

He pulls up to his house almost three hours after his suspension from school. His joyride has finally come to an end. Again, his house is quiet as he retreats to his room. He paces the floor. Back and forth, back and forth.

"This is bullshit!" He goes to his dresser and opens the second drawer from the top. His hand fiddles under the folded clothes and when his hand reappears, it holds a gun. Oh, Shit! He caresses the weapon in his hand, and as he does, his heartbeat slows, and his face relaxes. He reaches back into the drawer and pulls out a box of ammunition. He releases the magazine, and with fingers outstretched, plucks a bullet from the box and inserts it into the magazine. He continues the loading process until the magazine is full and then snaps it into the handle of the gun. With a devilish grin, he strokes the slate gray weapon in his hands, turning it a few times.

A car pulls into the driveway, and as soon as the car door slams, Zane's head turns to his bedroom door. For the first time, there's fear in his eyes. He eases the gun back in the drawer and covers it with the folded clothes before quietly closing the drawer.

"Zane?" A male voice yells from down the hall and then footsteps, each one louder than the one before it. "Zane!" Zane's bedroom door flies open and bangs against the wall.

"Suspended? What the fuck happened?" his dad, Steve, says red-faced. He's as menacing looking as he was when the boys were young, but there's an extra edge to him as well as some pounds. He's also lost a lot of his hair and what he has left on the sides is mostly gray.

Zane's large frame shrinks. His shoulders and head droop, as he peers submissively at his dad. Steve gets right in his face and shouts again.

"Of all the times to get in trouble, you pick now? Just before the most important game of the season? What the hell were you thinking?"

"I'm sorry, Dad. I . . . I didn't mean for this to happen," Zane says in a quiet yet frantic voice.

"You bet your brainless skull you're sorry. Three recruiters are coming to see you—three! And now you can't even play in the game." Steve's spit flies from his mouth. "You sorry piece of shit!"

Steve punches Zane in the face so fast Zane couldn't have seen it coming. Zane drops to his knees and places his hand on the tender area.

"Get up!" Steve says. Zane obeys, but as soon as he's on his feet and standing upright, Steve hits him again, causing Zane to fall back to the floor. Steve kicks him in the gut and then grabs him by his hair and bashes a fisted hand into Zane's face multiple times before letting go. Zane lets out a quiet, high-pitched cry each time he's hit.

"You're pathetic, you know that? A fucking loser," Steve says with one more kick to his side before backing away. "You let me down, let your team down."

Zane's in a fetal position on the floor and buries his head between his knees and chest.

"I'm sorry," Zane says.

"What was that? You're sorry? Well, you'll be sorrier when I kick you out of the house," Steve says and leaves.

Zane hugs his knees tighter until he's a ball on the hardwood floor and cries. His body convulses with each sob, and for the first time, I feel sorry for this boy who's tortured my own children. My motherly instincts want to pull him to me and hold him. But all I can do is watch this poor boy fall to pieces on the floor.

For over thirty minutes, he remains in a tight ball. His sobs have stopped, and now he's quiet except for a few sniffles. He moves to his feet but stays crouched, his arms once again wrapped around his legs in front of him. He rocks back and forth in the same calm manner a mother rocks a child. Slow, calming movement. The swaying motion increases and his muscles tense. He lifts his head from his knees, showing his swollen, wet, vacant eyes. His body trembles and each minute brings on another level of agitation. It's like watching Bruce Banner turn into the Incredible Hulk as veins pop and muscles twitch. He doesn't turn green, and he doesn't tear out of his clothes, but he's certainly not the same boy who was pummeled by his father.

His heartrate quickens as he lifts himself to a standing position. He touches his face but doesn't wince when he skims over a bleeding and bulbous cheek. He ambles to the dresser and opens the drawer, pulling out the gun again. Staring at the loaded weapon, his face twitches into an odd smile, one I've seen before in the movies, one reserved for cold-blooded killers.

He slips the gun into the waist of his jeans, pulls his T-shirt over it, and grabs a handful of bullets from the ammunition box, shoving them into his front pockets. Stopping at his desk, he opens a drawer and pulls out a black Sharpie. Taking off the cap, he writes "Fuck you!" on the mirror above his dresser before placing the cap back on the marker, returning it to the drawer, and walking out the door.

He descends the stairs and, with a quiet, yet determined stride, moves down the hall. I want to scream and warn everyone, but no one would hear me. I'm no use to anyone. Zane approaches the den and peers in. Steve sits on the couch, his back to the door, watching some sports channel. Still at the door frame, Zane pulls the gun from of his waistband and slowly raises it, pointing it toward his father's head.

"No, no, Zane!" I say.

He holds the gun up. His arm shakes. "Bang," he mouths before lowering the gun and placing it back into his waistband. Barely audible he says, "I'll be back for you. I need a little target practice first."

Zane's eyes are vacant blue orbs as he enters his car. Fear of what is to come propels me to stay as close to him as possible. His heartbeat has calmed, his breathing even, his shoulders relaxed. It's as though there's no one residing in his body as he goes through the motions of putting the car in drive and flying down the streets.

My terror increases as Zane turns into our neighborhood. Many of the homes are decorated for Thanksgiving while others already have their Christmas decorations displayed. Winnie, one of my neighbors, is wheeling her trash to the curb. Such a normal, daily task on a normal day.

It's hard to deny what I know. He's coming for Ivy. It's as though a pair of hands are tightening around my neck. I must get to Ivy, warn her, protect her.

"Zane, please don't do this." There's no response, not even a hint he can hear me. But I can't stop. "Zane, honey, you're upset. You need to settle down and think about this." No matter how hard I try, I can't stop the raging storm from heading directly for my home. "Oh God, no, no, no!"

Zane pulls up to the house and exits the car. I move ahead of him as fast as I can and enter through the closed door.

I yell for Ivy and Edward, but before they can answer, Zane rings the doorbell.

Ivy runs down the stairs.

"Ivy, it's Zane. He has a gun. Don't answer the door." There's a mild sense of relief that I got to the kids before they made the mistake of opening the door.

"He has a gun? Oh, God!"

There is a click and the door opens. Zane's in the entry.

"Kind of dangerous not to be locking your doors, isn't it?" he says with a smile on his otherwise blank face. He closes the door behind him and locks it. My relief vanishes and is replaced with a physical, pounding fear, like someone's hammering me into the ground with a hard rubber mallet.

"What do you want?" Ivy says, a slight tremor in her voice.

"I want you, of course."

I don't know whether to stay or get Edward. Someone needs to call 911. I rush up the stairs. Edward's still not acknowledging me, so I go to Jazzy's room.

"Jazzy, I need you to stay up here and call 911," I say in as calm of a voice as I can.

"What? Why?" Jazzy asks.

"Zane Goodman's downstairs and he has a gun. Lock your door and call 911, okay?" Jazzy nods, her eyes as wide as quarters. She grabs the phone and dials.

I enter Edward's room.

"Edward, Zane's in the house with a gun. Ivy's down there. Jazzy's calling 911. I'm going back down now," I say not waiting to see if he responds.

As I descend the stairs, Zane stands in the entry pointing the loaded gun at Ivy's face with his shaking hands. The scene in front of me seems so out of place. Everything looks so normal with the kid's backpacks by the door, the entry table basket filled with keys, and the lineup of shoes on the stairs. Yet, amid all that is right with my family, is something so horribly wrong—an angry, hurt boy with a gun, aimed at my daughter.

"You fucking ruined me, bitch," Zane says. "If it weren't for you and your loser brother, I wouldn't be in this mess. It's all your fault."

"I'm sorry, Zane. I didn't mean for you to get in trouble," Ivy says, her voice pleading. "Maybe if you put the gun down, we can talk."

"I don't want to talk. I want you to pay. I'm here to collect a debt. You ruin me, I ruin you. It's really rather simple."

"Why don't we go out? Get something to eat and talk?" Ivy asks.

"Go out? No, it needs to be bigger than that."

"Put the gun down, Zane," Edward says from the top of the stairs.

"Well, if it isn't Edweirdo," Zane says. "Are you going to try and save your pathetic sister?"

"Just put the gun down," Edward says.

"Naw, I don't think so."

"This doesn't need to happen. We can work this out." Edward raises his hands as if in surrender and walks down the stairs. Each step is slow as he keeps his eyes on Zane.

"Are you coming closer so you can get a good look at your sister when I shoot her?"

"Please, put the gun down," Edward says.

"No way. You know, I think I'll take care of you first so I can have my way with Ivy before I put a bullet in her head." Zane moves his hand and points the gun at Edward, who's halfway down the stairs.

"Or, on the other hand, maybe I should take care of your sister first so you can watch her die. That would be nice, wouldn't it?" He points the gun back at Ivy.

Edward looks right at me. He can see me, and his eyes are apologetic. The next movement is quick. Edward jumps from the middle stair, his arms outstretched in Zane's direction. He quickly covers the distance between them. Zane turns, points the gun at Edward and pulls the trigger. *Bang.* The sound is deafening. Time abates, giving me a slow-motion viewing as the bullet exits Zane's gun, cuts through the air and enters Edward's abdomen.

"Edward!" Ivy says with a panic-filled shriek.

Edward grabs on to Zane as he falls and pulls Zane to the floor. Zane hits the tile hard, knocking the gun from his hand. The gun slides a few feet away from Zane. He tries to break free from Edward, but Edward somehow flips Zane to his stomach and pulls his hands behind him.

"Ivy, get some rope from the garage," Edward says, his voice weak and out of breath.

"I'm not going to leave you," she says.

The color in Edward's face drains, and a blood stain grows rapidly on his shirt.

"Please. Hurry."

Ivy runs to the garage and moments later returns with some thick twine.

Edward has Zane pinned to the floor, but Edward's face is nearly white, and his eyelids flutter. Edward's shirt is blood-soaked. Ivy wraps the twine tightly around Zane's wrists and then ties them in a secure knot.

A piercing scream comes from Ivy as she catches Edward before he collapses to the floor.

"Oh God, no!" she screams. "Don't die on me, Edward, don't you dare!"

Chapter Twenty-eight

I crouch next to Ivy. Edward's heart still beats. But after a few more pulses, it weakens. Sirens sound in the distance. Edward's blood pools on the floor and flows into the crevices of the grout. Zane thrashes about like a fish.

Jazzy's at the top of the stairs, crying.

"Jazzy, go to your room and call Daddy. I'm here with Edward. He's not alone," I say.

The flashing red lights of the emergency vehicles bounce off the beveled glass of the front door.

"Ivy, you're going to have to open the door," I say.

"I can't let go of Edward."

"If you want to help him, the best thing you can do is let them in."

Ivy leans over and kisses Edward's forehead before carefully sliding him off her lap and onto the floor. She stands and opens the door as the police arrive. Her teeth chatter loudly.

The police grab hold of Zane and summon the paramedics. In less than a minute, a frenzy of activity erupts in the front of the house. Edward's heartbeat slows into a weaker *thump, thump*.

Ivy stands behind one of the paramedics and watches, her arms tightly wrapped around herself. "Mom, can't you do anything?"

"I'm sorry, Ivy. It's out of my control. He has to fight. Come on, Edward, fight."

"It should have been me. This is my fault," Ivy says.

"This is *not* your fault. Don't even think that."

"That bullet was meant for me, not Edward."

"He had a bullet for both of you."

"Miss, are you okay?" a cop asks Ivy when he notices her talking to the air.

"No, I'm not okay," she says.

Jazzy comes to the top of the stairs. She surveys the carnage below. Her mouth opens as she looks on with wide-eyed terror. Ivy runs up the stairs and embraces Jazzy, shielding her eyes from the scene. She leads Jazzy back into Jazzy's room.

Edward's heart continues to slow, each beat weaker than the one before it. I'm not afraid for Edward. Death's not something to be feared, but I don't want this to be the end for him. He's too young; he has too much life ahead of him. He deserves to live a long, happy life.

"Edward, hang on, sweetheart. Don't give up," I say in his ear.

Brad's frantic voice comes from outside. "My family's in there. Please let me in," he says. One of the cops escorts him through the doors. He sees Edward and rushes to his side.

"What happened?" he asks me, his eyes terrified, his heart racing. One of the paramedics goes into a short explanation of Edward's injuries as Brad crouches and places his hand on Edward's head. I talk over the paramedic.

"Zane came with a gun. He wanted revenge on Ivy and Edward," I say.

"Oh God. Where are the girls?" Brad asks, panicked.

"Upstairs in Jazzy's room. They're okay."

"How's Edward?" he asks.

"Sir, I'm sorry, but you need to step back and give us some room," one of the paramedics says.

"He's holding on, but he's been badly hurt," I say. "Why don't you go check on the girls? I'll stay with him."

"Okay," he says, reluctant. The fear in his eyes haunts me and reaches to the very depths of my soul, squeezing it until it aches.

He disappears up the stairs. I didn't want to tell him I don't know if Edward's going to make it much longer. His pulse is weak, and he's lost a lot of blood.

"Let's get him to the ambulance," one of the paramedics says as they secure him on the gurney and lift it. I'm right behind them and enter the ambulance, taking a seat next to one of medics.

Brad appears at the back doors of the ambulance.

"I'll be there as soon as I can," he says.

"Take care of Ivy and Jazzy. They need you. I'll see you at the hospital," I say.

They close the ambulance doors and turn on the sirens. I can barely hear his heart, and then, it stops. This can't be it. Brad and the girls can't lose Edward. There's a flurry of words and activity as they start compressions. And then, Edward's out of his physical body, sitting next to me.

"I don't look too good, do I, Mom?" he asks.

"Edward, you get back into that body of yours right now! That's an order."

"I can't."

"Yes, you can, and you will."

"Mom, maybe this is for the best."

"The best for who? For your father? Your sisters? You?"

"I feel so light, nothing's holding me down. I like this feeling," he says as he moves his arms and legs. "Is that how you feel?"

"I did at first. But after a short time, things began to hurt worse than when I was alive. What you're feeling now doesn't last."

"Mom, I'm sorry," he says looking into my eyes.

He grabs my hand, and for the first time, I feel his touch. An intense warmth flows within me, and I can't help but want to hold on to him and never let go.

"Edward, you have nothing to be sorry for."

"The day of the accident, I was the one you were texting. I was the reason you were at that intersection at that time. If it weren't for me, you'd still be alive."

"What I did was stupid. I knew better. It's no one's fault but my own. You're not to blame, do you understand?"

"That whole time you spoke to me, and I ignored you? I heard you . . . and I saw you."

"I know."

"I didn't want to believe it was you. I felt so guilty and didn't deserve your affection, so I just . . . pushed you out. I'm sorry."

"It's okay. I understand," I say, patting his knee and loving the way it feels to touch.

"No, it's not okay. All you wanted was for me to acknowledge you, and I didn't. I just didn't know how." He squeezes my hand. "I love you, Mom."

"Edward, I am so incredibly proud of you. The day you dropped Jazzy off and told her she wasn't a freak was when I knew how tremendously big your heart was. Well, I always knew, I just never got to see it." I lean into his body and he smiles.

"You heard me?"

"Of course. And the day you buried the rabbits? That was the day you became a man, and I knew you were going to be okay."

"I heard you that day. I was already planning on burying them. I knew Jazzy would've been really upset."

"You know, the day I found out I was pregnant with you, I knew you were destined for something big. You're special, and I've always believed you're an old soul." There is a short stretch of silence as we both watch the paramedics do chest compressions. "What you did in there, jumping on Zane? You're not the same fearful boy you were less than a year ago."

"Zane didn't give me much choice. I wasn't going to let him take more than he already has."

"Is that why you started using drugs?"

"Drugs?"

"The ones you took when you skipped school."

"I didn't take any drugs. I was running and lifting weights. I've been doing that almost every day. I knew I needed to be strong to protect myself from Zane. Why did you think it was drugs?"

"You were sweaty and red in the face and a little dazed. And that day you slept through picking up the girls . . . I guess I assumed the worst. I'm sorry," I say relieved. But I'm disappointed at myself for thinking that way.

"I couldn't sleep the night before. I was exhausted."

"Why did you sell your meds?"

Edward looks away for a moment and then looks me in the eyes. "I was going to buy a gun. For protection. I'm so glad I didn't."

"You did the right thing, Edward. And you showed me you can take care of yourself."

"I guess we really never know how strong we are until we're forced to be," he says. The smile that lights up his face tells me he believes in himself.

"It's not your time to go, sweetheart. You still have work to do."

"But I want to stay with you. I don't think I want to go back."

"What's going to happen to Ivy and Jazzy if you leave them? What's going to happen to Dad? They need you now. I know you don't think so, but you're the one thread that everyone's holding on to."

"Mom—"

"No, Edward, you have to go back. I promise, life will get better. You've already figured out one of the toughest lessons. Believing in yourself is what paves the way for a successful life. You deserve to experience it."

Edward fades. His grip on my hand weakens.

"Stay with me, Mom," he asks.

"I will. Always."

He disappears from my side, and the paramedics announce they have a pulse.

Chapter Twenty-nine

When we arrive at the hospital, Edward is whisked to the ER, and I stay with him. He continues to balance precariously on life's tightrope.

"We need to get him to the OR and stop the bleeding," a doctor says. I kiss Edward's forehead. "Hang in there, Edward. Just hang in there. I'll be back. I'm going to look for Dad."

Brad stands in the center of the open, chair-filled room, his face heavy with worry, each line a deeper crevice than I remember. He sees me and rushes over, a look of desperation stares at me. Should I sugar coat it or tell him the truth?

"I think he's going to be okay," I say.

"You think? How is he? What's happening? They won't tell me anything."

"He died, Brad, only for a brief time, but his heart stopped."

"Oh no. I can't lose him too." People in the room stare at Brad, probably wondering if they should move away from the crazy man talking to himself and crying.

"Let's find a seat in the corner. You're getting some stares," I say. He scans the room before moving.

"Sorry," he says to the people before he sits in a secluded corner of the room.

"I spoke with him. He understands he needs to stay."

Brad leans forward and rests his forearms on his legs. "I've been so tough on him. I made him pick up the slack from your absence, got angry at him. I wouldn't blame him if he wants to leave," he says in a whisper, barely moving his lips.

"You haven't been hard on him. You've been a parent. And you know what? He rose to meet your expectations and then some. He grew into a man because of you."

Brad's eyes question me. He didn't have the opportunity to see what I saw, to watch Edward transform more than I ever gave him credit for.

"He's an amazing young man, Brad. He has a lot to live for, and I hope I convinced him to fight." I pat Brad's leg, and even though neither of us can feel it, we can see it, and that's all we need. "I'm going to see how he's doing. I'll let you know if anything changes."

"Okay," he says. "Claire?"

His eyes, the ones I fell in love with more than twenty-seven years ago, are raw and intense. "Yes?"

"I couldn't have done all of this without you. Thank you."

I smile, but if what Gammy said is true, I can't take credit for any of this. It might appear that I've helped, but they've learned to adapt without my physical help. Together, my family is strong.

In the operating room, Edward's stomach cavity is open, and the hands within it are stitching something up.

"He's a very lucky young man. One more millimeter and he wouldn't have made it to the hospital alive," the surgeon says.

"He must have a hell of a guardian angel," a nurse says from behind her mask.

They put my son back together, gently placing parts in the

proper places before closing him up. The surgeons are so careful and precise, and I'm grateful for their attention to detail.

"He's a handsome boy, this one. I'm sure his parents are proud. I heard he jumped in front of a gun to protect his sister," the nurse says.

"The world needs more people like him." The surgeon says as he ties off the last stitch. "All right, he's all yours. Clean him up and get him to Recovery. I'll talk to the parents."

I trail the doctor out of the operating room, down the long hall and past the double doors to the waiting room, just as I did a month ago after I officially died. Brad springs from his chair and rushes to the doctor, meeting him in the middle of the room. Brad glances at me, and I smile. Immediately his shoulders relax.

"Mr. Blackwell?" the doctor asks.

"Yes."

"Is your wife here?"

"Yes, uh, I mean no."

"Is she on her way?"

"She died. It's just me now," Brad says.

"I'm sorry, I didn't know. Let's have a seat." The doctor gestures to some vacant chairs. "Edward's out of surgery. He's lost a lot of blood, and he suffered some severe damage to his internal organs, but we were able to stabilize him."

"That's good news," Brad says.

"He's not out of the woods. The next twenty-four hours will be critical, but he's a fighter."

"I know. He's like his mom."

I return to Edward and stand by his side. He looks vulnerable and young, all hooked up to a myriad of noisy machines. He's breathing on his own, but he's in and out of consciousness. A nurse tends to him, so gentle and loving like I would be if I were able. The nurse speaks to him even though he's asleep.

"That's a brave thing you did, Edward. Your sister's very lucky to have you," she says as she changes his IV and writes down his blood pressure from the machine. "You're going to be as good as new in no time."

What the nurse says is true. We're lucky to have him—I was lucky to have carried him in my womb, to feed him from my breast, and to see him turn into such a fine young man. I want everyone to know how incredibly special he is. Maybe now, people will see what I see.

Once Edward is situated in his room, Brad and the girls enter. Ivy's nurturing ways emerge as she strokes Jazzy's long, soft hair and kisses the top of her head. I smile at Ivy, letting her know how happy the sight of the two of them together makes me feel.

They move close to Edward's bed.

"He's going to be okay. Edward's going to fight to stay here with you," I say.

Tears shine in their eyes.

"Does he hurt?" Jazzy asks me. The nurse answers at the same time I do. Jazzy looks a little confused as to which person to listen to, but she looks at me.

"Not right now, Jazz. He's resting, and they've given him some pain medication," I say.

"Can I touch him?"

"Of course you can. He'd like that. You know, when I was in the hospital, I heard everything you said to me."

"Really?" she says, and I nod while the nurse twists her pink lips and glances at Jazzy out of the corner of her eye.

"I'm going to give you some time alone. I'll be at the nurse's station if you need anything," the nurse says before leaving the room.

Jazzy looks at Ivy who reaches into her purse and pulls out Pink Kitty. Jazzy takes it and places her stuffed animal on the pillow, next to Edward's head. "I brought this for you. You got to get better, Edward. I miss you," she says. Ivy wraps her arms around her little sister and hugs her.

Brad moves to Edward's other side and whispers in his ear. "I'm proud of you, son. Rest and get better."

I take in all I see. My family. The pride that swells within me is larger than its container. It spills forth like a waterfall. All their struggles, all their insecurities, all their false perceptions, are now so trivial, so unnecessary. As long as they have each other and believe in each other and in themselves, they can conquer all they face.

Edward's heart pumps strong and determined. It's an incredible sound; the thump, thump of your own child's heartbeat. From the day I heard it in the doctor's office for the first time to this exact moment, it never ceases to be anything but a miracle to my ears.

The nurse returns to the room. Time no longer feels limitless, which has me wondering how much more of it I have here. There's a persistent tug, like when the kids were little and they would pull on my arm, asking for attention. Is Gammy coming to get me? Of course, just like everything else, there's no written guide. The nurse gazes at Brad and the girls, her face full of compassion. She retrieves blankets and snacks for them, as though they are her patients too.

I'm drawn to the nurse. I follow her out of the room and

listen to her heart. It's a beautiful sound, and I can see her heart, not as an organ but rather as a vessel of love and kindness. It's large and full. I see her heart like I used to see beautiful people, admiring their full smile or the way their eyes twinkled when they were happy or how their face glowed. But now, I can see the heart the same way; perhaps what I'm actually seeing is her soul. While some are small and almost lifeless, this nurse caring for my family is radiant and perfect and pure.

Chapter Thirty

"Do you think Edward will be home for Christmas?" Jazzy asks as I sit with Brad and the girls at a table in the hospital cafeteria.

"Oh, I'm sure he will," I say.

"Good, 'cause I don't know if Santa would know to come to the hospital," Jazzy says.

We all have a much-needed laugh. I love seeing the girls' eyes light up when they laugh, so full of life that they sparkle like glitter in the sun.

"So, I'm just curious. What do I look like to you?" I ask all of them. I've never been able to catch a glimpse of myself, well, my ghostly self. Mirrors never showed my reflection. Jazzy speaks almost immediately.

"Oh, Mommy, you're wearing that puffy white skirt and pink top you wore at Easter. That was the day we climbed into the chick cage at the petting zoo, and all the baby chicks climbed over us, remember? They were so cute. I kept laughing 'cause their little feet tickled. That was one of my favorite days."

"That certainly was a happy day, wasn't it?" I say.

"No," Ivy says. "Hudson jeans and your pink Henley shirt

with your favorite boots. You wore that the day you took me to the American Idol concert."

"That was years ago. How could you possibly remember what I was wearing?"

"Because it was . . . like Jazzy said, one of my favorite days."

Now I'm curious as to how Brad sees me. I'm wondering if I'm in some sexy negligée or not wearing any clothes at all, wouldn't that be a hoot? He always said his best part of the day was snuggled up in bed together, naked.

"Brad?" I ask, unable to contain my smile.

He looks at me with a sheepish grin and gives me a wink but then waves his hand.

"You're wearing your wedding dress." He stares into my eyes. "Best day of my life."

"I guess I'm the way you want to remember me—attached to a favorite memory." I'm a little sad that Ivy's memory is from years ago. Ivy must not have any favorite recent memories with me in them. It's a regret I'll have to take with me. A regret I can't change. "Hey girls, why don't you go get some dessert?"

Brad hands the girls some cash and they run to the counter.

"I feel different. I'm lighter, like a weight that I didn't know was holding me down is somehow giving way," I say to Brad.

His eyes narrow. "What does that mean? Are you leaving us?"

"I don't know. Edward must be out of the woods now. He's going to be okay. You're all going to be okay."

"But we need you. *I* need you."

"I don't think you need me the way you think you do."

I move closer to him and gaze into his eyes.

"You're a wonderful father. I wouldn't have married you if I didn't think you would be."

"I don't know if I can do it alone. You were the one who took care of all the hard stuff. I know that now. While I made money to support our family, while I focused on my career, you held it all together."

I wasn't the perfect mother or the perfect wife, not even close. It was evident when I got to see my family from a different perspective, see the multitude of mistakes I've made, big and small. But, I'd like to think I learned from my failures, and that those failures were nothing more than part of life's journey.

"You're going to make mistakes. You're going to feel like the world is falling apart around you sometimes, but look at them." We both watch Ivy and Jazzy as they laugh and high-five each other. "They're great kids. *We* have great kids."

"They're pretty awesome. I guess I didn't know how wonderful they were until we were thrown into the fire," Brad says.

"It was a pretty large fire. But you all learned to put it out, *together.*" They did this all on their own. Even though I was present, I was left without any control. I couldn't protect them, but somehow, they protected each other. It's a humbling lesson, but one I needed. They never needed me to create a perfect world for them. All they ever needed was for me to believe in them and love them.

Jazzy and Ivy return to the table, carrying some cookies and ice cream bars.

"That's a lot of sugar," Brad says. His comment amuses me. Policing their sugar and junk food intake was always my job; now it's his. Everything's now *his* job.

"We couldn't decide, so we got both," Jazzy says.

"I think you need to save some of that for later," Brad says.

"But the ice cream will melt," Jazzy says.

"Duh. We have to eat that first. Then we sneak the cookies when he's not looking," Ivy says and bumps Jazzy with her elbow.

"Good idea," Jazzy whispers.

"Should we go see how Edward's doing?" Brad asks while the girls devour their ice cream. Jazzy wears more on her face than she's consuming. Some things never change.

As we exit the cafeteria, we see Bridget wheeling Grayson down the hall. He nearly disappears into the large rolling chair. There's an oxygen tank attached to the side of the wheelchair and a plastic tube feeding him air through his nose. Bridget's hair is in a messy bun, and dark blue circles droop below her tired eyes. She's wearing oversized sweatpants, a pink breast cancer walk T-shirt, and flip-flops, and if I didn't recognize the beat of her heart, I would swear it wasn't her.

"Bridget," Brad calls out when he sees her. He strolls over to her and Grayson and crouches in a catcher position. "Hey, buddy, how're you feeling?" he asks.

"Better," Grayson says, his voice hoarse.

"That's good to hear," Brad says, placing his hand on the top of Grayson's head and ruffling his hair.

Bridget's heart is complex as it beats. It holds so much—feels so much, just like Brad's. Love, contentment, relief, pain, fear. There's nothing bad in her heart. No bad intentions, no hurtful inclinations, no ulterior motives. The only thing her heart is guilty of is its loneliness and its search to cure the pain it causes. I never saw it that way before and never once thought of her as lonely. I should have taken the time to get to know her. If I had, I would have known what a good person Bridget really is.

"How's Edward?" Bridget asks. "I've been so worried about him since I heard."

"He's a fighter," Brad says. "He's going to be okay. He's going to get through this."

"What a relief." She places her hand on her heart and closes her eyes for a moment as though truly giving thanks, before opening them again. "I kept praying he'd be okay. Y'all have been through too much."

"Thanks for your prayers, they seemed to work," Brad says.

"They do work. I prayed for you, Grayson. Our whole class prayed for you, and you're doing better, too," Jazzy says.

"That's so thoughtful of you, Jazzy," Bridget says. "We need to get going. Looks like they're going to let Grayson go home today. Maybe we could all get together when Edward gets home, and things settle down a little?" Bridget says.

"I'd like that," Brad says.

Brad, the girls, and I return to Edward's room, but he's not there yet, and Brad gets a panicked look on his face.

"He's probably still in recovery. I'll go check," I say.

I leave the room, and as I move down the hall, I'm flooded in light. There's a strong pull, and for a moment I resist, looking back to Brad and the girls. If only there was a way to stay, to watch my children grow up, to grow old with Brad. But that's not possible, I know that. It's time to let go. It's time for all of them to move on. The light brightens, washing away my earthly surroundings. Gammy glides toward me, her arms outstretched.

"Claire, it's time," she says. I smile at Gammy's warm, inviting face. "You've had a long journey. It's time to come home now."

"I was just going to tell Edward—"

"Oh, dear Claire, there's no need. He won't remember."

"Yes, he will. I promised him I would come back. I need to say goodbye. He'll remember If I never come back."

"No. He won't. None of them will."

"What do you mean?"

"It's the price you must pay."

"What's the price I must pay?"

"They will never remember you as a ghost. To them, you were never here after you died," Gammy says.

"But all those talks. They were important, Gammy. I need them to know how much I love them and believe in them." I made such progress. How could all of that be erased? I feel like someone jumbled up the completed puzzle right after I snapped the final piece into place.

"Darling, you were here to find your own peace, not theirs. They'll find it, in their own way, in their own time."

Gammy cradles my face in her warm, tingly hands. Any shred of doubt about what I have or have not left behind floats away. It moves farther and farther into the distance until it disappears in a fine mist, and what I'm left with is a view of my family's hearts, so full—so full of my love for them.

"See? They know. And even though they won't remember, they will feel your love. Love, dear, transcends the boundary between life and death."

I understand now. It's like one of the mysteries of life has been revealed to me, and I accept it without question. I reach for Gammy's hands, and the moment we touch, warmth and peace and happiness envelop me. All my sadness, anger, frustration, and worry disappear; they're no longer a part of me. The ground vanishes as the surrounding light swallows me. I'm light, I'm unencumbered, I *am* the light, and I'm letting go. I leave with nothing, but the deepest, purest love in my soul.

Epilogue

Edward

I scan the room one last time before compressing my suitcase with my knee and zipping it closed. If only I could have fit my Xbox in somewhere—I'm going to go through some major withdrawal. There's a knock on my door.

"Yeah?" I say, checking my watch. They should be here any minute.

"It's me. Can I come in?"

"Sure."

Ivy saunters into my room and plops on my bed.

"It's so bare... and clean," she says, looking around the room.

"I guess I could have left the posters up, I'm not taking them with me." I pull my suitcase up on its wheels. I'm trying like hell to avoid eye contact with Ivy because I don't want to lose my shit in front of her. Since the shooting, Ivy and I have a connection that can't be defined by some title or described with words; it's a feeling—like the warmth and protection of a mother's arms.

"I can't believe you're really leaving," Ivy says in almost a whisper.

"Me either. Senior year flew by."

"I'm going to miss you, Edward, more than you know." Ivy's voice falters and I have to swallow down the ball of emotions stuck in my throat.

"I'm going to miss you too." I sit on my bed next to Ivy. "I'm glad we're close again."

"Same. I wish Mom could see us now. She wouldn't believe it," Ivy says with that little musical laugh that reminds me of when we were younger.

"Do you ever get that feeling like she knows? Like she can see us?"

"Yeah. For a while, I felt like she was watching us. Not in a creepy sorta way, but just making sure we're okay—like she did when we were little."

"After I was shot, I had a dream Mom was sitting next to me and . . ." I stop. It feels silly to share.

"What?"

"It's nothing, really."

"It's *not* nothing," she says as though she knows what I'm about to say.

"She spoke to me. We had the best conversation and then she ordered me to get back into my body. It was so real, Ivy."

Ivy nods and is silent for a short time. She must think I'm crazy. Wouldn't be the first time.

"Sounds like Mom," Ivy says. "I had similar dreams shortly after she died. They were so vivid. Do you think she was really here?"

"If I've learned one thing, it's to never underestimate the power of Mom. If she's found a way, she's probably watching us right now," Edward says.

"You're probably right."

"I think she'd just want us all to be happy."

"She'd be so proud of you, Edward, going to the Air Force Academy." Ivy bumps her fist on my knee.

"And she'd be proud of you, getting away from those A-hole friends and writing your own music."

We sit for a few minutes, enjoying the peace between us.

"Dad's going to be okay," I say.

"Mom would like her," Ivy says.

"She makes him happy."

"Bridget and Dad are just friends. It's not like they're going to get married tomorrow. They aren't even really dating," Ivy says.

"I know. But he's different since . . . since the shooting."

"We're all different. It's a good thing, Edward. Sometimes being different is a *very* good thing," Ivy says. She looks so much like Mom, the same broad smile and expressive eyes.

The doorbell chimes and my heart races. This is it; I'm leaving. I'm filled with excitement and worry. I'm excited my next adventure's about to begin and worried I won't make the cut. I try to push my doubt aside and stand straight. There's no way I'm going to let Ivy think I can't do this.

"Well, time to get going," I say.

"Edward?" Dad calls from downstairs.

"Coming." I glance at Ivy. "Keep in touch, Sis. Promise you'll call if you need to talk?"

"Promise," she says and then reaches over and hugs me so tight I can barely breathe. She sniffles and her pulse taps on my chest.

"It's not like I'm leaving forever. I'll be back."

"You better." She pulls herself away and wipes the tears from her face. "Need help with anything?"

"Can you grab that bag?" I ask. Ivy helps me carry my things down. Dad's at the bottom of the stairs, Jazzy stands next to him.

"They're here, Edward," Jazzy says.

"Got everything?" Dad asks.

"I sure hope so." I place my bag on the floor before returning to the stairs to retrieve my shoes from the third step. Dad's shoes are above mine, Ivy's and Jazzy's below. I can't remember when we all started putting our shoes on the stairs, but now, it's as though none of us can go without this daily routine. It's the way we check in at night, all the shoes on their respective stair indicating everyone's safe at home. But it also offers a sense of comfort I can't explain. There's something about all the shoes lined up that holds some sort of secret message we may never fully crack.

As I put on my shoes, I think about how far I've come, how I never imagined this day would arrive, the day I leave and go off to school. I'm headed to the Air Force Academy to follow my dream of flying those fighter jets. After Mom died, I realized I didn't want to sit around and watch life pass me by. I wanted to make something of myself so she'd be proud of me. But when I started to push myself and attend the recruiter meetings, I finally understood. It's not about Mom and Dad being proud of me—it's about being proud of myself.

My bullet wound is completely healed, but I still struggle to overcome the insecurity Zane pounded into me. I don't know if I'll ever be able to shake free of every wound his words and actions inflicted, but I'm not going to let him win by allowing those wounds to control my life. Bullies don't deserve that power.

"I'll miss you, Edward. But I know you're going to do great," Dad says and pulls me into a firm hug.

"Thanks, Dad."

"Can I ride in one of those planes with you?" Jazzy asks.

"It's going to be a while before they're going to let me fly one of those."

"Oh, man," she says.

"You're all dressed up. Where are you going?" I ask Jazzy.

"Ms. Bridget's taking me to tea. She said Grayson and Zach don't want to go to a tea, so she's taking me," Jazzy says, swishing her pink dress back and forth.

"That sounds like fun." I kneel and take hold of her small hands. "Take care of Ivy and Dad while I'm gone and keep working on your math—I'm gonna quiz you when I get home," I say, and give her a kiss. "I love you, Jazz."

"I love you too, Edward." Jazzy turns and runs up the stairs.

I give another round of hugs, this time finding it hard to pull away. We've all been through so much together it's hard to imagine not seeing them every day.

Jazzy barrels down the stairs with a pair of my shoes in her small hands. She places them on my step.

"What are you up to?" I ask.

"I'm holding your spot," she says. I narrow my eyes. "Because you're coming back. Besides, with your shoes here, I'll think you're still home."

I get it. We all get it.

Taking a few deep breaths to keep the tears away, I snag my suitcase and make the short stroll to the waiting van in the driveway. The rest of them follow behind.

"Call me when you get there," Dad says as I climb into the van. As I settle into a seat, the door closes, and the van edges down the drive. I turn and wave.

All three of them stand in the driveway, their arms around

each other, waving back. The only one missing is Mom. Before they disappear from my view, a butterfly circles above them and lands on Jazzy's head. They don't appear to notice. There's a ping in my chest, and then it fades. I miss her. But I truly believe she's with me, with all of us, in the softest of breezes, in the warmth of the sun's rays or in the flutter of a butterfly's wings. And that's all I need to move forward, to live on and to let go.

A Note from the Author

Bullying has become a growing problem in our children's schools and beyond. The number of children bullied every year is staggering, and the increased number of children taking their own lives because of it continues to climb at an alarming rate. As a mother of a bullied child, I have seen firsthand, the damage such thoughtless attacks can cause to both the physical and emotional health of a child. Once the damage is done, the wound inflicted, it's nearly impossible to heal without a scar.

A percentage of the proceeds of this book will be donated to various anti-bullying campaigns that find creative, effective ways to stomp out bullying. If you know of a student looking for funding to create their own campaign, please reach me through my webpage at www.jansteeleauthor.com.

Also, if you haven't yet, consider becoming an organ donor. According to Organdonor.gov, over 113,000 people are currently on the transplant waiting list as of January 2019. Every ten minutes someone is added to the list, and twenty people die each day waiting for an organ. One donor can save up to eight people. Thanks to modern science, we have the ability to restore and extend lives through organ donation.

Acknowledgments

Thank you to the wonderful Acorn Publishing team, Holly Kammier, Jessica Therrien, and Lacey Impellizeri. Your incredible, tireless support throughout this process kept me grounded and focused on the purpose of the journey. I am so grateful and proud to be part of such an amazing group of authors. Most of all, thank you for believing in my story.

Thank you to my editor, Holly Kammier, for pushing me to dig deeper and for keeping me to deadlines. Without your continual encouragement, this book would have never been ready!

Thank you to Tammy Greenwood, my long-time writing mentor. Your early encouragement and guidance along with your skillful teaching of the craft made me believe I could actually do this. Thank you also to all my Read and Critique groupies from San Diego Writers Ink: Shawna, Chris, Dave, Erin, Bridget, Julieta, Heather, Padma, Dale, Estee, and Chih. Your invaluable insight and (sometimes painful) honesty only helped me make the story stronger.

Thank you to the team of skilled writers at the Southern California Writer's Conference and the amazing workshops that have taught me more about writing than anything pulled from a book. I continue to "write more, suck less."

Thank you to my parents, my sister and all my friends who believed in me when I didn't.

The biggest thank-you goes to my husband, Scott, and my children, John, Julia, and Jessica. You are the reason I breathe. You are my greatest cheerleaders, and without your support and constant encouragement, the publication of this novel would not be possible. You have all made significant sacrifices to allow me this dream. Thank you for overlooking the messy house, the dinnerless nights, or my incessant rants about my characters (to name a few). I love you all so much!

About the Author

Jan Steele grew up in the burbs of Chicago and, after thirty-two years of shoveling snow, moved to San Diego with her husband and children. She has taught everything from Kindergarten through high school but found her passion for writing years later while living as an expat in Asia for four years. She is a contributing author of Chicken Soup for the Soul, Miracles and More (2018), an MFA student at UC Riverside, and shares a blog with her sister-in-law, www.killingjunecleaver.blogspot.com. You can also visit her at her website, www.jansteeleauthor.com. In addition to writing, she loves to travel, volunteer, watch college basketball (go Zags!) and gaze at sunsets.

CPSIA information can be obtained
at www.ICGtesting.com
Printed in the USA
BVHW081500090719
552976BV00004B/9/P